Haunted by the King of Death

Felicity Heaton

ETERNAL MATES SERIES

Kissed by a Dark Prince
Claimed by a Demon King
Tempted by a Rogue Prince
Hunted by a Jaguar
Craved by an Alpha
Bitten by a Hellcat
Taken by a Dragon
Marked by an Assassin
Possessed by a Dark Warrior
Awakened by a Demoness
Haunted by the King of Death

Find out more at: www.felicityheaton.co.uk

CHAPTER 1

Grave's fangs sliced into the supple female flesh beneath his lips. She cried softly into his ear, her body arching forwards to press against the full length of his. He flexed his fingers against her curves and drew her closer still, closed his eyes and breathed in deep, silencing the buzzing in his mind as the warmth of her chased the cold away.

The mark on his back tingled and he ignored it.

He pulled his fangs free, wrapped his mouth around the twin puncture marks and drew slowly on her blood.

His eyebrows pinched in a frown.

Not the sweet taste of nectar she had promised, but the bitter taste of ashes coated his tongue as her hot blood filled his mouth.

He swallowed it with a grimace and resisted the urge to snarl against her throat, focused instead on feeding and on her. The buzzing in his skull grew stronger, destroying the brief moment of calm, and his back began to burn, fire pulsing across it in a way that made him able to picture the mark on it as it chased along the lines.

Damn her.

Not the female in his arms, but the one who had done this to him.

Reduced him to this.

A snarl curled up his throat and he sank his fangs back into the female, felt her tense and heard her gasp, but didn't notice either as he gave his voyeur the same show as always.

A vision of fury and hatred.

Grave tore his teeth from the willing female's neck and shoved her back. She staggered but moaned, too high from his bite to care how he treated her, too deep under his spell. He tore the skimpy red dress from the brunette, exposing her breasts and the tiny excuse for panties, nothing more than a scrap of scarlet material. She whimpered as he palmed her full breasts and he smiled slowly as the buzzing in his mind, the burning on his back, grew stronger.

Oh yes, his voyeur was very aware of his actions, was focused on him now.

He hoped the bitch got an eyeful.

Scarlet spilled down his blood host's chest from the multiple wounds on her throat and he growled as he swooped on that trail, lapping it up and following the lines back to the puncture marks. She moaned sweetly, writhed and rocked in his arms, and he clutched her to him, planted both hands on her bare backside and dug his claws into the peachy globes.

He licked the wounds, each sweep harder than the last, and then let out a feral snarl as he sank his fangs back into her. She jerked against him, her keening cry echoing around the sparsely furnished drawing room. Ecstasy. He could feel it in her.

But he couldn't find it for himself.

Not anymore.

The bitch had made sure of that.

He pulled his fangs free and bit down again, and again, and each time the female shuddered and cried in pleasure, began to sob as she wriggled in his arms, the scent of her arousal permeating the air. The rougher he was with her, the more she got off on it, and he had chosen her for that exact reason.

If he had to do this, if he had to use something that haunted his every waking hour, and sleeping one, then he would make sure that the one sharing the moment with him witnessed just how brutal he could be.

Just what she had made him.

He tore into the female's neck, rending deep puncture wounds that spilled blood like a waterfall down her bare breasts, the warm liquid soaking into his black shirt and sticking it to his chest. His heart thumped a painful rhythm against his ribs, blood pumping hard and hunger at the helm as he drank from the female.

Gods, he wanted her.

She squirmed against him, moaning in sweet supplication, rubbing her bare curves against his clothed body.

He wanted to fuck her.

Just as he wanted to screw every female who acted as a blood host for him.

It wasn't going to happen though, and that knowledge only made him rougher with her as the buzzing in his mind and across his back mocked him now, a constant reminder that he hadn't been able to get hard for a female for almost a century now.

All because of the bitch in his head.

Raw anger surged through him and he drank deeper, courted the darkness in the hope it might take him away from this room, from this female and the other one who haunted him.

Humiliated him.

But his bloodlust was an uncooperative bastard, seemingly determined to see him suffer in other ways tonight, refusing to come to his aid when he needed it most, needed to drown in oblivion and forget everything.

Images of *her* filled his mind and his body instantly responded, his cock twitching in his black trousers and beginning to stir, and he knew *she* would have felt it in him. He groaned, slowed his drinking and rubbed against the female, making her aware of his hardening shaft. She moaned low in her throat and dropped her hand to the front of his trousers, palmed him and made him harder still.

He lifted his head from the female's neck and kissed up it to her jaw, heading for her mouth. She rubbed him harder, sending shivers tripping through him, and he seized her lips in a hard kiss, determined not to squander this rare chance. Her fingers tugged at his fly and he willed her on, wanted to feel her hot hand on his flesh, needed to finally find release with a female. It was going better than usual. He couldn't remember the last time he had been hard for a female.

Her hand found his shaft.

"Gods, take me, Lord Van der Garde," she whispered.

Not the voice of the female in his head.

He instantly deflated, his cock going limp and useless in her hand. He shoved her off him on a snarl and tucked himself away as he glared at her.

"You were told not to speak," he growled and advanced on her, and she backed towards the dark wooden door of the drawing room.

He scooped up her red dress and threw it at her as her back hit the deep green wall near the door. She hastily caught it and covered herself, her hands shaking as she fumbled with the material, her dark eyes enormous.

Flooded with fear.

Grave stalked towards her, wrestling with the darkness as it rose within him, demanded he deal with the female. She would speak. She would tell others in the town what had happened here, and he would be humiliated all over again.

She turned to her right, hand stretching for the gold knob on the door.

He kicked off and had her throat clutched in his right hand before she could reach it. Her back slammed against the green wall and he loomed over her, aware that his eyes had changed as the room brightened. She stared up into them, panting hard, her face paling and tears filling her eyes.

"I told you not to speak," he snarled again and leaned closer, made sure she got a good look at his fangs and his crimson eyes, was aware his would be the last face she saw if she dared to say a word to anyone.

As much as he wanted to kill her, she would be missed by the local bordello, and the trail would lead back to him. He hadn't worked hard to secure a position of respect in the area only to ruin it because one blood host whore didn't know her place.

"I'm sorry," she choked out and lowered her gaze to his chest. "I forgot... it felt so good... I forgot. It won't happen again, my lord."

Too right it wouldn't.

He eased the pressure on her throat and stepped back, drew down a deep breath to centre himself and then leaned to his left, twisted the doorknob and opened it for her.

"Return to me in two days. Remember your place and the rules next time."

She pushed away from the wall, her mouth opening and then closing, and he knew he had given her punishment enough for her crime. If he had to go without, then she would go without too. Normally he made sure she found release, but tonight neither of them would leave satisfied.

She lowered her head, nodded and then hurried away from him.

Grave stood there in the open door, fighting the rising silence in the room, the quiet that he despised almost as much as the female in his head, because it was in the times of solitude and silence that she had the strongest hold over him.

He pushed her away, not wanting to think about her now, and slammed the door behind him with enough force that one of the oil paintings on the plum wall of the corridor crashed to the dark wooden floor. He stormed along the hallway, heading away from the drawing room and back to his apartments on the other side of the building.

The buzzing in his mind lingered and he struggled against it, tried to force the connection between them closed. Hunger and need chafed at him, his pulse pounding with them, urging him into finding another woman in some dumb hope that this time he would be able to slake both of his thirsts.

He wrestled with them too, unwilling to give her that much power over him. He had to open his connection to her and use it just to get his fangs to cooperate when he wanted to bite a woman, and that was humiliating enough, showed him constantly the hold she still had over him all these decades later. He was damned if he was going to think of her in order to fuck a female.

Although, it had been easier tonight. Was there a possibility that her hold over him was finally weakening as they approached a century apart?

Could he finally break free of her?

The part of him that always refused to be silent warned that it wasn't going to happen.

Thousands of women since her and not a single one had gotten him hard. Not a single fuck since she had screwed him over.

He hated her. Loathed her.

Once he had loved her.

He took the steps on the curving white marble staircase in the black-walled grand entrance hall two at a time, ignoring the two men that he passed as they saluted him by pressing their left hands to the breasts of their black knee-length jackets and lowered their heads.

His boots were loud on the wooden floor of the first level, and then the next curving staircase that led up to the second, where his quarters were located. He banked left and the cream corridor passed in a blur as he lost himself to thought, nursing the anger that thundered in his blood.

He shoved the wooden door at the end of the corridor open, stepped into his apartments, and slammed it behind him. He pressed his back to it and exhaled slowly as he stared at his elegant red-walled drawing room and through the large arched doorway to the sumptuous four-poster king-size bed in his ice blue bedroom.

Calm flowed over him as he rested against the door, his heartrate finally slowing to a more leisurely and normal rhythm.

He pushed away from the door, feeling that calm collecting inside him, growing stronger as he meandered around his home in the bastion of the First

Legion of the Preux Chevaliers. A legion he captained and a home that was his sanctuary.

A place he kept free of females.

Including the damned one in his head.

He closed his eyes and attempted to shut her out, but the buzzing persisted.

The calm he had fostered began to slip through his grasp. He walked into the left side of the drawing room and paced between the outside wall of his apartment and the wall of his bedroom, the heels of his riding boots marking the quickening rhythm of his steps on the dark wooden floor as he passed behind the black leather couch that faced the white marble mantelpiece. His pale blue eyes skimmed across the sash windows beside the unlit fire whenever he turned, alternating between the two that flanked the fireplace. The view beyond the panels of glass was sombre and dark, reflecting his mood.

Hell.

He had never felt the true effect of the dark realm before her.

He had fought in the ranks of the Preux Chevaliers, had elevated himself to the position of not only the captain of the First Legion but the sole leader of the entire army through blood and broken bones, and a little deception, and had gloried in war, solidifying his reputation and that of the corps under his command. Never had a vampire achieved the power he held in his hands, and gods, he had ruled this realm.

Until her.

Grave shoved her out of his thoughts and quickened his pacing, attempting to work off the energy that boiled inside him. Energy he would have expended in wild sex and quenching his thirst just decades ago. Now, only one female tasted sweet to him, only one could give him what he craved, so he only had one outlet for it.

War.

On the battlefield, he found the thrill he had been missing since falling into her trap. There, he could find release of a sort, was able to bite his foes in the heat of a fight for his life and experienced the pleasure of sating his bloodlust, feeding the beast within him.

Gods, he could bite any male he wanted any time, but he didn't want men. He wanted to sink his aching fangs into female flesh, soft and supple, delicately laced with the scent of blood, and taste sweetness and life, not ashes and death.

Grave halted and looked down at his hands.

His palms tingled, not with the memory of the female blood host's curves but the memory of *her*. They yearned to learn her curves again, to traverse paths he had found the deepest form of pleasure in, and feel her cool satin skin beneath his. Against his.

He snarled and stalked across the room, shoving his fingers through the longer lengths of his short dark brown hair and pulling it back until his scalp stung.

He had to free himself somehow.

A mirthless laugh escaped his lips.

How?

He had tried everything imaginable to achieve that freedom he desired. He had even left fresh from a war in the Third Realm of the demons to seek assistance in a fae town in the mortal world, searching for an answer from the witches there.

No one he spoke with, no amount of research he did, produced the cure he needed.

His heart hammered against his chest and he growled under his breath as he took agitated strides across his apartment. There had to be a way.

The buzzing in his mind grew stronger.

Bitch.

She was pushing, shoving the connection between them open.

He pivoted on his heel and his guard slipped.

An image of her fluttered into his head.

His body grew instantly hard.

Grave threw his head back and roared at the ceiling, darkness swelling through him like an oily tide, fed by the sudden surge of anger that filled his blood.

He harnessed the darkness, used it as he always did to give him strength, and slammed the connection between them shut.

The second it closed, the moment he felt the buzzing disappear and the mark on his back settle, his right hand dropped and he groaned as he palmed his hard length through his black trousers. Hot pleasure shot through his veins like the sweetest drug and he drowned in it, ignoring the shame that lurked in a dark corner of his mind as he undid his fly and stroked himself.

He hated thinking about her, about how beautiful she was, ethereal and breathtaking, but images of her filled his mind, remembered moments of bliss in her arms that had felt so real at the time.

He grunted as he grew harder, signalling an impending release.

Grave tore his hand away and roared again.

He shoved his cock back into his trousers and paced harder, cursing her name a thousand times over in his mind.

Cursing his own name with it.

The shame he constantly fought to hold back flooded him. Not only shame that he was reduced to touching himself to get any shred of pleasure and release, but the shame of being stripped of his strength and weakened by something that had happened close to a century ago.

He was a warrior, tested in battle and undefeated.

Yet she had defeated him.

She had used the softest part of him against himself, a part that never should have existed in the first place.

His heart.

He wouldn't give up though. He hadn't lived for millennia working his fingers to the bone to elevate himself to his current position in order for it to end here, now. There was so much more for him to do.

He stopped behind the black leather couch.

But it felt as if a clock was ticking as his heart slowly beat, a steady thump that sounded like a marching drum leading him towards his doom.

He raised his hands before him, turning them palms upwards, and stared at them, gritting his teeth and causing his fangs to cut into his gums as the tingling in his hands grew fiercer. He shook his head, silently pleading them not to do it, not when he had convinced himself he had been seeing things on that battlefield in the Third Realm.

They shimmered and turned ghostly, so he was able to see the floorboards through them.

He curled his fading fingers into fists and snarled a vicious curse as they became solid again, damning the female who had done this to him.

The phantom who had crushed his heart.

CHAPTER 2

Isla was in trouble. She had been in the midst of a battle between the elf kingdom and a dragon shifter's army when her curved blades had fallen from her hands and she had collapsed. It had only been for a moment, but it had left her cold.

She was turning incorporeal again.

Part of her had known this day would come, and she had thought she would accept it, but now that it was here, she wanted to fight it. She had grown used to having flesh and blood, substance like her dearest sister.

Her hands shook as she raced up the white stone steps from the town at the base of the spire of rock upon which her sister's castle stood, her eyes fixed on the towering fortress above her that glittered like snow in the waning light from the elf kingdom. Her long white hair bounced against her back as she lengthened her strides, taking two steps at a time now as she pushed herself to go faster. The demon soldiers of the First Realm moved aside for her as she rushed from her meeting in the garrison, driven to seek Melia.

Afraid.

She needed her sister, needed to speak with someone about what had happened. If anyone had an answer to her problem, it was Melia. She had been foolish to keep quiet about what had happened to her in the battle, had been stupid to believe it would be a one-time occurrence and that she would be fine. She should have spoken to Melia after the battle, but she had been too afraid to tell her, was still too afraid of what she might say. She needed to cling to hope, needed it with a ferocity that astounded her.

She had never realised just how much she had grown to love her life, had grown to love everything about it.

Except perhaps one thing—the reason she had sought the mage and subjected herself to the spell that had given her a solid form.

She reached the plateau where the castle stood and hurried across the courtyard, passing the beautiful white fountain that was the centre of so many happy memories of better days, long peaceful ones where she had spent all the hours with Melia, walking with her while she rocked her son to get him to settle.

The demons guarding the curved courtyard stood to attention, rising from the stone benches that surrounded the fountain and bowing their heads as they pressed their hands to the chest of their black uniform jackets. She nodded at each of them and slowed her pace, trying to collect herself as she approached the grand arched entrance of the white castle.

A few of the large demon males lifted their heads, their blue gazes inquisitive as they followed her. She knew she wasn't acting normally. When she passed through the courtyard, she often spoke with the guards, seeing how they were and inquiring about the families of those who had one, and carefully avoiding mentioning mates around the males who wore thick torcs. The heavy twisted bands of pale gold and black, closed tightly around their necks, signalled they were widowers and had lost their mate.

Just as Melia had lost hers, the First King, Valador, in a battle close to a century ago.

A battle Isla had witnessed, a death she had seen, and shortly afterwards had forsaken her life as a true phantom, turning her back on her incorporeal form and the power it gave to her, in order to become flesh and blood.

In the name of revenge.

She had stepped into her corporeal life for that purpose, but she had come to love touching things, and the sensation of wind in her white hair or sun warming her bones through her blue leather clothes, and she didn't want to return to an empty existence so desperate for the feel of another beneath her hands, pressing against her body, that she would lure them to their doom.

Isla entered the arched hallway of the castle, her pace quickening again as the feel of eyes on her faded. Her steps made no sound as she flowed along the corridor, her blue eyes fixed on the arched white double doors at the other end of it, beyond the hallways and staircases that branched off from it.

She pushed one of the doors open as she reached them and scanned the enormous grand room on the other side. The spiky white throne on the dais at the far end of the aisle and the white stone pews that formed two columns down the length of the middle of the square room were empty.

Where was Melia?

As acting king of the First Realm of the demons, Melia was normally in the grand hall during the day hours, receiving many from the kingdom and hearing what they had come to say. Of course, there were slow days, when few showed up to discuss anything from their neighbours and other demon realms, to new crops from the mortal world they wanted to attempt to grow in their fields of black earth.

Perhaps this was a slow day.

Isla had been too preoccupied with her current problem and her business advising on the movements of the legions around the realm to pay attention to her sister's schedule today.

She backed out of the room, closing the door behind her, and turned back along the corridor, heading for the closest white stone staircase that would take her up into the castle to where those of higher ranks had their quarters.

She was close to the top of the staircase on the first floor when a male stepped into her path, the impressive breadth of his bare chest blocking her view of the corridor beyond him and thick legs like tree trunks encased in rich blue leather stopping her from passing him.

Isla looked up into pale blue eyes ringed with cerulean, set in a rough but handsome enough face. Pale golden horns curled from behind his pointed ears, showcased by the way he had drawn his long blond hair back into a thong at the nape of his neck. His firm mouth flattened and then the right corner twitched into a half-smile.

"Always in a rush, Isla. Do you never slow down?" His deep baritone was warm with his teasing, a familiar and playful note that she had always enjoyed hearing.

He had been her first real friend in this world, a male who had become like a brother to her, as close as Melia and just as beloved by Isla.

"Frey," she said, a little out of breath which didn't help. His smile became a smirk, as if he had heard it and had won their round of teasing. "Do you know where Melia is?"

He nodded. "With Tarwyn in his chambers. I have just been there, but now I must leave."

"Leave?" Isla frowned and he sighed, the sound speaking of the weariness she could see in his blue eyes now she was looking for it. "You must rest."

He shook his head. "I am afraid I cannot. The borders with the Fourth Realm are being tested and I must lead my men there."

As commander of their legions, she could understand why he had to go, but as prince he had a duty in the castle too, one he often neglected in favour of the possibility of a battle. There hadn't been a fight in the First Realm for centuries, not since they had signed a peace treaty and aligned themselves with the Second Realm and the elf kingdom.

Frey was old enough to remember the time before that treaty though, and she knew from speaking with him during long quiet nights at the castle that he longed for war. He had missed out on his chance at it, unable to attend the battle in the elf kingdom because of his duties as prince, forced to remain in the castle with Tarwyn to protect him.

Tarwyn was but a child, a toddler despite being near to a century old now. It would be another five centuries at least before he could rule under his mother's and uncle's supervision.

Isla couldn't openly wish Frey war, but she did so silently as she stepped up into the corridor, tiptoed and pressed a kiss to his whiskered cheek.

"Try to find some rest." She settled back onto her feet and clasped his thickly hewn right shoulder. "You look awful."

He chuckled and waved her away, and she paused to watch him heading down the stairs.

With his back to her, he reminded her of Valador. Noble, kind and gentle Valador. Frey had the same qualities as his older brother, but it was balanced by a thirst for war, a hunger for violence that many demons possessed. Valador had always been happiest away from the battlefield.

Frey was happiest on it.

When he disappeared from view, she headed along the corridor, passing the white wooden door to her room and then the one just up the hallway that belonged to Frey, and then banked left at the junction. She stopped at a room on the right and knocked softly.

After a few seconds, the door opened to reveal Melia's smiling face. Her blue eyes seemed brighter today, but they were troubled, as they always were after Frey's visits.

Sometimes, Isla thought that he stayed away from the castle as much as he could not because he wanted to avoid his duties as a prince but because he wanted to avoid paining Melia with his presence. They both knew that Melia saw echoes of her lost love in Frey.

Just as her sister saw echoes of Valador in her son.

Isla's gaze sought Tarwyn and found him sitting on a brown fur near the fireplace to the left of the room, his focus locked on the wooden animals in front of him. His dishevelled sandy hair fell across his brow in unruly curls and his tongue poked from between his lips as he concentrated, pale blue eyes fixed with determination on the toys. Isla had brought them to Hell for him as a present from one of her trips to the mortal realm, hoping they would be educational for him.

A moment with Frey had prompted it when he had called a bear a donkey when she had been showing him photographs of the time she had spent in the region of Canada and had then called a deer a bear. Of course, he had known a wolf when he had seen one. No surprise since werewolves made the free realm in Hell their home. She had expected the demon to know a bear though. He must have fought in at least one battle involving shifters of their kind.

So she had purchased the wooden zoo animals when she had seen them in a store.

To this day, part of her still wondered if she had done it to educate Frey too, intending for him to play with them with Tarwyn and learn the difference between a bear and a damned deer and donkey.

"He seems well today," Melia said in a hushed tone, her voice a soft melody in the quiet white room.

Isla knew Melia wasn't talking about the boy she watched, but the man who had just left.

"Impatient," she said in response and Melia's pale lips curled into a faint smile. "He wants war."

Her sister glanced across at her and sighed softly, her shoulders shifting with it. "He has not forgiven me for making him remain in the castle while we answered the call of the elves."

"He will in time. He's stubborn."

Melia looked away from her. "Like his brother."

Isla's heart ached for her sister as she drifted into the room, the long white skirt of her corseted dress gliding across the wooden floor in her wake, the pure colourless fabric matching her fall of hair that draped across her slender shoulders.

Isla closed the white door and stepped into the room, wishing there was something she could say to take her sister's mind off Valador, even when she knew it was impossible. Melia saw him every day in their son.

Tarwyn lifted his head, noticing her at last. He was on his bare feet a second later, rushing across the room to hug her legs. His cerulean trousers blended with hers and matched her corset, but where hers were traditional leather, his clothes were soft cotton more suited to a child. He tipped his head back and beamed up at her, his blue eyes sparkling, and began prattling away in the demon tongue about his animals and Frey's visit.

She listened to him for a while, aware that Melia was watching them from near the arched window. She petted his messy head of blond hair, teased the small horns that were growing in nicely now he was nearly one hundred, and looked at her sister. Melia smiled back at her, the hurt in her eyes gone, replaced with affection and warmth.

Tarwyn took hold of Isla's hand and tried to pull her towards the fur rug.

"I will play soon. I must speak with your mother first," she said in the demon tongue and he huffed and pouted, but released her and went back to his toys.

Isla waited for him to sit back down before she crossed the bedchamber to Melia.

Melia's gaze was on Tarwyn again, a softness in it that made Isla want to sigh and wish for her own child.

Tarwyn was a little miracle, probably the only child of his kind in existence. Phantoms normally bred other phantoms, but the spell that gave Melia substance had allowed her to bear the offspring of her mate, bringing not a phantom but a demon into the world.

"You seem troubled today. What is wrong?" Melia said in English and Isla realised her sister had stopped looking at Tarwyn and was staring at her now.

She wasn't sure where to begin.

She searched for a starting point, and the courage to tell Melia what she had done and what was happening to her. Her sister wasn't going to be happy with her. Isla had kept the true reason behind why she had chosen to become corporeal hidden from her sister. Melia had a kind heart for a phantom, a quality that had made her perfect for Valador.

Isla lacked what her sister had been given by the gods. She had kindness in her, but not as Melia did. When faced with someone who had wronged her, or brought harm to her kin, she was as cruel and lethal as any other phantom. Cold. Heartless.

Melia's sky blue gaze drifted down to her left hand and Isla stilled as she realised she was playing with the braid that hung from her temple on that side. The crystals at the end of the plait were warm beneath her fingertips. She looked down at them, the crimson stark against her pale skin.

A reminder.

She had found the crystals the night she had broken from Grave, had run headlong into the darkness and hadn't stopped until she had been close to collapse, surrounded by an unfamiliar town and strange faces, leagues away from the comfort of his arms.

She had found a place to rest and an elderly woman at a stall in the market had tried to sell her craft to her, and Isla had seen the crystals and silver wire.

She had braided a length of her long white hair on her left temple, close to her ear, and had woven an intricate knot with the silver wire, slipped the red crystal on and then made another knot below it. On the right side, she had done the same with a blue crystal.

Red for the vampire in her heart.

Blue for the phantom she would become again.

A reminder that one day, everything she loved in this world would slip from her grasp, and it was no one's fault but her own.

"Isla?" Melia drifted closer and her eyes slipped shut as her sister's hand came to rest gently on her shoulder, and warmth spread from that spot despite the coolness of her sister's skin. "Speak to me."

Isla opened her blue eyes and clutched the red crystal in her fist.

Her vampire mate.

She still dreamed of him every night, and still used the connection between them to keep an eye on him, and still hurt when he used it to get back at her, to show her things she didn't want to see.

Things that broke her heart.

Things that made her feel guilty.

When she had broken from him, she had convinced herself that she had done the right thing and she had felt nothing for the vampire, no real feelings anyway. She had tried to escape what she had done to him, but she had found she couldn't, and over the decades she had started to feel guilty about what she had done.

She had seen in her dreams, and in the things he showed to her, that her actions tormented him—her betrayal and the knowledge that the clock was constantly ticking for him. He lived his life waiting for the inevitable day when he would become incorporeal—a phantom male. He wasn't alone. It hung over her too.

Her freedom was about to be snatched from her and she was starting to feel there was nothing she could do about it. She didn't want to go back to being a ghost.

She didn't want that life for Grave either.

She held her hands out in front of her and stared at them.

"Isla." Melia's soft voice had gone dark, a thunderclap in her mind that warned her sister knew something was wrong, something terrible.

She looked up into her sister's eyes, found love and despair in them, and forced the words out.

"My hands faded on the battlefield."

Melia shook her head and stepped closer, seized both of her shoulders and held her so tightly that it hurt. She savoured the pain, because it made her feel whole, solid, as if she wasn't about to disappear from this world others enjoyed without appreciating what they had been given by the gods and drift back into the cold world of the phantoms, denied the pleasures others took for granted.

Her sister's expression turned grave.

It only worsened when Isla gave herself another push.

"I am not the only one this will be happening to," she whispered and her sister closed her eyes, lowered her head and sighed.

"What have you done?" Melia lifted her head again, canting it to her right, and looked back into her eyes, her eyebrows furrowed and blue gaze filled with a mixture of sympathy and anger.

"Valador… I saw him fall… I saw the male who claimed his life and I-I… I took vengeance on him." She wasn't sure she could say any more, not when Melia's pretty face was shifting towards horrified.

"I told you of the phantom mage who had made me corporeal because I believed that you sought substance purely so you could be with me and Tarwyn when he was born," Melia snapped and the air in the room chilled, the light sucking from it, turning it shades of grey instead of white. "Valador would not have wanted such a thing. If I had known your plan, I would have stopped you."

It wasn't the response Isla had expected and she staggered back a step, slipping from her sister's grasp and shaking as she battled the surge of guilt and shame, and the pain that always came with it. It beat fiercely in her heart.

"I saw the vampire kill your husband… I wanted to avenge him." As any phantom would have, but the look on her sister's face said that it hadn't been what she had wanted.

Being corporeal had affected Melia's mind, had softened it and destroyed her phantom nature. It had made her weak.

"*Vengeance*, Sister. I wanted vengeance and I took it. I am a phantom," Isla barked and regretted it when Melia only sighed, the sorrow remaining in her eyes, leaving her feeling that she was trying to justify what she had done when she didn't honestly believe she had done the right thing.

It had felt like the right thing at the time, when she had been a phantom.

But then she had fallen in love with the vampire.

"All you have done is doom yourself and now I will lose both my husband and my beloved sister." Melia's words were softly spoken but they fell like lead around her, striking hard and shaking her.

"I can fix it," she said.

Melia was silent for so long that Isla's nerves kicked up a notch, her heart pounding erratically against her chest as she struggled to find a way to undo what she had done. Was it possible?

"You will need a mage," Melia said at last and relief swept through Isla but lasted only as long as it took for her sister to speak again. "They are rare now, and you must try to find the one who performed the spell on you. He may be able to fix it... but..."

Isla swallowed hard. "But?"

Melia looked down at her feet. "It will be best you take the vampire with you."

"No," Isla snapped and sliced her hand through the air between them. "No."

It wasn't going to happen. Grave hated her, probably wanted nothing more than to kill her. His reputation before she had tricked him into becoming a phantom had been deadly enough, should have warned her away, but now he was second to the Devil in the list of most feared males in Hell.

Going anywhere near him would be a death sentence.

"You have done more than merely trick the vampire into becoming a phantom. You are bound to him. The mage's spell would have made it happen. To make a phantom flesh and blood requires a powerful bond... and that bond must be periodically renewed. I had thought your bond to me was enough... but now I see how wrong I have been. It is your bond to the vampire that gives you substance." Melia drifted closer again and fixed her with soft blue eyes filled with fear laced with love, and something else.

Something that chilled Isla's blood and sent a shiver down her spine.

"I will bond with another man," Isla blurted and Melia shook her head, causing her long white hair to sway across her bare shoulders.

"That is not possible, and you know it. You are bound to the vampire and the vampire to you. If he does not help you, you will both fade."

That chill grew stronger, the shiver fiercer. "I do not wish to become incorporeal again."

Her sister's expression turned pained, flooded with sorrow. "You will not become incorporeal, Isla... you will fade."

Fade.

Fade was the phantom way of saying die.

Isla swallowed to wet her suddenly dry throat and slowly shook her head as she looked at her sister and realised her sister knew first-hand that the danger was very real.

"How long do you have?" Isla whispered, unable to get her voice to work as her throat tightened and heart ached at the thought of losing her sister.

Melia smiled sadly and looked off to her right, at her son, a wealth of love in her eyes. "I will live long enough to see Tarwyn grow into a man and then I will join my love on the other side. I am only able to be here now because of my bond to Tarwyn. He has his father's blood and that is keeping me corporeal. I am not sad, for I knew what was to come when I bound my life to my love's."

Her sister was going to choose to fade.

Isla's knees weakened and she had to lock them to keep standing as that knowledge crashed over her, battering her and stealing her strength.

Her sister was going to choose death over life.

Isla wanted the opposite, and that desire flowed through her stronger than ever as she thought about what her sister was going to do. She refused to make such a choice for herself and she refused to condemn Grave to death too.

He was going to kill her the moment he set eyes on her rather than hearing her out, but Melia was right and she had to at least attempt to convince him to work with her to find a phantom mage. If she could just get him to listen to her, she was sure she could make him see reason.

She almost laughed out loud at that.

Grave had lost all reason when she had betrayed him. He had become a vampire bent on hunting her, hurting her, and she was proposing to walk right into his hands and place her life into them.

He was going to live up to his reputation, the name Hell had given him and one he justly deserved.

The King of Death.

CHAPTER 3

Grave kicked off hard, his left boot skidding on the loose black earth as he propelled himself to his right. He rolled across the ground, evading the meaty fist that had been aimed at his head and came up on his feet. Behind him, the demon male turned on a snarl and Grave dipped his body low and swept his left leg out in a swift arc, catching the male across the back of his knees as he launched another attack.

The large demon hit the earth with a thud and a growl, and Grave sprang to his feet, scooped up his fallen blade and brought it down in a fast arc, little more than a blur of silver cutting through the low evening light of the Seventh Realm.

It sliced through the demon's neck just as easily.

Blood sprayed in a burst of crimson and then dwindled to a steady trickle that pumped in time with the male's heart as it slowed to a halt.

Grave breathed hard, the scent of blood overwhelming as it drenched the churned earth and the bodies strewn across it. Several of his men had fallen, their corpses resting in tangled heaps beside those of their allies, the demons of the Seventh Realm, and their enemies, the demons of the Sixth.

He licked his bloodied fangs, savouring the rich tang of his victims. The darkness within him pushed harder and he embraced it, savoured it as he savoured the blood. Nurtured it.

Asher, his second in command, a male with ice blond hair stained crimson in places, halted beside him for a heartbeat, long enough to check on him and give a brief nod before he kicked off, a blur in the falling darkness.

The male knew better than to coddle him in battle, or question him, although it had been clear he had wanted to do both.

With a low snarl, Grave stalked forwards, prowling through the fallen demons and vampires, his scarlet eyes locked ahead of him on the battle where it had moved back towards the border.

They were winning, driving out the demons of the Sixth Realm who had dared to invade the Seventh.

The battle still raged, hundreds of demons of the Sixth Realm, marked by their golden-brown horns, chestnut hair and golden eyes, clashed against his men and the demons of the Seventh. The sound of war filled his ears, and his heart, the constant din of battle axes and swords striking and agonised bellows as warriors fell mingled with shouts of victory.

Gods, he loved war.

Courted it almost as fervently as he courted his bloodlust.

Foolish were the vampires who feared it.

He licked his fangs and bit back a moan as he thought about sinking them into demon flesh together with his claws, tearing apart his foes to sate the dark hunger riding him.

A dark hunger that gave him strength, power to defeat any foe he met in battle. Bloodlust that had given him the reputation he had fought for and deserved. A reputation that meant more to him than anything else.

Two large demons of the Sixth Realm cut down one from the Seventh and turned his way, slow smiles curving their lips as they saw he was alone. Fools. They thought they could end him?

He laughed as he flexed his fingers around the black and red hilt of his katana, the sound so out of place in the midst of battle that it gave the demons pause.

Grave used it to his advantage.

With all the preternatural speed of his kind, he closed the gap between them and had his blade buried hilt-deep in the gut of the demon on the right before the male had even seen him. The male let out a garbled cry and the other one turned on him, raising his double-axe to cut Grave down.

He left his blade in the stomach of the first demon and spun to face the second. The axe came down fast and he grunted as he raised his right arm above his head and the thick black handle struck his forearm. Pain splintered in a ring where it had hit, warning of a fracture. Grave paid his body no heed and snarled as he shoved upwards, knocking the axe and the male's arm up with it.

The demon staggered backwards and Grave sprung forwards, sank the claws of his right hand deep into the demon's fleshy left shoulder and bit down hard on the right side of his throat. The male roared and grabbed him, and Grave's fangs tore through his neck as he was ripped away.

He flew through the air and landed hard on a corpse with a grunt.

Bastard.

He licked his fangs and pushed onto his feet, coming to face his foe again.

One of his men was there already, battling the demon male, and Grave growled low in his throat at the sight, the darkness that flowed through his veins growing blacker as his mind whispered dangerous words, taunting him with the fact someone had stolen his prey.

He had been weak again, and now someone had taken what was his.

He hunched forwards and roared out his fury, and both the demon and the vampire stopped with their axe and sword in mid swing.

He would kill both of them. The demon for the fun of it and the vampire because the impudent bastard had stolen his prey.

No one took what was his.

No one.

He ran at both males and the vampire was gone in a flash, disappearing from the fray like the pathetic creature he was. He would deal with him later. He snarled as the demon swung the axe at him and threw himself feet first under the blow, skidding across the ground and ending up next to the first demon.

Grave grinned.

He wrapped his fingers around the hilt of his sword and slowly pulled it free of the corpse as he rose onto his feet.

His senses warned of the demon behind him.

He took his time wiping the blade clean on the corpse's leathers.

Could almost feel the fetid breath of the second demon on the back of his neck and hear the whisper of death as the axe sliced through the air aimed for his head.

Fool.

Grave dropped to his knees and the demon's axe cut through the air above him. He twisted as he shoved onto his feet and arced his blade upwards, cutting across the demon's broad chest. The male bellowed and stumbled back two steps before recovering and swinging the axe again. Grave dodged right but the blade nicked his shoulder, cutting through his black shirt, and the scent of his own blood laced the air, strong on his senses.

He saw red.

In a blur of speed, he came around behind the demon and drove his sword forwards, piercing deep into the male's side, a wound meant to slow rather than kill.

This one had cut him, and that meant this one died by his fangs.

The male staggered forwards and tried to turn, but Grave leaped on his back and tipped him off balance. The demon landed face first on the bloodied black earth and Grave slammed into his bare back. He grabbed the demon's left horn and yanked his head back as he struck hard, sinking his fangs into the right side of his throat. The male struggled, bucking wildly, and Grave bit deeper and raked his fangs through the male's flesh, cutting long grooves into his skin. Blood poured from the wound, flowing so quickly he almost choked on it as he tried to swallow it all, his bloodlust demanding he didn't waste a drop.

He gulped it down and groaned as the demon's struggles weakened and his heart began to falter. There was no sweeter thrill than this for him, not anymore. War. Gods how he craved it.

Each blow that bruised his flesh, shattered bone and tore muscle.

Each dance with death.

He would wage war for free, but the Preux Chevaliers traditionally worked for the highest bidder, and who was he to turn down a tidy sum of gold?

He had been raised an aristocrat, born to one of the most powerful pureblood vampire families, and as an aristocrat he had grown accustomed to a certain level of comfort and convenience, and that required money.

He wasn't an elite, those born to a family with lowly turned humans in their ranks or sired by such a creature.

He was an aristocrat.

A pureblood.

As all in the Preux Chevaliers were.

They were the most powerful of their kind. Faster, stronger, superior in every way to an elite. Bred from the purest blood, able to trace their ancestry back to the elves.

But with pure blood came what many in the vampire world viewed as a terrible curse—bloodlust.

He released the demon when his heart gave out and sat back on him, breathing hard and grinning as his blood thundered in his veins, pleasure rolling hot and sweet through him.

Pleasure his bloodlust gave to him.

Pleasure that had become his everything.

Only a fool would deny themselves the ecstasy of sating their bloodlust. With every step closer to the edge that he took, that ecstasy only grew more intense, more satisfying, until he was chasing the next high, aching for it to be better than the last.

His crimson eyes scanned the battle that had moved further from him, nearing the black mountains that formed the border between the Seventh Realm and the Devil's domain, the path the demons of the Sixth had taken to avoid entering the Fifth to reach the Seventh.

He gave himself another minute to savour the high of his kill and then lumbered onto his feet, pulled his blade free and cleaned it on the dead male's dark gold leathers. He could feel his bloodlust fading again, satisfied for now, but it would soon rise again, returning to embrace him and deliver him another high, and another victory.

Grave prowled through the corpses towards the battle, itching with the need to hurl himself into another fight, to feel fists striking his flesh and cracking his bones. The darkness that had been ebbing away began to flow back again, slowly filling his veins as he stalked towards his next victim, hungry for more.

Itching for another fix.

He singled out the male he had decided led the Sixth Realm demons, one who stood at least three inches taller than the rest and he had caught barking orders at the others. He wielded his broadsword with devastating skill, cutting down a demon of the Seventh and injuring one of Grave's men in the process. The demon commander whirled to face three vampires who had come up behind him, and Grave snarled as he spotted his second in command among them.

"Asher," Grave barked and the blond looked in his direction. Grave shifted his gaze from him to the demon and snarled, "Mine."

Out of the corner of his eye, Asher bowed his head and signalled to his two men, and together they backed away from the demon as he turned to face Grave.

The male shoved bloodstained fingers through his wild chestnut hair, preening it back from his face, and smirked at him. Crimson coated every inch of his broad bare chest and had soaked into his deep gold leathers, forming dark veins across the material. The demon flexed the fingers of his other hand around the hilt of his broadsword, a blade that matched Grave in height, and stared him down, his golden eyes glowing brightly in the darkness.

"Come, Little Vampire." The warrior crooked a clawed finger, his English sounding rough with his demonic accent, and grinned again, flashing fangs as his horns curled from behind his pointed ears, twisting around like a ram's. "Let us see who is the true King of Death."

Grave readied his blade and pressed the ball of his right foot into the black earth, preparing to launch at the male and do just that.

Darkness rolled over the land, visceral power that pressed down on him and chilled his blood.

Around him, the battle stilled, warriors frozen in position, locked in combat for a heartbeat before they all broke apart and turned as one towards the black mountains.

Grave looked there.

A male stood on a huge rock at the base of the mountain, just metres beyond the edge of the battle. He towered over them, black eyes surveying every warrior below him, gold elliptical pupils flashing as his gaze shifted quickly from one male to the next. His stance was casual, the black gauntlet covering the lower half of his right arm resting on the hilt of a huge black broadsword that stood beside him, the point buried into the solid rock, but Grave had the feeling this male hadn't come to the edge of the Devil's domain just to watch them fight.

The demon straightened and curled his clawed fingers over the pommel of his sword as his black eyebrows pinched low and his broad lips flattened.

Grave watched him closely, wary of the newcomer. He was young, appearing little more than in his early twenties to mortal eyes, but that meant nothing when it came to demons, especially those of the Devil's ranks.

This male could easily decimate both sides of the warriors gathered before him.

It was rare for one of his kind to leave the Devil's realm, although as far as Grave could tell, the male still stood within the threshold of his dark lord's lands.

The sensation of death and power that he exuded seemed to grow stronger as he searched the faces of the warriors, and many of them began backing away from him, some of the Preux Chevaliers included.

Grave remained where he was, beyond the line of demons and vampires now forming between him and the newcomer.

The young male ran the claws of his left gauntlet around the curve of his polished black horn and then ran the pad of his thumb across the pointed tip. They looked as if they had been sharpened, made even more deadly.

The longer Grave watched him, the stronger a sensation within him grew, a feeling that he knew the male even though he also felt sure he had never met him before.

He was oddly familiar.

But then, most demons looked the same to him.

The male's broad bare chest shifted in a deep sigh and he moved his left foot, his shoulders twisting as he went to turn away.

His eyes landed on Grave.

He stilled and narrowed his gaze, and his demeanour darkened, the sense of power that flowed from him becoming a crushing wave as he turned back to face him and lifted his left hand.

Pointed right at Grave.

"You," the male snarled through sharp fangs and Grave had half a mind to point a finger at his chest and blink hard.

Instead, he remained perfectly still and held his calm façade even as a question pounded in his mind.

What had he done to deserve the bastard's attention?

He scowled as the ranks of warriors between him and the demon parted, all three factions quick to clear the way, removing themselves from the firing line.

Grave bared his fangs at Asher, daring him to back away any further than he already had.

So a demon of the Devil's ranks had come to them looking for a fight.

It wasn't the first time he had fought a demon of his kind and it wouldn't be the last. He had fought older, stronger demons from the Devil's domain than this one and lived to tell the tale.

He would mount the bastard's head on his wall.

Or his entire carcass on the towering metal spikes outside his palace.

The demon pulled his black broadsword free of the rock and dropped to the earth, the obsidian armour on his lower half rattling as he landed hard. He straightened and the warriors around Grave backed off another step. Asher wisely remained where he was, his sword at the ready and his crimson eyes locked on the demon.

Grave calmly walked forwards, into the gap between the two groups of warriors. The situation was turning strange, with warriors who had been fighting to the death just minutes ago now united in silence in the face of a potential new enemy.

An enemy that had singled him out for some damned reason.

"What do you want?" Grave barked and the male's black eyes darkened.

"You," he hissed and stalked towards him, crossing the threshold between the realms.

Grave arched an eyebrow. "Any reason why? I was in the middle of a battle so I would like to know why you chose to disturb it and by the looks of things ruin my chances of getting paid for the job we had undertaken."

"A job," the demon spat and flexed black clawed fingers around the hilt of his obsidian blade. "For a price you will do anything... kill anyone?"

He nodded.

Maybe the demon had come to buy the services of the Preux Chevaliers.

That thought died when the demon disappeared only to reappear right in front of him, launched a hand out and grabbed him around the throat. He choked as the demon lifted him from the ground by his neck and kicked out, striking hard with his boots, battering the male's legs.

He sensed Asher rush forwards.

"Retreat," Grave bit out when the demon turned his black eyes on his men, his elliptical pupils little more than gold slits burning in their centres, and he felt the male's intent to attack.

Whatever he had done, he could find a way out of it, but he wasn't going to put his men in the firing line for no reason. He was their captain, their commander, and he was damned if they were going to die because of him.

"Retreat." He squeezed that word out again and relief poured through him when he heard Asher barking orders to his men and sensed them moving back, drifting into the distance.

The lands around them emptied, leaving him alone with the demon male.

"How very noble," the demon said, his voice a low purr laced with darkness, fury so strong that Grave could almost feel it sliding over his skin, tugging at his bloodlust. The male's eyes slid back to him and narrowed again as he studied him, tilting his head to his left. "Odd that you have such an approach with your subordinates when you do not extend that nobility to others."

To others?

Grave frowned and grasped the male's wrist and hand in an attempt to lessen the pressure on his throat.

The male snarled and tightened his grip in response, and Grave choked as his head felt as if it was going to burst and he swore he could feel his trachea collapsing.

He kicked out again and the male snarled, twisted towards the mountains and hurled him at them. Pain exploded across his back as he slammed into the rock on which the demon had stood and he breathed hard as he collapsed onto the black earth, wheezing as he fought for air.

"Where was your nobility when you murdered my family?" the demon growled and the ground shook with each word, causing small chunks of rock to break off the boulder at Grave's back and rain down on him.

He closed his eyes and flinched as one struck his temple and he felt the sting, smelled the fresh blood as it bloomed to the surface of the cut.

He had murdered the demon's family?

"I came only to deliver a message... this time." The male's voice was so loud that Grave tensed, his eyes shooting open.

Boots filled his vision.

A face filled it a moment later as the demon hauled him off the ground by his throat again and shoved him against the rock. A face filled with fury, twisted in pain and hatred, darkened by anger. Razor sharp fangs flashed between his teeth as he snarled and his black horns flared further forwards, so close to Grave's face as the demon leaned towards him that he leaned back, pressing the back of his aching head into the rock.

"I came to deliver a warning."

Grave swallowed as best he could. He wasn't sure he should be thankful about the fact he was going to survive this encounter, not when the air around him had slowly turned ominous, a sense of doom steadily growing within him.

"I have spent my years well, Lord Van der Garde," the male hissed in his face and smiled slowly. "My dark master gave me access to his seers... gave me knowledge and power. I know of Night and Bastian... your brothers... I know of your cousins, Snow and Antoine... I know of their family."

Grave tried to shake his head. No. He wouldn't let this bastard target his family because of something he had done.

He lunged forwards and cracked his forehead against the demon's, and the male grunted and reeled backwards from the force of the blow, his grip loosening. Grave broke free and shoved his hands against the male's chest, and then darted around him, gaining space and freedom.

He would kill the bastard right here and put an end to his threat.

He ran across the black earth, crimson eyes furiously scanning it for a weapon, any weapon.

The air behind him shifted and the ground slammed into his face, and he cried out as his right scapula shattered under the force of the demon's blow.

The male leaned over him, bringing his mouth so close to Grave's right ear that his left horn stabbed into the nape of his neck.

Grave stilled, heart pounding as he felt the press of the male's horn against his spine. One wrong move and the male would kill him with it, he knew it.

He gritted his teeth and bit back the growl of frustration that wanted to burst from his lips. As soon as the male gave him space, he would find a way to break free again. He had to bide his time. He would find a way to break free and he would find a blade, and he would cut the bastard's head off.

"Such anger," the male whispered into his ear. "Imagine how I feel... imagine seven hundred years of waiting... yearning to kill you and your kin as you killed mine before my very eyes... taking my family from me... leaving me to die in that castle... nothing more than a helpless babe."

A shiver ran down Grave's spine.

He remembered that night, and he hadn't been alone in leading the attack on the black castle at the edge of the Devil's lands. Snow had been with him.

It wasn't possible the demon had been at the castle though.

They had been thorough, had checked every room, every damned nook and cranny to ensure they had killed the entire family of demons. It had been part of the contract they had been carrying out for the Preux Chevaliers. The

Seventh King of demons had wanted the noble family eradicated because they had been sending the more powerful Devil's demons to raze their lands and kill their people.

It had been a message to the Devil, a warning to remove his cherished elite from the borders of their realms, and it had worked.

But this male had survived, and now he was sending a message to Grave, one he couldn't dare to ignore.

"Next time our paths cross… I will be delivering the heads of your entire family… one by one."

The demon stilled and Grave could feel his eyes on his back, close to his hand where it pressed into his broken right shoulder, keeping him pinned face down on the black ground.

Grave gasped as the male ripped the shirt from his back and squeezed his eyes shut as claws raked lightly over his skin, tracing a pattern between his shoulder blades.

"A mating mark," the demon murmured and continued to follow the lines of it.

Grave swallowed against the bile rising up his throat, fought the flood of vile oily darkness that pulled at his bloodlust as the male stroked his claws across his flesh and his power flowed over him. Into him.

Power that Grave knew he wasn't strong enough to overcome on the battlefield, not as he was now, weakened by the very mark the male had noticed.

"This is unexpected." The demon moved his hand to the back of Grave's head and shoved it down against the rough ground, and he grimaced as pain splintered across his skull. The male leaned closer again and smirked. "Unexpected but not unwelcomed. I will take my time with the female when I find her. Perhaps I will even keep her alive for a while… to serve me."

Grave snarled and flashed his fangs, unable to keep still any longer. No one touched Isla. No one but him. He was going to be the one to end her, not some demon. Her life was his to take in payment for what she had done to him.

The male pressed harder on his head and he ground his teeth against the pain, stilled beneath the demon, fearing he would crush his skull if he kept fighting him even when he knew the demon wanted him alive.

Wanted him to suffer.

"I will send you to your death soon enough… but first you must witness the bloody end of your family… and you will die with the knowledge that your mate is forever in these hands." He brought his claws close to Grave's face and Grave flinched away, unable to stop himself from reacting.

The demon's smile grew wider. Darker.

And then he was gone.

Grave remained face down on the earth, breathing hard as he battled the sudden flood of emotions, feelings he hadn't experienced in a very long time.

Fear. Despair.

He rolled onto his back and stared at the dark grey sky of Hell, and the mark on his back warmed, began to tingle as a connection started to open.

He slammed it shut on her, unwilling to allow her to see him like this, shaken and afraid, fearing for his life and that of his family.

He had already lost too many of them.

He pulled down a hard breath, curled his fingers into fists until his claws bit into his palms, and then roared his fury at the sky, stopping only when his lungs burned and head turned. His fangs bit into his gums as he snarled, fury obliterating his fear, darkness destroying the despair.

He was the King of Death, second only to the Devil in this dark realm. A lowly prince of demons was no match for him.

Grave would hunt him down and kill him before he could lay a claw on any of his family.

If the male wanted war, then he would have one.

CHAPTER 4

Isla lingered in the shadows, her right shoulder pressing against the dark stone wall of the building beside her in the middle of the large town in the free realm of Hell, a place that many species called home.

Including vampires.

Her blue eyes remained fixed on the towering creamy yellow walls across the expansive square in front of her, never moving from them. She used what senses she had to track those who passed between her and her point of focus, ensuring no one dared anything while she studied the fort that was home to the First Legion of the Preux Chevaliers.

And their captain.

Grave.

The town had grown since she had last been here, almost a century ago, continuing to spread outwards with the fort at its centre, becoming a bustling hub thanks to the sheer number of people who came to seek the aid of the Preux Chevaliers. She had passed more inns than she could count during her journey from the nearest portal, and walked along cobbled streets packed with stores selling everything imaginable. The people of the free realm were certainly entrepreneurs, taking advantage of the popularity of the mercenary vampires to line their pockets with coin.

Two vampires emerged from the arched entrance in the golden wall of the fort and she tracked them for a moment before returning her gaze to the barrier before her.

She wiped her palms on her blue leathers and took a deep breath to steady her shaky heart, exhaling it hard in an attempt to expel her nerves.

Inside those walls stood another town, a cluster of yellow rendered buildings that were more at home in Italy than they were in Hell. She smiled as she recalled the first time she had set eyes on the bastion of the First Legion, and how Grave had reacted with horror when she had pointed out that it was strange for a vampire to choose such a sunny colour for his home.

Sunny.

Gods, how many times had she teased him with that word after that?

She had slipped it into comments on everything from his palace to his disposition, and every time he had reacted so beautifully, turning horrified pale blue eyes on her that had gained a ring of crimson around the outside of his irises, a warning she had pressed his buttons again.

Her smile faltered and then died as she reminded herself that those days were long gone, and she was the one who had destroyed them.

Maybe if she had realised before completing her plan and leaving him that everything had been real, including the feelings in her heart, things might have been different. Maybe if she had been braver, had found the courage to return to him despite knowing how angry he was with her, how deeply he wanted to kill her for what she had done to him, she might have been able to fix things.

She looked down at her hands.

She definitely wouldn't have been fading if Melia was right and the bond between them needed to be periodically strengthened in order to keep her corporeal, and him with her.

Those hands shook and she lowered them to her sides and clenched them into fists.

Her gaze returned to the walls that looked so innocent, belying what was beyond them, tricking her into thinking it was a place of peace, not a haven for close to two thousand vampires of the most dangerous degree.

Including one vampire who wanted her dead.

It was only the morbid display of power that stood outside the gates that gave any hint of what the bastion contained.

She eyed the six tall rusted metal spikes that were set into the flagstones at a forty-five-degree angle and the corpses that had been impaled on them, dangling high above the ground. A warning to any who saw them.

Her stomach turned.

Some of them were demons, including one she recognised as being from the Fifth Realm. There was a bear shifter too, still in his animal form, and on the far right was what looked like a sorceress. The other three had rotted too much for her to tell what they had been.

The First Legion had been busy.

Pools of crimson lay below the fresher corpses, and empty shallow dips were beneath the rotten ones, a sign of how often the spikes were occupied, so frequently that the blood that dripped from them had worn down the black stone.

She pulled down another deep breath to quell her nerves and stepped out into the main square.

A passing vampire male eyed her and her courage failed and she slinked back into the shadows of the alley. She couldn't do this. She hadn't seen Grave in the flesh in decades and she wasn't strong enough to face him now.

Isla gritted her teeth and scolded herself.

She was strong enough. She had to do this. Both of their lives were on the line.

Thoughts of how he would react rushed through her mind, none of them good, and she shook as she took another step back, away from the fortress.

He hated her. Wanted her dead.

She closed her eyes and steeled herself, using the same mantra she had since leaving him.

He had deserved it.

He had killed her sister's beloved, leaving their son fatherless.

She had only done what any phantom would have in her position. She had taken revenge on the man who had destroyed her sister's world.

Isla kept telling herself it but the conviction she normally felt when she chanted it was nowhere to be found today. The cold remained, the sense of shame that lurked inside her heart still there despite her efforts to expel it.

She had only meant to use her corporeal form to tempt Grave into her trap, seducing him so he would fall foul of the effects of kissing a phantom, an act that would condemn him to becoming incorporeal. A phantom's kiss was their most devastating weapon, one used to turn someone of the opposite sex into a phantom too so they could mate with that person. Some phantoms chose to devour the soul of that victim afterwards, and others left them to drift through eternity incorporeal and unable to touch anyone.

Her stomach rumbled at the thought of eating and she pushed her hunger aside, unwilling to use the excuse of finding a suitable soul to feed on in order to escape facing Grave. She would feed afterwards.

After she had seen him and begged him to do the right thing and help her.

After she had seen him.

Gods. She shivered at the thought of being in his presence again, at the thought she would finally be close to him once more, able to smell him and see him with her own eyes, to feel him near her.

She should have left after kissing him, should have made her escape that night as planned.

She had tried, but Grave had been too addictive, weaving a spell that had held her captivated by him.

His savage beauty, his lethalness that was countered by how attentive and tender he had been to her, all of him enchanted her. Every facet.

There wasn't a part of him that she hadn't fallen in love with.

His spell had been thorough, and she believed that perhaps she had cast one upon him too. Not the spell she had meant to cast, one solely to make him suffer as a phantom, but the same spell he had cast upon her.

Had he loved her?

Was there any part of him left that still felt something for her or had she destroyed it all?

The months she had passed with him had been bliss, but the birth of Tarwyn had been a reminder the phantom part of her hadn't been able to ignore. When she had held the babe in her arms the first time, had gazed down at his face and seen Valador in him, and how devastated Melia had been by the birth of her son when she should have been happy, should have had her mate there with her, she had been filled with rage and had directed it at Grave.

The way he had reacted when she had told him she was a phantom and it had all been a lie designed to turn him into a phantom too fuelled the belief that he had felt something for her, his hurt so phenomenal she had experienced it too, hadn't been able to breathe because of it.

But that hurt had quickly morphed to fury and a terrible rage of his own, a determination to make her suffer. He was slowly taking his own form of revenge on her, and now there was a part of her that couldn't blame him for it.

Even when a small fragment of her, her deepest phantom instincts, took pleasure in how he still suffered with the knowledge he would become a phantom too, that his actions on the battlefield had a consequence and he was paying for taking Valador from her sister.

Isla stared at the grand archway in the wall, able to glimpse the elegant sandstone flags of the courtyard through it and a hint of the corner of one yellow building.

How many times had she wanted to see him again?

Now she stood on the threshold of his home, knew he was there because the black flag of the Preux Chevaliers stood proud at the top of the pole above the gates, signalling the First Legion were in their barracks.

She stood on the verge of seeing him again, and the part of her that feared him was slowly losing ground against the part of her that ached for him.

Their decades apart had been cold and lonely, filled with that constant ache in her heart, a need to be close to him again.

Whenever that ache grew too fierce, she found herself reaching for him, forcing open the connection between them so she could see him, could know what he was doing and spend time with him in her own way. She knew he didn't like it. He had told her that countless times, looking in a mirror at his reflection and cursing her.

The sensation that had come over her shortly after she had taken up position opposite his fortress grew stronger, and she knew he was aware of her and she wasn't welcome. The bond between them relayed it to her, but she clung to the tattered shreds of her courage, determined to see this through.

To face him.

If he didn't have his men turn her away at the gates anyway.

She palmed the smooth wooden hilts of the two curved short blades strapped to her lower back, snug against the blue leather of her corset, and courted the idea of fighting her way in if they tried to deny her entrance.

Probably not a wise idea.

She wanted Grave to listen to her, and harming his men would only give him more reason to kill her.

The two guards outside the gates changed with another pair dressed in fine black knee-length jackets, tight trousers and riding boots.

Gods, Grave had looked so good in his uniform, the material fitted closely to his body and accentuating every inch of it.

She shook that image away and pushed off, crossing the expanse of black stone flags between her and the gate before she could lose her nerve again. Her heart accelerated as she neared the arched entrance, thundering against her ribs.

The two vampire males at the gate eyed her but didn't stop her from passing.

Isla let out the breath she had been holding and slowed her pace as she crossed the threshold and entered the home of the First Legion. On the left and right sides of the elegant square, yellow plastered buildings with terracotta roofs and black shutters formed a line, and through the gaps between them, she saw similar buildings beyond them.

Ahead of her.

She swallowed hard as she faced the palace beyond the grand white marble fountain.

It was as beautiful as she recalled, the same colours as the other buildings within the fortress, but different in style. The façade stretched across the huge square, three storeys high, with rectangular black-shuttered windows only two metres apart, the white stone casings that surrounded them a stunning contrast against the yellow render. Between each window, a white flat stone column stretched the height of the floor, appearing to hold up the matching pale stone band that ran across the top and bottom of each level.

Words carved in Latin decorated the band across the top of the ground floor, centred above the arched entrance.

Nulla Misericordia.

Isla made her way past the fountain, focusing on the gentle sound of the water to calm her rising nerves, and strode towards the entrance. Vampires passed her but none of them stopped her from advancing. In fact, most of them didn't look at her at all.

She wasn't sure that was a good sign.

Was Grave luring her into a trap, or did he really want to see her?

She passed under the arched entrance of his palace and her pace slowed again as the four sides of the building towered above her in its bare courtyard. The inside was darker, with the two upper floors painted in a more sombre shade of yellow that was closer to grey, and the casings of the windows, the bands that delineated each level and the flat decorative columns all made of black marble.

The ground floor was different too, set back under the building, with rows of narrow arches supporting the upper floors and thick black columns between them.

She kept an eye on the guards who loitered in the shadows under the arches, aware of their eyes on her.

Her nerves started to get the better of her as she crossed the courtyard, her body and mind responding exactly as whoever had built it had intended. It was a building made to intimidate, to unsettle the visitor and set them on edge.

It captured the nature of the one who had ordered it perfectly, creating a vision of power and importance, but elegance too.

Grave.

Isla rubbed her damp hands on her leathers as she stepped up onto the raised path that ran beneath all the columned sides of the building and through the double-width black-framed doorway. Her eyes took a moment to adjust to the darkness on the other side, but she kept moving forwards, afraid that if she stopped she would run away.

Oil lamps flickered around the square entrance hall, illuminating the huge gold-framed paintings hanging on the black wall and the imposing white marble staircases that ran up both walls to meet in a curve at the first floor.

A second set of curved marble staircases ran from beside the top of the first ones, sweeping back towards the wall behind her to join with the second floor, and high above her an enormous chandelier hung in the open space between the two floors.

Isla kept an eye on it as she passed under it, her boots silent on the white marble tiles. She never had trusted it. It seemed too large and weighty to hang from such a slender chain.

She walked straight ahead, through another double-width doorway beneath the staircase, and her steps slowed further as she entered the corridor between the entrance hall and the audience room.

Isla turned her gaze towards the black marble floor, keeping her eyes off the grotesque display of mounted heads that lined the obsidian walls. She had dared to look at them once, had been horrified when she had found herself somewhat captivated by the gruesome collection and the way the light from the oil lamps flickered across them, a dancing of shadows that made them come alive.

Another trick meant to intimidate, designed to strike fear into the hearts of those who desired to make a pact with the vampire mercenaries of the Preux Chevaliers and their infamous leader.

Isla lifted her head as she cleared the corridor and her heart almost stopped in her chest.

Grave lounged on his ebony throne on the raised black platform opposite her in the pale-walled room, his scarred chest bare between the two open sides of his black dress shirt. A crystal goblet hung from between his long fingers and he raised it slowly, bringing it to his lips. He lazily sipped the blood, painting his firm lips crimson, his ice blue eyes on her the entire time.

She fought to find her voice as she stood before him in the bare room, but it wouldn't come as he stared at her, cold and silent, as grim and dark as Hell itself.

His malice rolled through her, his hatred filling the room.

Scarlet ringed his frosty eyes.

The silence seemed to stretch into forever, thickening with each second that she stood in it without saying anything. She didn't know what to say. She didn't know how to break the silence.

What could she say?

There were a thousand things but nothing at the same time.

The longer he stared at her, the stronger a feeling within her grew, until she was close to looking away from him, unable to hold his gaze as her insides churned.

Guilt.

The man before her was so different to the one she had tricked into kissing her, so much darker, and it was her fault. She was responsible for the changes that had taken place, turning a passionate and attentive vampire into a powerful, dark and deadly monster.

And now she had to ask the monster she had made for a sliver of compassion, for his help.

She didn't deserve it, but she still dared to hope that he would give her the help she needed because he would fade too if they didn't do something about their bond.

His eyes narrowed on her and glittered with ice as he lowered the goblet to rest on the arm of his throne.

"Come to finish the job, Isla?" His voice darkened as he eyed the handles of the two blades strapped to her lower back. "I can see no other reason you would crawl back to me."

The phantom instincts she tried so hard to contain got the better of her and she took a hard step towards him. "You deserved what you got."

"Did I?" He chuckled mirthlessly, a bitter hollow sound that she didn't like, not when she had heard him truly laugh with joy. "I seem to always get what I deserve."

She wasn't sure what he meant by that, but the distant look in his eyes and the feelings she could sense in him said it wasn't directed at her. Something was troubling him. She glanced at his chest, at the fresh healing scars on it, and the ones on his handsome face too. He had been in a battle again. Had something happened there?

He idly swung the goblet back and forth, his pale eyes locked on it as the blood sloshed side to side.

"It is nice to still be able to hold things." His gaze slid towards her and darkened, his voice little more than a snarl as he glared at her. "Would you not agree?"

She fought the urge but her eyes still dropped to her blue boots.

"We have a problem," she whispered.

"No, I have a problem. More than one but let us focus on the one that stems from you." Grave's grim tone had her lifting her head again, pinning him with a look she knew conveyed every ounce of curiosity running through her blood because he scowled at her in the way he always did when daring her to say something when he wanted her silent. He stood sharply and the goblet in his hand came flying at her so fast she barely had time to dodge it. It exploded against the wall behind her and she flinched. Grave growled. "You get to go back to being the phantom you are. I fail to see how that is a problem for you, Isla. You can lure more men to their doom with that pretty smile and those wicked curves. You must have grown bored of being stuck in this world, bound to one male... unable to get your fill of—"

"We will not become phantoms," Isla interjected, unable to bear any more of his barbs.

He fell silent, stood there before his throne staring at her again, staring right through her in that way he had perfected, reducing her back to the meek female she hated with all of her heart but couldn't seem to stop becoming in his presence.

She looked down at her boots.

"If we do not become phantoms... what do we become?" His calm and collected tone sent a shiver through her, a warning that she was treading on thin ice. "What will this do to us?"

This male was at his most dangerous when he was like this, outwardly unaffected by anything, but inwardly churning with anger, with darkness that ruled him and began to show in his eyes as the scarlet gained ground against the pale blue.

Fire and ice.

Grave was made of them. A beautiful contradiction. Two elements that shouldn't be able to live together but somehow he made it work, harnessed both to his advantage.

Savage bloodlust.

Ironclad calm.

Isla tipped her chin up and faced her fears head on, because all he could do to her was exactly what was going to happen to her anyway if he refused to help. "It will kill us."

His handsome face turned sombre, lips flattening for a moment, before his expression darkened and eyes narrowed on her.

"And I am meant to believe this?"

Isla frowned back at him. "Believe what you want. It is the truth, Grave."

"Do not speak my name," he barked, so loud that it echoed around the room and she tensed, instinctively took a step back towards the door as his rage poured over her and shone in his scarlet eyes. "You do not have the right to speak it. Not anymore."

Isla lowered her eyes and they caught on his chest, on a chain around it and a pendant she could see now that he had stood, causing it to fall from beneath the sides of his black shirt.

The delicate silver Celtic knot nestled in the valley between his pectorals.

The ancient symbol was one of protection, designed for a loved one.

A phantom symbol.

A gift that she had given him.

A spark of hope ignited in her chest.

Grave lifted his hand, slipped his fingers beneath the pendant and raised it, drawing her eyes up with it. They jumped back to his face when the pendant reached his chin and she searched his eyes, aching for a sign that whatever feelings he'd had for her still existed somewhere inside him and that he would help her.

"I wear this," he said in a low voice, soft and almost tender as he gazed at the symbol of her affection. "I wear this to remind me of your lies... a reminder of what you did to me, in case I am ever foolish enough to forget it... to relinquish my mission to make you suffer."

The spark of hope inside her stuttered and died.

His face blackened and he curled his fingers around the pendant as he scowled at her, the red bleeding from his eyes, leaving them icy cold blue again.

"If death is the price you must pay for what you have done, so be it, Isla." He turned away from her, stepped off the platform and walked towards the open door in the back right corner of the room.

Isla took swift steps towards him, panic rising to swallow her as he stepped through the doorway.

Her entire body tensed when he slammed the dark wooden door in her face.

Her knees wobbled but she refused to collapse, forced herself to stand tall.

She had been a fool to hope Grave would help her. She never should have listened to her sister. Melia didn't know him like she did. Now she had wasted another day in which she could have been hunting for a phantom mage.

But worse than that, she ached more than ever for Grave.

Isla pressed her right hand to her chest and closed her eyes, focused on the mark on her back between her shoulder blades, near her heart. It warmed, tingling on her skin, but then the connection that had been opening slammed shut in her face just as the door had.

She turned away from it, lifted her chin and let her hand fall away from her heart.

If Grave wouldn't help her, then she would track down a phantom mage alone. She would do all in her power to stop what was happening to her, and to Grave.

She would save him somehow.

She owed him that much.

She couldn't undo what she had done...

Isla stilled.

Or could she?

CHAPTER 5

Grave stood at a window in the huge library on the top floor of the palace, staring down into the courtyard, watching the slender female as she appeared from the building and stormed across the sandstone flags.

Her steps slowed as she neared the fountain and she looked back at the palace, an expression on her face that called to him.

There had been hope in her stunning blue eyes when she had spoken with him, but now there was nothing but despair and pain, and he enjoyed it, but gods, he hated it at the same time.

He cursed her in his mind and tried to tear his eyes away from her, tried to force himself to turn his back on the window and stop watching her, but he couldn't stop looking at her and couldn't walk away.

He had barely kept his cool and refrained from standing as she had swept into his grand hall, had barely leashed the hot bolt of lust that had burned through him on seeing her again.

She was as beautiful as he remembered.

Even with their apparently joint problem diminishing her slightly, she was still radiant. Ethereal. Breathtaking.

Dangerous to him because of it.

He had thought he was over her, that during their time apart the things she had done had destroyed any and all feelings he'd had for her, leaving his heart free of her. Leaving him cold and immune to her.

He had thought wrong.

One single glimpse of her. One single breath of her sweet scent. One single word falling from her lips.

It was all it had taken to pull him back under her spell.

He despised her for that, and hated himself too.

He turned on a snarl as she disappeared from view beyond the main gate of the fortress and began pacing along the bank of windows. Fury rolled through him with each hard step, anger at her for daring to walk back into his life and at himself for turning her away, and being foolish enough to hope she might fight harder, might have come back when she had stopped at the fountain rather than walking away.

Gods, had he really wanted her to come back?

He squeezed his eyes shut, growled through his clenched teeth and shook his head. No. He hadn't. He really hadn't.

A quiet voice whispered that he had.

Grave crushed it out of existence.

He paced harder, trying to work off some steam and purge her from his life again.

But her scent lingered in his lungs, her beauty still branded on his mind.

He grabbed the nearest wooden chair and roared as he sent it flying across the library. It smashed into the bookcase lining the far wall, shattering into pieces and knocking several books to the floor with it.

Grave grabbed another, and then another, and when chairs weren't enough to satisfy the need to destroy everything because he couldn't destroy what he really wanted—his feelings for Isla—he tipped one of the ebony desks over and unleashed his fury on it, attacking it with claws, fists and booted feet until it was little more than a scattered pile of tinder on the wooden floor.

His chest heaved as he breathed hard, head bent and heart pounding, anger still thundering in his blood.

He stilled when someone halted outside the double doors of the library. Waited.

Asher wisely moved on, and Grave waited for him to pass beyond the sphere of his acute senses before he staggered backwards to the window and slumped onto the seat there, the back of his head smacking against the glass panes. He grimaced as his healing right shoulder ached under the pressure of his weight and shifted into a more comfortable position.

He stared at the destruction he had wrought, feeling nothing, not a single care about what he had done.

Not when his heart still beat for Isla.

He had thought he was free of her. He had thought he was stronger and able to see her without her affecting him, without feeling anything for her. He had thought that whatever he had once held in his heart had died when she had shattered that organ, but the sight of her had robbed him of his breath and her scent had made him hard as steel in his trousers, aching for her.

He was never going to be free of her, not so long as they were bound.

She would always affect him, no matter how much he hated it.

Grave tipped his head back, pressing it into the glass, and closed his eyes, breathing out a deep sigh as resignation filled him.

"Damn her," he muttered, raised both hands and ran them over his dark hair, clawing it back.

He couldn't think about her right now, not when he had more important things on his mind, things he had almost foolishly revealed to her with his careless words. He had caught the look in her eyes, the intense curiosity.

He lowered his right hand to his chest and rubbed his thumb across the pendant around his neck.

Just as he had witnessed the spark of hope she had felt on seeing he still owned the trinket she had given him.

And he had done all in his power to crush that hope.

Grave looked down at the intricate knot, recalling what he had said to her—he wore it as a reminder of what she had done to him in case he was ever foolish enough to forget it and relinquish his mission to make her suffer.

The reality was so much worse than that.

He couldn't bring himself to part with it.

Gods, he had tried.

He had cast it into a valley in the Sixth Realm once and turned his back on it, only to end up scouring the black lands for it, desperate to find it again and have it back in his possession. It had taken him five days of searching, five days without sleep or blood.

When he had finally found it, he had experienced such a powerful surge of relief that his knees had given out and he had sat in the middle of the valley, clutching it tightly in his fist, close to tears.

He curled his lip.

There might have been one or two tears.

The metal warmed as he traced the knot, following the lines of it, the weight of it soothing in his fingers.

He hadn't taken it off since that day.

He should have known from that alone that seeing Isla again had been a bad idea, that he wasn't over her at all. If he didn't have the strength to part with a stupid trinket, how the hell had he expected to have the strength to see her and feel nothing?

Imbecile.

He huffed and released the pendant.

Was it possible she had spoken the truth though? She was fading too, and rather than becoming phantoms, they were dancing with death?

A few days ago, he would have leaped at the chance to hear what she had to say, to bleed her for any information she had that might help him or even use her just to save himself, but now all he could think about was the pressing need he felt to save someone else.

The mark between his shoulder blades warmed and this time he didn't close the connection to her, but he did hold things back from her, only allowing her to feel his negative emotions, the anger and frustration he felt.

Not anger and frustration born of her and her visit.

These emotions were born of the demon prince and his threat.

Grave turned his head to his left, looked into the courtyard below and then beyond it to the wall and the grand gate, and the dark stone buildings of the town outside. Was she still out there or had she already moved on, using one of the portals to teleport somewhere else in Hell?

The part of him that refused to give up and die, the piece that clung to his feelings for her, hoped she found the solution she was looking for and managed to save herself.

He ignored it, pretending it hadn't said a damn thing, but it was impossible when the same voice whispered poisonous words in his heart, words that rekindled fear in his veins and had him coming to his feet.

The demon prince wanted her as his prize.

And wanted his entire family dead.

A family that wished the same thing for him, but one he was bound to in blood, obliged to warn despite their feelings for him.

He turned towards the window and studied the darkening horizon with a growing sense of dread. He had given himself a day to recuperate, a day in which he had locked himself in this library with three of his men and uncovered the record of the attack on the demon castle in the archives, arming himself with all the information he could muster because he knew he would need it if he was going to convince some members of his family to listen to him.

Now, he couldn't delay any longer.

He focused on the mark on his back, felt it warm against his skin and start to tingle, and pictured Isla standing before him as she had in his grand hall.

Beautiful, enchanting Isla.

She had spoken about him getting what he deserved, and he wasn't sure what she had meant by that, but there was a chance it was about to happen, and he couldn't dispute that he probably did deserve it after what he had done to this person.

The one he intended to warn first.

Would she feel it when his eldest cousin, Snow, killed him in a fit of bloodlust?

CHAPTER 6

Grave stood beneath the columned portico of an elegant sandstone building in London, staring at a pair of darkened glass sliding doors that seemed so out of place on the old theatre and waging war with himself for a change as he debated whether or not to knock. He glanced over his shoulder, turning his ice blue gaze skywards, and cursed the faint pink tinge on the clouds that signalled what his body was already telling him.

Dawn was coming.

He had delayed long enough, dragging his feet during his preparations and his journey to the nearest portal, putting off entering it by thinking up ridiculous excuses about leaving his legion without their commander when Asher was perfectly capable of leading them in his stead, and then finally accidentally missing several vacant taxis when he had exited the portal in London.

Now, he could delay no longer.

It was either knock on the door and face his cousins, or leave now to find somewhere to wait out the day.

He blew out his breath.

He had faced enemies far more powerful than himself, had battled legions of shifters, demons and even dragons, but facing his family felt like an insurmountable task, one he dreaded, one that left him feeling death had finally caught up with him and was firmly on his heels, a shadow looming at his back waiting to strike him down.

Grave slowly raised his right hand and rapped his knuckles against the glass. Hard. When no one showed up within two minutes, he knocked again.

The doors slid open.

"You are late. Aurora is—" The immense white-haired male cut himself off and scowled at Grave, his pale blue eyes glittering with ice as his eyebrows dipped low above them. "What the fuck are you doing here?"

Red seeped into the edges of his cousin's irises and his pupils began to narrow, starting to turn elliptical. Fangs flashed between Snow's lips as he snarled low in his throat and advanced on Grave, the sheer size of him and the threat he had issued enough to have Grave backing off a step.

Snow hadn't courted his bloodlust.

It had been born in the fires of Hell, and wasn't something Grave wanted for himself or wanted aimed at him. He had danced with his, had stoked it and somehow mastered it, controlled it when normally the affliction controlled its victim.

As it controlled Snow.

Images flashed across Grave's mind, disjointed and dim memories of a night he would never forget, one that haunted him despite his best attempts to push it forever from his mind.

Blood coated everything. Splashed up walls. Ran down broken furniture. Bathed battered bodies.

The corpses of his kin.

His aunt. His uncle.

His parents.

Snow had killed them all in a fit of bloodlust, turning their peaceful lakeside chateau into a scene straight out of a hellish nightmare.

War erupted in Snow's eyes, the ice fighting the fire as he fought with himself, his powerful body visibly shaking. His cousin's muscles strained against his black t-shirt, trembling beneath the tight material as he curled his fingers into fists at his sides.

"Go away," Snow bit out, voice a deep pained growl, and staggered back a step. "You are not welcome here."

The glass doors slid shut.

Grave pulled down a deep breath and tried to silence the voice in his mind that told him to leave. He would, but not yet. He needed to warn his cousins, even when his presence only pained one of them.

He knocked again.

"Fucking hell, what are you doing here?" A light female voice cut through the quiet morning air and he whirled to face the owner, his right hand reaching for a sword that wasn't there.

The black-haired mortal standing on the steps below him arched an eyebrow at him, her golden eyes eerily bright in the low light.

He should have come armed, but he had feared tipping his cousin over the edge.

Beside the female, a bare-chested demon brute towered, his dusky horns curling around the curve of his pointed ears and beginning to flare forward as he glared at Grave, seven foot of pure muscle and menace. There were other reasons not to attack the mortal female. She was mated to the demon king who was looking at him as if he was searching for a reason to tear out his entrails.

Charming considering that Grave had gone to war on this demon's behalf, risking his life and those of his men to assist him in his fight against the Fifth Realm of demons only a few months ago.

The door behind him opened again and he spun on his heel, heart leaping into his throat as his claws extended and he prepared for a fight.

That same heart plummeted into his stomach when he found himself facing a slender female with dark hair that tumbled in gentle waves around pale shoulders and green-to-blue eyes that felt as if they were peering down into his soul, pulling out all the darkest memories it held.

All of his sins.

Behind her, Snow loomed in the shadows, his all-black clothing a stark contrast to her fair skin and white dress. His right hand gently rested on her left shoulder, a possessive and protective gesture that warned Grave this was the female Snow had chosen as his mate, the one he had heard about.

Aurora.

An angel.

Or former angel.

Though she hadn't chosen to turn into a fallen angel, she had chosen to fall from grace for his cousin.

Grave eyed the male, seeing only the brutal vampire he had witnessed on the battlefield countless times and the one who had slaughtered almost all of their family, destroying their bloodline.

He closed his eyes when a sharper image of his mother flashed across his eyes and gritted his teeth as he looked down at her where she lay in his arms, broken and dead, ripped from him.

On the heels of that soul-destroying memory, another more brutal and devastating one followed, hitting him hard now that his defences were down.

His sister.

His little sister.

He stood on the paved drive of another remote chateau, his back to the building and eyes on the snow-white dress that fluttered in the night breeze on the grass, near a pair of black heeled ankle boots and a delicate black-and-red lace choker.

Gods, he relived her terror and her pain, the fear that she too had bloodlust because of their family's insistence on keeping their bloodline pure, that they had bred into her the same terrible disease that had caused Snow to take most of their family from them. She had been inconsolable, convinced that she would one day lose control and harm her family.

She had been the gentlest creature the world had ever seen, pure of heart and kind of soul, unable to hurt anyone even to feed from them.

She had done the unthinkable.

Unbearable.

She had walked out into the morning and disappeared.

Bastian and Night believed her dead, because her young body wouldn't have been able to withstand even weak pre-dawn light. Grave couldn't bring himself to believe that she was gone. He didn't feel any sense of loss, not as he had when he had held his mother.

He stared at the clothes, studied them closely. Even a full day in sunlight wouldn't have been enough to disintegrate her body, and there was no evidence that she had burned to death, nothing but her clothes.

She wasn't dead.

Was she?

The same terrible darkness he had experienced in that moment welled up in him again, his eyes shifting to reflect the blackness pumping through his veins, an undeniable thirst to maim and kill, to spill blood in order to unleash his rage and his pain.

"Aurora, take Sable and Thorne inside," Snow said, his deep voice swimming in Grave's ears as memories swamped him, pushing at his control and giving his bloodlust a stronger hold over him.

Gods, he needed the pain and the high of victory, needed to fight something to make those two things happen.

He flicked his near-black eyes open, pinning them on his cousin, and breathed hard, his heart thundering against his chest as he fought with himself rather than surrendering to his need to battle his own flesh and blood.

He had sworn he wouldn't, never again, not after the night he had confronted Snow about what he had done and had come dangerously close to killing him.

A slave to the very disease that had caused his cousin to murder their family.

Bloodlust.

It rode him hard now, at the helm, controlling him when he was used to controlling it. Oily darkness rushed through his veins, drowned out any good thoughts, any glimmer of light, replacing them with a crushing need to kill.

"Leave," Snow bit out again and Grave forced himself to shake his head.

"Cannot," he gritted and dug his emerging claws into his palms, grimaced at the hot sting of them cutting into his flesh, and snarled through his fangs. "I must speak with you."

Snow folded his arms across his broad chest.

"What the fuck is he doing here?" Another familiar male voice shattered the tense silence and Grave slid his black-to-red gaze towards the newcomer, a male with short dark brown hair and ice blue eyes that matched Snow's and his own.

Antoine. His younger cousin and keeper of Snow, despite what Snow had done to him.

How was it Antoine and Snow could forgive each other, but neither would forgive him?

"I must speak with you both," Grave ground out and advanced a step, his fury rising to stoke his bloodlust to startling new heights as he faced his cousins.

Both males blamed him for the things Snow had done during his service with the Preux Chevaliers, but Snow's memories of his time in Hell were muddled, twisted by his bloodlust.

Grave hadn't had the heart to tell him as much when they had last met and Snow had turned on him, thrown vicious barbs detailing everything he had apparently done while they had served together, essentially making out that he had been the one to awaken Snow's bloodlust. The male was so desperate to weaken the hold his guilt had on him that he had fabricated events in order to lessen some of the weight on his heart.

He wasn't sure what would happen if Snow realised what he had done, and he didn't want to find out.

So he had taken the blame.

All to stop his cousin from slipping deeper into the hold of his bloodlust.

Grave looked over his shoulder at the lightening sky and then back at his cousins where they stood side by side in the dark entrance hall of the theatre, Snow standing at least two inches taller than his younger brother. If it wasn't for their eyes, many wouldn't believe they were siblings.

Snow's white hair was wild, brushing the nape of his neck and his jaw, and his black t-shirt and jeans, and heavy soled black leather boots, made him look more like a biker or a goth than a respectable owner of a vampire theatre.

Antoine matched that image perfectly. Neatly clipped brown hair, clean shaven square jaw, and expensive dove grey tailored shirt tucked into an equally expensive pair of crisp black slacks, topped off with polished Italian leather shoes.

They couldn't have looked more opposite to each other if they had tried.

The back of Grave's neck prickled in warning.

"Let me in," he said in a calm tone despite his desire to snap at his cousins as his nerves began to get the better of him again, entwining with his bloodlust to make him more dangerous than ever.

The sun was perilously close to rising now and he wasn't sure whether the buildings around them would give him much cover. There were alleys between them all, and the road at his back was wide enough that the sun could easily hit him if it rose at either end of it. He looked around again, trying to chart the position of it.

"I would not be here if it was not important," he barked and advanced another step. Antoine flashed fangs at him and Snow scowled and moved a step towards him, coming to block his path into the building. He flicked another glance at the sky. He was almost out of time. Time he might not have to find shelter if he didn't convince his cousins to allow him inside right now. "It concerns all the family."

Snow's face shifted, softening as he frowned at him.

"Twelve-eighty-nine. A demon stronghold on the borders of the Devil's domain and a mission to eradicate the threat contained in it," Grave said and Snow's arms fell to his sides, his frown melting away and his expression turning curious.

The crimson in his cousin's eyes faded as conflicting emotions flickered in them, and he knew Snow was remembering the mission.

"I am listening." Snow eased back a step, but didn't clear the doorway.

It was a start, but Grave was damned if he was going to have this conversation on their doorstep when the sun had just broken the horizon and he was in danger of being exposed to it. He was old enough to withstand it for a short time, but he didn't want to test how much immunity to it his two thousand years would give him.

Images of dreams he'd had of his sister screaming as the rays of the sun devoured her flesh burst across his mind and he snarled.

"Let me in." He put some force behind those words, letting his cousins know it was a demand and not a request. "The sun…"

"No." Antoine shook his head.

"You can come in," Snow said over him and ignored the frown Antoine turned on him.

Grave was quick to take his eldest cousin up on his offer, stepping inside the double-height foyer of the theatre and ignoring the look of pity mixed with guilt that Snow tossed his way. His eyes rapidly adjusted to the dimly lit entrance, and he held back the sigh of relief that wanted to burst from his lips as the doors behind him slid shut, blocking out the toxic UV light.

In the quiet of the theatre, he could hear Aurora and Sable talking in the distance, their voices drifting from an open door to his right beyond the elegant staircase that curved upwards towards the first floor, giving access to the private boxes of the theatre.

Antoine huffed and walked towards the door, his shoes loud on the pale marble floor. Snow lingered in the middle of the red and gold foyer, the crystal chandelier directly above him and his back to the double doors beneath the balcony, watching Grave with ice blue eyes that hid whatever he was feeling.

As Snow stared at him, crimson began to ring his irises again, gaining ground against the blue as rapidly as it was losing it in Grave's own eyes as they transformed back and his bloodlust eased enough that he could bring it back under control.

"Come, Snow," Antoine said and whatever dark path Snow had been treading, causing his eyes to turn scarlet, he stopped walking it and looked across at his brother as his irises cleared. "If we must speak with him, we should do it somewhere a little less public."

A frown flickered on Snow's brow, drawing his white eyebrows together, as he glanced back at Grave, but then he nodded and joined his brother at the plain wooden door. Antoine watched him pass, and stepped into Grave's path as he tried to follow and pressed his left hand to Grave's chest. It was cool through the material of his black dress shirt and he looked down at it, and frowned at the delicate gold band around his ring finger.

Antoine was mated too?

"Upset him, and I will be the one to kill you," Antoine hissed and Grave stared him down, using the scant inch difference in their height to his advantage.

He tipped his chin up, straightened his back and wanted to mention that Snow was the one who had done nothing in this world but upset him, and no one gave a damn about that. Everyone was always in Snow's corner.

The fiend had destroyed their family, had torn Grave's parents from him, but no one, not even Grave's own damned brothers, despised Snow for it.

Not as he did.

Antoine's hand fell from his chest and he turned away from Grave, disappearing into the gloom of the black corridor. Grave stood on the threshold, fighting with his feelings again, emotions he hadn't experienced in centuries, born of a time that had finally been growing distant to him but now felt as if it had been only yesterday.

When Antoine's footsteps grew as distant as he wished his memories were, Grave turned down the corridor and followed it as it gently sloped downwards. Light flooded it at the other end and he squinted as he entered a bright black-walled double-height room.

"This is private enough," Antoine said and Grave looked around at the room.

On the far wall, a staircase led upwards, and below it was an area with four red couches surrounding a wooden coffee table.

On one of those red couches sat Aurora, Sable and Thorne, deep in conversation.

Grave frowned at them.

This area wasn't private at all.

He turned a scowl on his youngest cousin, but Antoine countered it with a look that said he didn't care and that he had chosen this place on purpose.

He knew how uncomfortable the presence of the females made him and was enjoying it.

Grave glared at Sable when she stopped talking and turned to look over her shoulder at him, her golden eyes dark with malice. She shot to her feet and came to face him.

"You're quiet today. Cat got your tongue?" Sable taunted and he ignored her.

He had found her spirit amusing when he had been on her side in the war against the Fifth Realm, but that amusement had been tarnished by the fact that she was apparently powerful enough to paint the walls with his blood and entrails if they fought.

She might carry angelic blood in her veins, but she was still beneath him, a weak creature undeserving of his attention.

He turned his cheek to her and she huffed and muttered foul things beneath her breath about 'kicking his arse'. Out of the corner of his eye, the demon king Thorne gently took hold of her arm and somehow convinced his hellion bride to settle back down on the couch and continue speaking with Aurora.

Grave's gaze shifted to the ex-angel.

Snow snarled low in his throat beside him, a warning that shot through Grave and had his eyes instantly leaping away from Aurora to him. His cousin's red eyes narrowed on him, elliptical pupils nothing more than thin slits in their centres, and then the larger male stalked away, heading towards the slender petite female.

Grave couldn't bring himself to watch as Snow fussed over her, and she turned dazzling green-to-blue eyes on him, her rosy lips curving into an affectionate smile as she stroked his bare forearm and spoke with him.

A sudden, powerful urge went through Grave.

A need to leave.

He took a step back towards the corridor, his heart beginning to pound as he found his eyes caught on the two couples, his blood starting a slow burn as he saw the love play out between his cousin and Aurora.

He had never thought Snow capable of love, or that anyone could love him.

But it was there for him to see as Snow petted Aurora, and she lovingly caressed his cheek, luring him down for a reassuring kiss.

Grave took another step.

He had never thought himself capable of love either, or that anyone could dare to love him, but he had fallen in love and he had believed she had loved him too.

But he had been sorely mistaken.

Isla had played him for a fool.

She didn't love him and now he believed she was incapable of such feelings where he was concerned.

He had felt her fear when she had come to him.

No one who feared someone that much could love that same person.

Grave went to turn away, but a hand locked around his left wrist, stopping him from escaping, and he looked down at it and then up at its owner.

"There's something different about you," Snow said in a hushed voice, one meant for his ears only, and Grave didn't like the way his cousin's eyes searched his, as if hunting for the difference he had sensed and determined to find it no matter how deeply Grave wanted to hide it. Snow's now-blue eyes narrowed on his. "Four centuries I served with you in Hell, and you were merciless… constantly getting us into trouble… but you were not so cold and emotionless… not even after—"

Grave looked away, not wanting his cousin to speak about what he had done to their family, not when he was already feeling weak, liable to be overcome and ruled by his emotions. He stared at the dark floor of the backstage area, slowly pulling himself together, trying to shut out his cousins so he could find his balance again and master his feelings, locking them down again.

Snow didn't give him a chance.

"You knew how to laugh," his cousin whispered close to his face and Grave closed his eyes, hoped to the gods that Sable hadn't heard that titbit because she would use it against him whenever their paths crossed. Damn. Almost anyone he knew would use it against him to shatter the image he had perfected, the illusion of a male born of darkness, emotionless and cold, a King of Death who ruled with an iron fist and had no weaknesses. Snow tugged him closer still. "You showed concern for your comrades."

He still did, but only those who looked closely enough would see it.

He tried to break away from his cousin, but Snow crowded him and Antoine closed in too, hemming him in against the black wall near the exit.

"Bloodlust hasn't robbed you of your feelings or driven you to rage and kill," Snow husked in a pain-filled whisper that tore at the softer emotions his cousin believed didn't exist in him anymore. "You are driven by a stronger force now… what happened to you?"

Grave slid a wary look towards the red couches visible in the narrow gap between his two cousins. Sable appeared to be listening to Aurora, but Grave knew better. She was listening to his conversation with his cousins.

So no matter how fiercely he wanted to tell Snow what had happened, he wouldn't do it. He couldn't expose a vulnerability around so many who might seek to exploit it and use it against him.

Something in the region of his heart ached, because he knew that Snow was going to take this the wrong way and would be less inclined to listen to him, and more liable to go into a rage.

Grave braced himself for the latter.

"Nothing happened."

CHAPTER 7

"Nothing happened."

And exactly that did happen.

Grave waited, sure his cousin was just building up to tearing into him, but Snow remained quiet and thoughtful, watching him with knowing ice blue eyes that left Grave feeling he couldn't hide anything from him, as if he was stripping back his heart layer by layer to reach the diseased part and expose it.

"I don't buy it." Snow shook his head, causing the long silver-white lengths of his hair to sway, and released Grave. "Sell me another line. Something happened to you and now you're here."

His cousin eased back and folded his arms across his chest, causing his biceps to bulge beneath his tight black t-shirt. Intimidation tactics. Snow was only an inch taller than Grave, but he was bigger in build, something he had always used to silently threaten Grave ever since they were youths. It might have worked back then, but it didn't work now. They were the same age, as powerful as each other despite the difference in their builds. If they clashed, it would be bloody, and beautiful, but neither would emerge the victor.

Grave glanced at Antoine where he stood sentinel beside his older brother, his arms crossed too and a dark edge to his expression as he glared at Grave that warned if Snow fought, he wouldn't be alone. Antoine would fight beside him.

An unfair advantage.

No bastard would fight on his side.

He drew down a deep breath, held it and then released it slowly as he reminded himself that he hadn't come here to fight. Gods, standing before his cousins made something painfully clear. Snow was right. He had changed.

He viewed everyone as a threat now. A potential fight. A potential death. Was he that eager for the sweet oblivion of pain and his bloodlust that he would fight his own family?

He cursed Isla's name for what felt like the millionth time, blaming everything on her. She had been the one to change him. That smile and laugh Snow remembered wasn't a figment of his warped imagination, a twisted memory that had never happened. They had existed once. He had been capable of good as well as bad.

Isla had ripped out the heart that had housed those softer emotions though and replaced it with a damaged shadow of that organ, one that didn't know how to do or feel such things.

Snow's steady gaze held him, demanding an answer.

Grave would give him one.

"A demon from the Devil's domain attacked me during a battle between two other demon realms," he said and Thorne perked up, turning his head slightly towards him, so Grave could see his left horn and the crimson eye that slid his way. It wasn't unexpected. King Thorne had a realm to defend and protect, and had only recently won a war. It was natural for him to be concerned about wars in the other realms. Normally when one demon realm lost a war, they turned their anger on a different one. "He intervened and delivered a message to me."

Snow poked him in the right shoulder and Grave grimaced as it burned, clenching his teeth against the lingering pain.

"More than a message," his cousin said with a frown. "As if I wouldn't notice you were injured."

Grave had hoped he wouldn't, but he had underestimated his cousin. They had served together for four centuries, had been assigned to the same legion, and he should have known Snow would have uncovered all his tells in that time together, learning to detect when he was trying to hide things. Vulnerabilities. Perhaps he could make it work to his advantage.

"The night we attacked that castle on the border, we did not kill every demon." Grave rolled his shoulder, easing the tightness that had been building in it. His cousins knew of his injury now so there was no point in hiding it anymore. He pressed his left hand to it and rubbed it. "An infant survived."

Snow's face darkened again. "A babe?"

He nodded. "No longer a babe now though. He is strong, and he wants revenge, Snow... on those who led the charge... and their families."

Antoine bit out a curse. Snow's glacial blue eyes began to blaze like fire. His brother noticed it and placed a hand on his left shoulder. Snow looked down at him, some of the red clearing from his irises but not enough to erase the murderous edge from them. Grave knew the thoughts pinging around his head, the hunger to hunt and destroy, all in the name of protecting his kin.

Snow would help him, he knew it.

"If this demon comes for Snow and our family, we will handle it." Antoine's deep voice echoed around the room with authority that dared anyone to challenge him.

Grave took him up on it.

"This demon—"

A loud crash from above cut him off and had everyone turning towards the stairs against the far wall of the double-height room. Sable, Aurora and Thorne came to their feet. Antoine broke away from them and Snow let out a low growl that sounded more animal than vampire.

Footsteps echoed down the staircase and then a male appeared in view, pursued by a brunette female with a young boy in her arms.

Dogs.

Grave curled a lip at the two werewolves and was about to ask what the hell Antoine and Snow were doing allowing such a couple to stay in their theatre when he caught the scent of the male.

He smiled slowly.

What was Kincaid's pup doing here?

Kyal growled over his shoulder as the female shoved him in it, causing him to stumble and have to grab the railing to stop himself from falling down the steps. His bright blue eyes flickered gold as he flashed fangs at her and then he lowered his head, his expression gaining an air of regret, and turned away. He tunnelled his fingers through his rich brown hair, clutched it and looked as if he was on the verge of doing something amusingly stupid.

Like attempting to calm the angry bitch at his back.

Was he the father of the boy she held so close to her that his black clothing blended into hers?

Did Kincaid know his son had sired offspring?

Grave's grin widened.

Gods, he could imagine the coronary the old werewolf warrior would have if he discovered that. It would be beautiful. Grave would pay to watch him rip into his heir. Every account he had uncovered pointed to Kyal leading a sheltered life, shut inside Kincaid's estate in Scotland, but the dog had clearly disobeyed at some point and slipped the leash.

Kyal reached the bottom step and turned to face the female, and her hazel eyes narrowed on him in a way that warned him not to speak. Whatever he had done, it looked as if he was going to be paying for it for a long time to come.

The werewolf male shoved his fingers through his hair again, causing the golden streaks in it to catch the light and shine brighter, and huffed, his shoulders shifting beneath his khaki t-shirt.

"Just go," the female snapped and Antoine and Snow were on the move, heading towards Kyal.

It seemed the pup was about to be shown the door.

Kyal opened his mouth to speak and she shook her head, her ponytail swaying across the shoulders of her black long-sleeved top. He closed his mouth, cast her a pained look and then shut his eyes, lowering his head at the same time. When he turned away from her, Snow and Antoine halted a short distance away, both males watching the werewolf closely.

The female pursued him a few steps.

Grave frowned as a scent hit him. The boy in her arms.

He was a vampire.

A second male hurried down the steps behind the female, one with wild short black hair and green eyes that matched the infant the werewolf held. A vampire too. He carried a second child wearing a pink dress.

Grave pulled down a deep breath to catch her scent and wasn't surprised when she smelled like a dog.

A vampire and a werewolf had produced offspring? What the hell were his cousins up to in this theatre, besides attempting to destroy their family name by harbouring such people?

Kyal proved himself to be an idiot after all.

He turned back towards the female and tried to close the distance between them, but Snow's hand came down hard on the scruff of his neck and stopped him in his tracks.

"Leave quietly, Kid," Snow growled in his ear and Kyal looked up at him, and disappointment went through Grave when he saw that the werewolf had some sense after all.

He had hoped the pup would do the opposite and give his cousin a reason to kick him out.

"Protect the babies." Kyal turned back to the female. "No one can know about them. I won't tell anyone about you, but you have to be on your guard, Kristina. I'll return if it becomes dangerous for you."

The black-haired vampire now standing behind the female Kristina bared his fangs on a growl.

"It's okay," she said without taking her gaze off Kyal, her voice as cold as her flinty hazel eyes. "The werewolf is leaving."

Kyal shirked Snow's grip and turned away, and paused as he came face to face with Grave. He stood there a moment, blue eyes impossibly wide, filled with recognition and shock, and then they narrowed and he flashed fangs at Grave and stalked off.

Grave watched him go, curious about why the male had come to the theatre and what trouble he expected to come for the one called Kristina. The babies weren't Kyal's, so why did he feel a need to protect them?

"Kristina," the black-haired vampire called and air swirled in the room as Snow and Antoine suddenly moved, and Grave whipped back to face them.

Snow caught the female werewolf before she could hit the floor and Antoine carefully took the boy from her as Snow eased her down onto her knees. The boy reached for her but Antoine bounced him in his arms, cradling him gently as he talked nonsense to him.

Aurora took the baby girl from the black-haired vampire and he went to Kristina, kneeled beside her and gathered her into his arms, littering kisses across her brow as he stroked her dark brown hair, smoothing it.

"I'm fine," she muttered and pushed at the vampire, and he huffed and eased back, and then helped her onto her feet.

She protested but he held her as she dusted down her dark jeans with trembling fingers. Grave arched an eyebrow. Females. Always saying they were fine when they were far from it.

If females were a little more honest, perhaps the world would be a better place.

One where his heart was still in one piece.

"Who was that?" Snow said.

Before Grave could say the werewolf was the son of the warrior Kincaid, Kristina stared up at Snow with shock written on every line of her face and spoke, silencing Grave and the entire room.

"My brother."

It wasn't possible. Kincaid only had one child. If he had more, Grave would know of it. He had enough spies keeping an eye on the werewolf leaders, tracking their movements, to be well informed of their personal lives.

"You're an only child," Snow whispered and the female looked unsure.

Antoine flicked a glance at Grave, and then at Sable and Thorne, and Grave knew what was coming. This was family business, and Antoine was still intent on treating him like a stranger, shutting him out.

Would he shut Snow out if he knew the truth?

Grave doubted it.

"I'll take Kristina to our room so she can rest." The black-haired vampire took hold of her arm and led her towards the stairs. She wobbled with each step and when they reached the staircase, the male scooped her up into his arms. She pushed against him and he sighed. "You always have to fight me. For once, just rely on my strength."

She looked up at him, hazel eyes bright with unshed tears, dark eyebrows furrowed high on her forehead, and then buried her face against his neck and gave a subtle nod of her head. The vampire brushed his lips across her hair and carried her up the stairs. Aurora and Antoine followed, carrying the two children.

Grave tracked them, curious about Kyal and his relationship with the female, until he felt someone's eyes boring into him. He slid Sable a bored look. She could glare stakes at him all she wanted, he wasn't going to rise to whatever bait she intended to throw at him.

He turned away from the huntress and found Snow watching him again. His cousin stared at him in silence for so long that he began to feel uncomfortable and was actually glad when Antoine returned.

"Is he still here?" Antoine looked from him to Snow and crossed his arms, causing his dove grey shirt to tighten across his shoulders and chest. "I thought I made it clear we would deal with the demon if he tried anything."

"Tried anything? He has threatened your family. He knows of your mates," Grave snapped and took a sharp step towards his cousins. "He named them and all of my family too. He means to kill us all and you talk as if your pathetic friends you treat more like your family than your own damned flesh and blood are strong enough to defeat him."

Snow bared emerging fangs. "They are our family."

"And I am not... Night and Bastian are not?" Grave stalked another step forwards and flashed his own fangs at his cousin.

"You are right," Antoine said and Grave shifted his gaze to him. The bastard smiled coldly. "Night and Bastian are our family. We should warn them."

Before he could pick one from the hundred retorts spinning around his mind, Antoine turned away from him.

Snow moved to do the same.

Grave lunged for him and froze when his left hand went straight through Snow's forearm.

Snow stared wide-eyed down at his arm and then up into Grave's eyes. Blinked. Grave didn't dare move or speak. If he pretended that hadn't happened, his cousin might think he had imagined it.

"I will help."

Those three words falling from Snow's lips felt as if they had sealed Grave's fate and in the short span of time it took for Antoine to turn back towards his brother, an incredulous look on his face, Snow had grabbed Grave by his arm and was dragging him towards a door in the wall that had been behind him.

Snow shoved the wooden door open and pushed him inside what looked like an office. The second Antoine appeared, blocking the doorway, Snow's hand closed around Grave's throat and he grunted as the cream wall of the office slammed against his back. Snow's face filled his field of vision.

"What's wrong?" Antoine quickly shut the door.

"Grave is holding out and not telling us everything." The pressure of Snow's grip increased and Grave had trouble breathing as he stared into his cousin's ice blue eyes.

"The two problems are not related," he wheezed.

"I don't give a fuck if they're related," Snow barked. "What happened to you?"

The look in Snow's eyes and the force and heat behind his growled words stole Grave's voice. He could almost fool himself into believing his cousin actually cared about him.

He placed his hand over Snow's on his throat, touching him this time, and pulled it away from him. His feet hit the floor again and he busied himself with straightening out his shirt, tugging the cuffs down to his wrists and shutting out the looks both of his cousins were giving him now. He didn't need their pity, not when they didn't really give a damn about him and had been willing to let him face a demon alone just a few seconds ago.

"It is my problem. Not yours. You made it perfectly clear that I am not considered a member of this family. It was a mistake to come here. I will deal with the demon and this alone." He pivoted on his heel but Snow stepped into his path, blocking his way to the door.

Antoine closed in too. "Dealing with what exactly?"

Snow talked over his brother. "Is this what happened to change you?"

Grave hated that soft look in Snow's eyes. It made his skin crawl and made him itch with a need to escape, to be alone again, free of scrutiny and vampires who poked their nose into his private business. He should have known better than to attempt to touch his cousin, but it had been a knee-jerk reaction, one he hadn't been able to contain, and now Snow had latched onto it and he wasn't going to let it go easily. Snow never had been well versed in personal boundaries. When they had served together, his cousin had been constantly meddling in his private affairs, winkling answers out of the other vampires or anyone else involved if Grave refused to tell him.

"Back off and let it go, Cousin. I have it under control and that is all you need to know." Grave tried to step around him.

Snow's palm slammed into his chest, knocking him back against a mahogany side cupboard. His backside hit it and he scowled at Snow as he pushed onto his feet.

"Bloodlust?" Antoine frowned at him, his pale blue eyes showing a flicker of concern too now.

Great. Now both of them were at it. He wasn't in the mood for this. He had come here to warn them and he had. He didn't need to stick around and suffer an inquisition into his private life.

He had a demon to hunt.

"No. Something worse," Snow snapped, deep voice loud in the small office, and leaned his back against the door. If Grave had to forcibly remove him from it so he could leave, he would, and his cousin should know as much. He took a step towards him, but Snow spoke again, stopping him cold. "How bad is it? Do Night and Bastian know?"

The blood in his veins froze at the thought of Snow telling them and he could only stare at his cousin, fighting to find his voice and lie to him by saying that he had told them about his problem in order to stop Snow from informing them.

Snow threw his hands up in the air. "How can you not tell them? They're your brothers."

He didn't have a good answer to that question. There were countless reasons he was keeping his situation private, but only one that Snow would understand.

"I did not wish to worry them. I will fix it."

A vein in Antoine's temple throbbed. "Fix fucking what?"

Snow looked down at him. "Grave's hand went straight through me."

"What?" Antoine's blue eyes widened.

"It is not a problem." Grave looked away from his cousins and curled his lip at the oil paintings hanging on the walls, depictions of colourful sunsets and landscapes. What sort of vampire decorated their office with such scenes? Daylight was hardly something a vampire should enjoy looking at. It was synonymous with death after all. "I am dealing with it. Let it go."

Snow grabbed him again and slammed him back against the wall near the door. "No. Tell me what happened. Is it a witch's curse? We have a witch. She might be able to fix it."

Grave closed his eyes.

Snow was a rabid dog with a bone and he wasn't going to let it go.

The bastard had had a thing about family since killing most of their one, an obsession with protecting them that didn't quite mesh with Antoine's since it turned out Snow still included Grave in the circle of people he considered family.

He slowly opened his eyes and looked into Snow's, catching the pain that danced in them, the desperate need that a part of Grave was familiar with and understood.

Snow needed to repent, and now he was turning Grave's sins into his own.

He sighed and another war ignited inside him, a battle between doing what his pathetic heart desired and shoving his cousin away, keeping him at a distance.

The weak part of himself won.

"A woman tricked me."

CHAPTER 8

It wasn't the whole truth, but it was as close as Grave could come right now to confessing what had happened to him and hopefully it would be enough for his cousin.

"I will deal with her and what she did after I deal with the demon."

He hated the look in Snow's eyes, the pity. He dared a glance at Antoine and could almost fool himself into thinking that Antoine felt sorry for him too.

"I will help you track this demon down." Snow held up his hand when Grave went to speak. "You are in no condition to fight him alone."

Fantastic. He wanted Snow's help, but at the same time he wanted to keep Snow in the dark about the full details behind his problem. He had intended to lure the demon to somewhere in the mortal plane and then contact Snow so they could deal with him together, but now Snow was bent on venturing back down to Hell with him to hunt for the demon.

Isla was still down there, searching for a phantom mage. What if she couldn't find one, highly likely considering how rare they were now, and showed up on his doorstep again?

Snow would find out all about what had happened.

He debated telling his cousin now and getting it over with, but he couldn't. Snow had said that he had changed, but the reality was that Snow had changed too. He was no longer the male that Grave had been able to confide in, the one who had fought in his corner whether he was in the right or whether he was in the wrong. Only a few minutes ago, he had treated him as if they weren't family, and now he was acting like a big brother to him?

"No." Grave pushed him away and stalked across the office, getting as far away from his cousin as he could in the small space. He stopped near a set of filing cabinets in the corner behind the huge mahogany desk. "I do not need your help."

"You never do," Snow muttered and shook his head. "But you are getting it whether you like it or not. What happens when you are fighting this demon and your problem occurs?"

He would die, and that would be the end of it.

"I will not let you go alone."

For a moment, Grave thought Antoine had been talking to him, but then he looked at the brunet male and found him staring at his brother, his dark eyebrows drawn down into a determined frown and blue eyes daring Snow to refuse.

Snow huffed. "What about Sera... and the babe?"

Grave could only stare at Antoine as the male looked down at his feet, reeling from what Snow had announced. Antoine had a child and he hadn't informed the family. If he had, word would have filtered down to him. What reason could Antoine have for keeping the child a secret?

"You have offspring?" he said and Antoine looked across at him.

"A baby girl, and she is none of your business."

That was rich considering his cousins were determined to get their noses firmly stuck into his private business. What came around, went around. If they wanted to probe into his life, he would probe into theirs.

"Did you inform the family?" He stepped around the desk, directly into line with Antoine.

The look that crossed his face confirmed his suspicions had been correct and Antoine had kept the birth from them.

"Why not?" He ventured a step towards him, curious now. The birth of a child was something to celebrate.

"Sera is elite." It was Snow who spoke, but Grave couldn't take his eyes off Antoine as that sank in.

Antoine had muddied their bloodline by mating with an elite vampire, one born of a turned human.

Or worse.

"No… you did not." He didn't need to say anymore. The guilty look on Antoine's face was answer enough.

Antoine hadn't mated with a vampire born of a turned human parent. He had mated with a turned human.

What was the world coming to?

"Millennia of our family being born of pure blood and you dare to tarnish our name with such a mating?" Grave curled his fingers into fists to stop himself from grabbing Antoine and shaking an answer out of him.

Their family had been held aloft for generations, respected by all, even the other aristocrats.

He could feel it all crumbling around him as he stared at Antoine in disbelief.

"Pure blood that has given us nothing but grief, Grave. Remember that." Snow stepped in front of Antoine, shielding his younger brother with his formidable build, and Grave looked up into his eyes.

Red ringed them, a reminder that he didn't need.

He knew first-hand the terrible result of their family's determination to keep the bloodline pure.

Bloodlust.

The fire that had set alight his blood dwindled and died as he looked at his cousins and thought about everything. His reaction to discovering the mother of Antoine's child was a turned human was wrong to a degree, a knee-jerk response that was the result of everything his parents and relatives had bred into him during his upbringing, hammering it into his head that keeping the bloodline pure was the most important thing in the world.

His cousins were right.

It wasn't.

His sister still might have been in his life if it wasn't for bloodlust. His parents. His uncle. His aunt. Everything he had lost, he had lost it because of that terrible disease.

For the first time in his life, he felt it was a bad thing. Purity had brought them nothing but grief.

Gods, who was he to judge anyway?

He had mated with a phantom.

It was all the more reason to keep it from his family. If they knew... he didn't want to think about it.

They'd all had the same ideas bred into them, all of them raised to believe that muddying their bloodline was tantamount to a sin.

How would Bastian react if he knew what Grave had done?

"If I do not go with you... it is too dangerous for you to go, Snow." Antoine's deep voice, softly laced with worry and affection, pulled Grave from his thoughts.

His younger cousin placed a hand on Snow's shoulder and Snow turned his head towards him, looking down at him as he stepped out from behind him.

Antoine wasn't talking about the dangers of the realms of Hell or those who lived within them. He was talking about it being dangerous for Snow's state of mind, that entering Hell with Grave and assisting him in something related to the shared dark part of their past might send him deep into his bloodlust.

Snow should have sought to master it as Grave had, harnessing it instead of allowing it to rule him, using it rather than fearing it. If he had, perhaps then he wouldn't have to worry about losing control.

He mentally chastised himself. He had no right to think poorly of Snow because of his inability to master his bloodlust, not when he was partly responsible for the hold it had over his cousin. An unfamiliar sensation squirmed in the pit of his stomach. He didn't normally do guilt, but it was a feeling he couldn't extinguish when it came to Snow and his predicament.

When Snow had been nearing the end of his term with the Preux Chevaliers, he had confided in Grave that he didn't want Antoine to have to serve after him because he feared it would awaken bloodlust in his younger brother. Grave had taken advantage of Snow's love for his brother, seeing it as a chance to gain something he desired—rulership of the Preux Chevaliers.

He had convinced Snow to help him take out all of the superior officers so he could take the first step in seizing control, promising that Antoine wouldn't have to serve if he was in charge.

He couldn't have known what would happen, that the battles they waged against the commanders and their loyal men would give Snow's bloodlust such power over him, and eventually lead to him losing control and killing half of their family while lost to the darkness.

He held his tongue, aware that Snow was already struggling and he was only thinking about entering Hell again. Fire warred with ice in his eyes, a constant state of flux that had Grave on the verge of telling him Antoine was right and it wasn't a wise idea.

The only thing that stopped him from refusing Snow's help was a sudden tingling in his fingers that warned they were fading again.

The attacks were either getting closer together or it was the stress of the situation causing them to fade. Either way, it wasn't good news. He focused on the mark on his back and felt it warm as he thought about Isla. Was she close to finding a mage?

He doubted it.

"Snow," Antoine started but Snow shook his head.

"Remain with Sera and the babe. Your family needs your protection."

Antoine scowled at him but it was short lived. His shoulders sagged beneath his grey shirt. "You are my family too, Snow."

It chafed that Antoine didn't mention Grave was his family. It seemed he had been right before and only Snow viewed him as kin now.

"I do not need your help," Grave bit out and tipped his chin up, standing a little taller as both of his cousins looked his way. "I only came to warn you... but now I am not really sure why I came at all. I should have sent word through a messenger. I apologise for disturbing you."

He tried to get past Snow but the male blocked the door, pressing his back to it again and refusing to budge even when Grave tugged on the handle near his hips.

"You came because we're family." Snow's words made him falter, his anger fade a little, enough that he stilled with his hand on the doorknob, the heart that had been cold for longer than he could remember warming as his cousin's words sank into it. "Deep inside you know that... we all do. No bullshit excuses now, Grave. You came because you knew I would help you... and I will."

Snow's right hand came down on his shoulder, and Grave stared at the doorframe beyond him, struggling to mask the sudden feelings that welled up inside him, softer ones he fought to banish before anyone saw them.

Was Snow right?

One look into his cousin's eyes, one glimpse of the warmth in them, gave him the answer to that question. He had come here personally because he had secretly hoped Snow would help him. Snow was powerful, his strength and skill as a warrior matching Grave's own, and with his body unpredictable he needed his cousin's assistance.

He just hadn't quite believed Snow would offer it.

Part of him wanted to keep refusing, afraid that if Snow entered Hell again and fought beside him it might give the bloodlust a stronger hold over him again and he might end up hurting Antoine and his family.

"Snow," he started but his cousin shook his head, determination flashing in his icy eyes.

"I've made up my mind. You're stuck with me whether you like it or not." Snow held his hand up when he tried to speak again. "I mean it, Grave. Whatever you have in your head, it isn't going to happen... I swear it. I'm stronger now I have Aurora. She can soothe my bloodlust and calm me. I won't hurt my family if I go to Hell with you, but I might if I don't. I'm not the sort of guy who can stand by and do nothing when the people I love are in danger and you know that. If I don't do this... if I don't go with you to stop this bastard before he can leave Hell... and he shows up here and hurts my family, then I will lose my fucking mind and gods fucking help anyone near me if that happens."

Snow did have a point. He was liable to go on a bloody rampage if the demon attacked Vampirerotique and he hadn't attempted to stop him in order to protect those he loved, more so than if he was back in Hell, reliving his past in that dark place as he helped Grave track the male down. Maybe it was better they killed the demon before he could find this theatre and their family.

Better for everyone.

"At least press your brothers for help." Antoine's hard voice cut into his thoughts like a shard of ice this time, destroying any warmth that had been flowing through him.

Not a chance. While Night would help him, Bastian would laugh if he discovered the only thing to drag Grave out of Hell and back to the family was an enemy made in service to the Preux Chevaliers, a legion he had captained before Grave, and a woman.

There was a soft knock at the door.

Snow stepped away from it and it opened a crack to reveal Aurora. Her stunning green-to-blue eyes warmed as she spotted her mate and pushed the door open all the way. Grave noted that Sable and Thorne were gone, and hoped they hadn't heard too much of his conversation with his cousins.

"What is happening?" Aurora's soft melodic voice sent a shiver down Grave's spine and he edged away from her.

"There is a demon threatening the family and Snow has decided to help Grave with it by going to Hell." The dark edge to Antoine's expression as he looked directly at Aurora, and ignored Snow's warning growl, told Grave that the male was attempting to get his brother into trouble with his mate.

The dark-haired female turned sorrowful and concerned eyes on Snow. "Is this important to you?"

He nodded. "Grave needs my help and I must give it. I am partly responsible for this demon targeting us."

Aurora looked from Snow to him, and another shiver went down his spine. Her green-to-blue eyes were eerily bright, almost glowing as she studied him. He didn't like it. He backed away another step and tried to drag his gaze away from hers, but it was impossible. It was as if she had cast a spell on him, had power over his body and could command it against his will.

He cursed her in his mind. No female had power over him.

Yet he couldn't tear his eyes away from hers.

He wasn't sure how Snow could bear being around her. It pained Grave as he looked into her eyes, seeing nothing but purity and goodness. He could feel it seeping into him, burning him, and he itched to scrub his hands over himself. Such a pure being shouldn't look at him. Wretched. Despicable. He was darkness made flesh. Her gaze bore into him and he gritted his teeth as he fought to look away from her. The extent of his sins pressed down on him for the first time, a weight his body couldn't bear, and he hated it.

Just as he was close to shoving past her to escape her steady gaze, she shifted it back to Snow.

Grave exhaled hard and slowly pulled himself together as all eyes in the room turned away from him.

"I will go with you," Aurora said and all Hell broke loose.

Snow and Antoine's voices merged into one as they argued with her and Grave had to admire the way she fought back, refusing to let the males coddle her, even when he agreed with his cousins. Hell was no place for a former angel, especially one who hadn't fallen entirely from grace to become like the fiendish fallen angels who called Hell home. When the argument grew heated, and Snow looked close to losing control to his bloodlust, visibly torn apart by the idea of his precious angel going somewhere so dangerous for her, Grave stepped forward and shocked the room, and himself at the same time.

"I promise I will not allow anything to happen to him."

He wasn't sure what had possessed him to make him promise such a thing, whether it was the thought of Snow being overwhelmed by his bloodlust or Aurora risking everything to be with her mate, or something he didn't want to consider.

All three of them stared at him in silence for what felt like hours, and then Aurora smiled at him. Positively beamed. His skin crawled. She was too good. Too damn pure. He wanted to rip that smile off her face so she couldn't turn it on him again.

Grave tamped down that vile hunger and managed to wrestle it back under control. He wouldn't harm her. He could see that she meant the world to Snow and that she was good for him, and he was glad.

One of them deserved a shot at sanity and kicking their bloodlust, and Snow definitely deserved it more than he did.

Maybe he would just fade gracefully from existence.

No one would miss him.

The three realms would be a better place for it too.

Snow lifted his head and looked over the top of Aurora's right at him, his blue eyes narrowing as his white eyebrows pinched hard above them. Grave had the oddest sensation that Snow had heard his thoughts and that look was meant to warn him that there was no way in Hell he was going to allow Grave to fade away.

He wished he had that much fight left in him, but coming here to the theatre had made him realise some things. He was tired, and he had never felt so cold and alone as he did now. No, that wasn't true. He had felt cold and alone for decades.

Since Isla had betrayed him.

"Who is she?"

Grave snapped back to the room and stared at Snow. "Who is who?"

His cousin's gaze was unflinching and merciless. "The female who did this to you."

His first instinct was to dance around things and ask 'did what to me?' but he didn't see the point when Snow crossed his arms over his broad chest and set his jaw, making it clear that he wasn't going to give up. Dog with a damned bone. Typical of his cousin.

Grave sighed and gave a pointed look at Aurora.

Snow shook his head. "She's staying."

He huffed again. Stubborn bastard.

The weight of their gazes pressed down on him and he struggled with the words, with his feelings, all of his usual confidence draining away as he considered what he was about to do. He wanted it, but he feared it at the same time. No one knew about what had happened to him, and he hadn't realised how much he needed to confide in someone until he had set eyes on Snow again.

Gods, he felt pathetic.

He blamed Isla for this weakness and then immediately took it back, and that only made his mood worsen to the point where he was close to snapping at his cousin to leave him alone and turning his back on his family.

Again.

He shut out Antoine and Aurora, focusing solely on Snow, and swallowed his pride.

"She is my mate."

Antoine chuckled, the sound out of place in the thick silence. "You are a fated mate for someone? Poor bastard."

Grave shrugged. "Thank you."

Antoine shook his head. "I wasn't talking about you. I was talking about the female. What did she do to deserve you as her mate?"

"Brother," Snow warned but Antoine ignored him and kept grinning at Grave.

Grave considered punching it off his face but settled for glaring at him as he thought about Isla and what she had done to him, and fury kindled in his black heart, slowly spread inky tendrils through him and tugged at his bloodlust.

"Maybe it is because she is a callous bitch?" he barked and felt nothing when Aurora flinched and backed towards Snow, and the male growled at him in warning. He pinned red eyes on Antoine and advanced on him, his breaths coming harder as everything Isla had done to him swam in his mind, stoking his rage to new heights. "She pulled me into a bond, spinning lies and false feelings, making me believe that she was in love with me too, and then she betrayed me. Fucking phantoms."

He knew he had said too much when Antoine's smile disappeared, his expression turning sombre and deadly serious.

"A phantom?" Antoine pushed him in his left shoulder, and the bastard was lucky he had chosen wisely and hadn't touched his healing right one or he would have ripped his throat open with his fangs. "But you are solid. A male who mates with a phantom becomes incorporeal like them."

Grave growled. "Not if she is corporeal at the time. She had some mage do a spell on her to make her solid... apparently it is wearing off."

Snow raked blue eyes over him. "You are becoming a wraith."

"What happens when you become one?" Antoine had moved through serious to concerned, and Grave wasn't sure how to process that. He couldn't remember the last time his younger cousin had looked as if he gave a damn about him. "Something tells me you're not just becoming a phantom, Grave."

Grave looked away from him and blew out his breath. There was little use in lying now. He had started and he would finish telling his cousins everything, because it was lifting some of the weight from his shoulders and some of the black clouds from the horizon ahead of him.

Even when it gave fear a hold over him too.

He had thought about what was going to happen, but talking about it to someone made it feel more real, and more unavoidable, and his need to escape the future that seemed set out for him was so strong that he could barely breathe.

Gods, that part he kept denying kicked off again, wishing Isla would find the mage, and this time it pushed him to find her and help her, to place this problem before his other one.

He looked at his family, torn between hunting the demon and hunting down a mage. Saving them or saving himself.

Either way it would be saving Isla.

Her name was poison in his mind, but a balm to his heart, and he didn't understand how he could both hate and love her at the same time.

She hadn't only betrayed him.

She had condemned him.

"I will not become a phantom," Grave said, little more than a whisper but his voice seemed loud in the silent room. "I am fading."

"Dying," Snow snapped. "Say it straight, Cousin. You are dying."

Grave nodded, and damn, it felt as if he had just taken a step closer to that fate, had made it real by accepting it.

"I will not let that happen," Snow echoed his thoughts and Grave had to admire his cousin's tenacity. Dog with a bone. "We will find someone to fix this first and then we will tackle the demon."

Grave wanted to refuse, but he didn't have the heart, and sense said that it was the right course of action. The demon hadn't attacked anyone yet, and attempting to fight him when he was weakened by his condition was a death sentence, and he preferred to remain alive.

"I know some places we can begin looking for a mage." As he said those words, fear slowly tightened its hold on him, sinking claws deep into his heart.

Isla was looking for a mage too.

He didn't want to think about what might happen if they crossed paths again, not because Snow would be with him and was liable to attack her, and that would trigger an episode of bloodlust in Grave that he knew he wouldn't be able to control, but because he wasn't sure whether he was strong enough to see her again.

He wasn't sure he was strong enough to resist the feelings he still had for her.

Lost in thoughts of Isla, he barely paid attention as Snow and Antoine laid out a plan. It was only when he found himself standing in a small bedroom on the second floor of the theatre, staring down at a single bed, that he became aware of the world again.

Aware of something other than his mate.

He stripped down to his black boxer shorts, lay on top of the dark grey covers, and rested his hands on his stomach. A twinge shot through his right shoulder. He grimaced and rubbed it, stared at the ceiling as he worked to soothe the knotted muscle, and lost himself again.

The mark on his back warmed, and he didn't close the connection Isla was forging between them. He allowed it to blossom and thoughts of her to come with it, to fill his mind and steal him away from the world, filling the quiet hours of day as sleep eluded him.

Someone knocked on his door, pulling him away from her at last, and he frowned as his senses warned the sun was setting and he hadn't managed to sleep at all. He dressed and opened the door, and Aurora was there. She dropped her gaze to his riding boots and twisted her hands in front of the waist of her white dress.

"Snow is ready."

Grave eyed the fresh set of marks on her throat. Snow was ready and fed by the looks of things. His stomach growled at the thought of blood and he swore he would find some soon. His healing injuries demanded it almost as fiercely as his bloodlust.

Maybe he would drain the mage dry after the spell was done.

He followed the petite raven-haired female down to the backstage room where Snow was waiting, deep in conversation with Antoine. A pretty blonde stood beside him, rocking a small bundle of black in her arms, a contrast against her blood red dress that had Grave's stomach rumbling again.

An unruly tuft of pale hair poked out of the black cloth.

"Bop." The female tapped the baby on its nose and it wriggled and laughed. When it stilled, she did it again. "Bop."

Grave edged closer and tried to get a look at his new relation. The female lifted her head and he waited for her to frown at him or say something to drive him away.

"I don't think we've met," she said, surprising him with a bright smile that reached her forest green eyes. "I'm Sera and this little bundle is Helena."

She tilted the baby towards him and Grave canted his head as he looked at her, into pale blue eyes and at white-blonde hair that were a painful reminder but one he couldn't look away from.

"It is a coincidence." Antoine's voice sounded distant to his ears.

Helena wriggled again, pulled a face of sheer frustration as she tried to escape the blanket, and Grave still couldn't stop staring at her.

"Sera insisted."

"I like the name," she shot back, a touch of malice in her tone now. "You never gave me a valid reason not to call our daughter Helena."

"It was my mother's name," Grave said, his own voice sounding as if he was listening to it from afar. "She looks like her."

"I know." She tucked the baby close to her chest and tapped her nose again, eliciting another laugh. "I thought it was an honour to her, like your brother Bastian is named for Antoine and Snow's father."

Snow placed a hand on his shoulder, snapping Grave out of his stupor, and he looked across at his cousin where he stood beside him. Pain filled his cousin's blue eyes and Grave shook his head, silently telling him that he didn't need to apologise.

After everything they had been through in Hell together, all the missions that had fuelled the rise of their bloodlust, they had a bond that was stronger than blood.

It was that bond that had Snow coming to his aid, just as Grave would always go to his when he needed him.

He only wished he had been home that night when Snow had needed him most, not far away in Hell, bent on taking command of the Preux Chevaliers, caring only about his own life and neglecting his family.

Snow slipped away from him, returning to Aurora, and Grave looked away as she showered affection on him. He was finding it hard to keep his thoughts off Isla as it was. Watching Snow with Aurora would only give his phantom more power over him, until she haunted his every waking moment.

"It is an honour," he said to Sera, not wanting her to feel she had done wrong by choosing a family name for her child.

In a way, he was glad she had picked his mother's name, because the babe was beautiful enough to bear it and perhaps it would help her grow into someone as kind and caring as his mother had been.

He bowed his head to Antoine and Sera, and little Helena, and led himself to the main foyer of the theatre. It was quiet, dark and cool, a thousand miles away from the busy palace he called home, where the temperature rarely ventured anywhere near cold.

And his home was a million miles away from the world of snow he had grown up in, a frigid and icy landscape where summer had been mercifully short and winter had been long, and filled with days where the sun refused to creep above the horizon.

"Ready?" Snow's deep voice transported him back to that world, to a time when he had been young and carefree, and they had been on the verge of venturing forth from their castle for the first time, heading for the mortal villages to find females to feed from, among other things.

Grave nodded and spoke in the old tongue, echoing the words he had said then. "As I will ever be."

Snow chuckled and walked forwards, and Grave paused to watch him. He wore his hair the same, overlong and messy, but gone were the thick fur cloak, tunic, trousers and fur-lined boots, replaced with a figure-hugging pair of black jeans, heavy soled leather boots, and a black t-shirt.

He still had the gait of a warrior though.

Snow paused on the portico of the theatre. Grave joined him and frowned as he sensed his cousin's hesitation, the fear that flowed through him as he eyed the mortals coming and going along the street and then the evening sky.

"Don't get out much?" Grave looked across at him.

Snow shook his head and cracked a smile. "Just a short stint now and then to test me."

"And how often does it go horribly wrong?" Grave couldn't resist asking that question, mostly to tease his cousin but partly because he wanted to know just what he had signed up for.

His smile widened. "Seven out of ten times. Aurora is getting good at teleporting me quickly back to the theatre and calming me."

Grave needed to look into angels more. Teleporting was a handy ability, one he hadn't realised she would still possess after leaving her home.

"Maybe she should have come with us, if she can teleport and soothe your bloodlust."

Snow growled, flashing fangs at him. "She is an angel. She cannot enter Hell without suffering greatly and you know it."

He did know it, and he regretted suggesting it as he saw the pain in Snow's eyes and the male glanced back over his shoulder into the theatre, a look of longing on his face. He hadn't considered how difficult this would be for his cousin, not only going to Hell but leaving the woman he loved behind. Vulnerable. A demon was targeting her too.

Just as he was targeting Grave's mate.

Grave shook that thought away.

Isla had never really been his mate. Everything had been a lie and he wasn't sure why he couldn't make himself remember that. Anger began to push to the surface again, fury that he was sure would never die, just like his feelings for Isla. He breathed to calm himself, slowly settling his feelings and mastering his rising bloodlust, pushing it back into submission.

He clapped a hand down on Snow's shoulder.

"Well, at least if you lose your head in Hell, you won't be alone. We can go on a bloody rampage together." Grave flashed a toothy smile at Snow.

Snow let out a laugh.

"It will be like old times."

CHAPTER 9

Isla couldn't escape Grave. Whenever she closed her eyes, he was there. Whenever she let her mind wander for a moment, he was waiting. She stared at the horizon, not seeing the cragged range of black mountains. She saw Grave.

She saw him lounging on his black throne, shirt undone to expose the tantalising ridges of his stomach and chest, tempting her fingers and lips, making her yearn to chart the paths she used to take across his body and relearn them, and all his secrets. She still remembered just where to kiss to make him laugh, or lick to make him moan.

She remembered everything about her vampire.

He was branded on her mind.

On her heart.

Her very soul.

She looked down at her feet and slowly shut her eyes, and heaved a sigh. It only made it harder to see him now, and witness the contrast between the male he had become and the one he had been before she had turned on him.

Isla cursed the phantom instincts that had made her do such a thing to Grave, and to herself.

She had been happy with him, had known true love for the first time and had experienced a deeper sort of love for her too, one that surpassed anything the males she had seduced with her phantom wiles had ever shown for her.

She eased down onto a rock on the gently sloping north side of the valley, stared off into the distance again and couldn't hold back another sigh.

She hadn't been prepared for that at all.

When Melia had mated with Valador, Isla had visited her sister and seen her flesh and blood, witnessed the love they shared and watched as they had exchanged tender caresses whenever they had thought no one was looking at them. She had thought she understood what they had, had honestly believed it no different to what she had with the males she seduced other than it would last longer.

She hadn't realised how wrong she had been until she had been made flesh herself and had gone after Grave.

Had fallen in love with him despite his flaws, and the things she knew he had done.

Isla propped her right elbow on her knee, rested her chin on her upturned palm, and fought the memories of those days.

Those halcyon days.

Lost forever.

She reminded herself that what she had done had been the objective of her mission, and everything else that had happened had been wrong, but her heart reproached her and twisted it around.

Falling in love with him, and making him fall in love with her had been right, and what she had done to him, using those feelings against him, acting like a phantom, had been wrong.

When had she started to hate her true nature?

She closed her eyes again. She knew the answer to that question in her soul.

In her heart.

She had begun to hate it the moment she had started falling for Grave, and she had grown to despise it when she had turned on him.

Now he haunted her, was more a phantom than she was, determined to make her suffer in the name of vengeance.

Gods.

Another flash of him reclining on his throne burst into her mind and she rubbed the bridge of her nose. It didn't stop a second image from exploding into existence, this one in time with the mark on her back tingling. The mortal realm. A beautiful country house. The image stuttered and faded.

It was always the way it happened. She would see something from her past, something she had witnessed with her own eyes, and then seconds later she would see through his in the present. Heat pulsed along the lines of her mating mark. Not her doing. Grave was in control of the connection between them, and was responsible for the flashes of him in her mind.

Was he aware he was doing it?

He did it to taunt her, to hurt her, normally, but whenever she had seen through his eyes over the past day, she had seen strange things. The world of mortals. A male with snow white hair and blue eyes that reminded her of Grave's. Then an elegant black vehicle with dark windows. Now a stunning house.

Isla felt certain that he wasn't aware that he was revealing these things to her, giving her glimpses of a journey he was on.

Where was he?

In all the years she had known him, he had never left Hell. He had even confessed that he hadn't left it in centuries before the day they had met, had been resolute that his place was here and not there.

What had made him venture forth from Hell to a place he had seemed to never want to set foot in again?

She shook away her curiosity and studied the valley below her. She had her own mission and her own journey, and it was time she continued it. She had rested long enough.

She stood and dusted the backside of her blue leathers down as she tried to focus on her mission to find a phantom mage, recounting the information she had gathered, all in an attempt to push Grave from her mind, but it was harder now that she was tired. Her small breaks weren't enough to restore her energy, and she hadn't fed in days, but she couldn't stop now.

She was close. She could feel it.

Her eyes stopped on the town a league from her that hugged the foothills of the mountain range that formed a border between the free realm and the elf kingdom. Light shone down on it from the realm of the elves, but the mountains partially blocked it, so half of the town was illuminated and the other side was dark, lit by the glow of lamps.

Isla started down the slope, and managed to keep her focus fixed on her mission for most of her journey to the town, mulling over everything she had been told about the phantom mage she was tracking. Several accounts had placed him in this town, all from people spread around the various villages and settlements in the free realm. He had to be here, or at least be known here. If he had moved on, she might be able to find information about him that would point to his new location.

She reached the edge of the town.

Images flashed across her eyes, overlaying onto the dark stone buildings, and she staggered back as a bloody scene played out before her and sudden pain stabbed through her heart like a hot lance.

Not born of her connection to Grave this time.

Isla blinked hard, reeling and breathless as her heart slammed against her chest, blood thundering in her veins, sending adrenaline shooting through her so fast that her legs trembled and hands shook.

Melia.

She broke into a dead sprint, eyes darting around the town as she rushed into it, desperately seeking a portal. There had to be one.

Another series of images blasted through her mind and her heart missed a beat.

Crimson on white flagstones.

The courtyard bathed in red.

She shoved people out of her way as she sensed a portal nearby, ignoring their shouts and curses, hot tears blinding her as she raced towards it. She had to reach Melia.

The castle was under attack.

Pain went through her again, agony that tore her heart apart and stole her breath.

Pain that wasn't her own.

"Melia!" she screamed as she spotted the tell-tale shimmer in the air just beyond the other end of the small town and sprinted harder, pushing herself past her limit.

Her muscles burned in protest, but she couldn't slow.

She had to reach her sister.

She skidded on the black earth, sliding into the portal, and chanted the words and her destination.

Darkness swallowed her.

She was running again before it had even evaporated, sprinting through the too-quiet streets of the white citadel, her eyes leaping up towards the spires of the castle that towered above her on the plateau.

The stench of blood hit her hard as she reached the arched doorway in the thick white curving wall that opened onto the steps that swept upwards to the castle, together with another scent that she recognised as a phantom, because it was a smell that seemed to follow her kind everywhere.

Death.

Her hands snagged the two blades strapped to her lower back and she pulled them free of their dark blue leather holster as she took the steps two at a time, tears spilling onto her cheeks as her feet carried her past the broken bodies of the guards. She shook her head and clung to hope in her heart.

Hope that her sister wasn't gone to the afterlife with those poor souls.

She spared a glance at one of the soldiers near the top of the winding staircase and quickly looked away. Whoever had killed him had torn him to shreds, ripped right through his black uniform to sever flesh and bone.

What beast could have done such a thing?

Isla stopped dead as she hit the courtyard, her grip on the wooden hilts of her curved blades loosening as she stared at the carnage. Blood sprayed up the thick stone walls of the castle, splattered the fountain in the centre of the courtyard, and drenched the flagstones as it pooled beneath the dead demons.

A whole legion. Close to one hundred males.

All of them dead.

A chill raced over her as she walked through their bodies, boots skidding on the blood, despair filling her heart and turning it cold.

Freezing it.

A slow burn began as she curled her fingers around her blades, her teeth coming together hard as she looked upon the dead and a dark hunger began to blaze in her heart.

Vengeance.

Whoever had done this, they would pay.

That black need faltered when she looked at the arched entrance of the castle and she swallowed hard, her blood chilling again.

Melia.

She stormed towards the doors and along the corridor, picking up pace as she neared the arched white double doors of the grand hall. Pain beat through her, agony so fierce that she could hardly breathe, but it also gave her relief.

Melia was still alive.

She ran towards the doors. Towards Melia.

Isla shoved the battered doors to the grand hall open, hitting them so hard that one flew off its hinges, and she stumbled into the room.

Where was her sister?

She had to be injured, badly if the pain Isla could feel through their connection was any indicator, but whatever had happened to her, Isla could fix it.

Her gaze caught on something on the raised dais, beside the white spiked throne of the First Realm, resting there in a pool of blood.

Her blades fell from her hands, clattering on the white flagstones.

She blinked hard, sending hot tears tumbling down her cheeks as she drifted forward, drawn towards them.

Wooden zoo animals.

Isla shook her head, her eyebrows furrowing as she refused to believe what she was seeing. It was a nightmare. A nightmare. That was all.

She glided to a halt at the foot of the dais and stared down at the blood-splattered toys that were worn at the edges, the varnish rubbed away by tender small hands and too much play.

No.

Even as she refused to believe it, her numbed heart knew it was true, and she squeezed her eyes shut against the pain that cut her like a thousand blades, each of them piercing that heart.

When she opened her eyes again, they rested on a smear of blood that streaked across the white stone, leading towards her right. She followed that line, fury rising inside her again like a phoenix from the ashes, burning so fiercely yet she couldn't feel it as she tracked the trail of blood.

She couldn't feel anything as her eyes lit upon her sister.

Melia kneeled in the corner with her back to Isla, blood covering her, streaking her white dress and hair. Her soft voice reached to Isla, a song in the phantom tongue that she hadn't heard since they were children.

A lullaby.

Isla's throat tightened, her lower lip wobbling as she fought the tears, the sorrow that chilled her at the same time as it filled her with fire.

Melia turned, looking over her shoulder at Isla, all the pain in the world in her blue eyes. Agony that echoed inside Isla.

Isla stopped sharply, a gasp escaping her before a sob followed it as Melia turned more towards her and she saw Tarwyn.

"No… no… no… no!" She staggered a step forwards and her legs gave out, sending her crashing to her knees on the white flagstones, but she didn't feel the pain as it shot through her.

The agony in her heart eclipsed it.

Tarwyn's beautiful eyes stared heavenward, his little face and white shirt covered in blood, but it was the vicious cut across his small throat that arrested her eyes and she couldn't pull them away from it.

So brutal. So merciless.

He was only a child.

What kind of monster would do such a thing to a child?

Isla broke down as Melia stared at her, curling forwards into her knees and sobbing against them, her entire body shuddering as she became deeply aware of what was to come.

She had lost her nephew.

Now she would lose her sister.

She lifted her head and silently implored Melia not to do it, to stay with her. She was the only light in this dark world, Isla's only warmth and comfort. She couldn't lose her too, not when it felt as if everything she loved in this life was being torn from her piece by piece.

The light in the room faded as anger welled up inside her and reflected in Melia's cold blue eyes.

Those eyes lowered back to the boy she held and she drew him closer to her, clutching his lifeless form to her chest, and began singing softly again.

No.

Isla reached for her, desperate to find her voice, to find the one thing she could say to make her sister stay with her, even when she knew it was impossible.

Melia was bound to Tarwyn through his father's blood.

With his death, she would fade.

She would disappear forever.

Isla couldn't bear it.

The thunder of footsteps came from behind her but she didn't tear her eyes away from her sister.

A deep male voice barked orders in the demon tongue, sending men to scout the castle, and she wanted to tell him it was pointless. Whoever had committed this atrocity was gone, and now all they could do was mourn.

Mourn and plan their revenge.

Whoever had done this, she would make them pay. She would make them suffer. They would know her wrath.

"What happened?" the male asked, his voice softer, a thickness to it that spoke to Isla of his pain.

A question she desperately wanted to ask. She needed the answer to it, so she could hunt and destroy the one responsible.

She looked up as the male paused beside her, his large hand coming down gently on her shoulder. He wobbled in her tear-filled vision and she blinked to clear it, but new tears came as she saw the ones in his pale blue eyes. His golden horns curled from behind his ears, twisted around like a ram's to reveal his rage. His pain.

Frey.

His eyes glowed in the low light as he looked from her to Melia and his hand shook against Isla's shoulder. She could see the fight to contain his grief written in every tight line of his handsome face, but somehow he was winning that battle when she had lost hers. He was holding himself together when she was falling apart. Gods, she envied his strength, wished she could be like him, could contain the pain ripping her apart and destroying her.

"I never should have left the castle," he bit out. "I am sorry."

Melia slowly shook her head and continued rocking with Tarwyn. "It is not your fault. It is mine. I should not have left him alone with his nurses. I should not have ventured down to visit the families in the town and left my own family defenceless. It is my fault."

Melia turned her head towards Isla, her eyes as dark as midnight.

"It is all my fault... I never should have told you how to become corporeal... I should have known what you would do..." Melia looked back down at Tarwyn and brushed a strand of pale hair from his brow. "I never should have idly stood by and allowed you to bewitch the vampire..."

Isla shot to her feet, her head spinning and sending the room twirling with it as she struggled to take that in.

"Did he do this? Did Grave do this?" Her gaze jumped to Tarwyn and the gruesome slash across his throat, and her mind leaped to recall all the dead demons in the courtyard. She couldn't believe it. Grave was vicious, bloodthirsty, but she had never seen him attack a child. Her eyes widened. The flashes of his journey. "He was not here. I know that. Grave was not here at the castle."

She had seen him at a house of mortal fashion just seconds before she had seen the castle.

"He did not need to be," Melia whispered and stroked her son's forehead. "His name is fitting. Wherever he goes, death follows in his wake... in his shadow... and he brings it to those he has never even met... through others."

Her sister raised her head and pinned cold eyes on her, and Isla swallowed hard, wanted to deny that but she couldn't find her voice, not when Melia was looking at her that way, as if she knew something and was afraid to tell her.

"How is he responsible?" The phantom side of her was already pushing, demanding she take revenge upon him and the one he had somehow sent to destroy this most beloved part of her world.

Melia's eyes hardened and the words that left her lips cut Isla to the bone and she couldn't breathe through the pain.

"The vampire is not responsible... you are."

"No." Isla shook her head. "No!"

It couldn't be true.

Melia gently caressed Tarwyn's horns, her eyes back on him. "It was my fault for telling you how to gain a solid form... it was my fault for not seeing what you intended to do and stopping you from seducing the vampire... and for that I have paid the ultimate price. I have paid for allowing you to mate with a vampire. I saw the one who did this. I came upon him in the courtyard as he was leaving."

Her sister pressed her hand to her side and Isla looked there, swallowed hard as she noticed the blood on her dress was fresh, still flowing.

"He knew what I was... but I was not what he was looking for... so he kept me alive to deliver a message."

"A message?" Isla staggered forwards a step.

"The vampire took family from a demon prince and now that demon prince will take everything from him... beginning with his family."

Ice prickled down Isla's spine, a feeling building within her, mixed with dread.

"But Tarwyn and the demons of this realm are not Grave's family... I do not understand, Sister. Why did he attack us?"

Melia slowly drew her eyes away from Tarwyn and Isla shuddered as her sister fixed them on her, feeling the cold in them race over her skin. "It is a tactic of war... to ensure your victory, target that which would weaken your enemy the most first."

Her.

Isla's knees buckled. Frey caught her in his arm, the warmth of it not a comfort as reality crashed over her and all she could feel was infinite cold. She didn't have the strength to stand, so she hung limp in his arm, head and heart reeling from the blow.

She was responsible.

The demon prince Melia spoke of wanted to repay Grave by taking his family, and what better way of weakening the vampire was there than targeting his mate first?

The demon had come for her, in order to take her from Grave, and instead he had taken everything from her.

The ice in Melia's eyes melted as she looked up at Isla and Isla tried to push out of Frey's arms as her sister began to fade before her eyes. Frey held her closer and she wasn't strong enough to break free of him, no matter how fiercely she struggled.

"Stay," Isla husked, voice thick with the pain beating hard behind her breast as she stretched an arm out to her sister. Her hand shook in the air between them. "Hold on. I will find a phantom mage to save you."

Melia began to shimmer, her form losing colour to turn as white as snow.

"I cannot live without you." Isla shook her head, her pale eyebrows furrowed and tears spilling down her cheeks, hot against her cold skin.

Melia smiled softly and it only made the pain grow fiercer inside Isla, until it felt as if it would consume her.

"I cannot," Melia whispered. "My place is now with my love and my son."

Isla's lower lip trembled and she kept shaking her head, silently pleading her sister to stay even when she knew all she could do was watch her fade away.

She couldn't take it as Tarwyn's body slipped through Melia's to land on the bloodstained floor and her sister's voice no longer reached Isla's ears as her mouth moved.

She heard the words echo in her mind instead.

"I love you, Isla... dearest sister... and I forgive you. Do not fade... do not allow your foolish pride to stand between you and living... not when you love your mate. I would give anything for another day... another minute with Valador and Tarwyn. Another second."

Melia's voice grew quiet in her mind and her form faded from ghostly white to little more than a shimmer in the air.

And then nothing.

Isla screamed out her agony as the connection between her and her sister shattered.

Grave flashed into her mind, facing her this time, and he stopped and seemed to look right at her, and then she was falling through the air.

She reached for him, desperate to touch him, desperate to feel his arms around her, but the distance between them grew and then darkness yawned around her.

It swallowed her.

CHAPTER 10

Something was wrong.

Very wrong.

Grave stopped dead on the golden gravel of the driveway, a spike in adrenaline halting him in his tracks, and he felt sure someone was about to attack him. He looked around him but only his cousin was there beside him, like a wraith in the darkness.

He pressed his hand to his chest. His heart pounded against it.

What the hell was wrong with him?

He tried to shake the feeling away, putting it down to nothing more than the stress of everything that had happened over the past week, but it refused to go.

A tremendous burst of agony blasted through him and he gritted his teeth and dug his claws into his chest through his black shirt. Damn.

"What's wrong?" Snow said beside him, concern in his deep voice.

Grave looked at his white-haired cousin and shook his head. "Nothing."

Snow arched an eyebrow at that, but didn't press him, and he was glad as he slowly breathed through the pain and struggled to figure out what had just happened. Was it the bond? Was he going to fade?

He shook that thought away, refusing to let it take root and seize control of him.

Nerves and fatigue were getting the better of him, making him weak. Making him want to see her.

Gods, he would rather be facing her than what awaited him.

He looked up at the huge Georgian house, the sensation of dread only deepening as he scanned the two levels of sash windows that punctuated the sandstone façade, meeting in the centre at a double-height portico, with towering Grecian columns that supported a triangular pediment with a beautiful carved frieze set into it.

Golden light shone from most of the windows and from the lamps on the walls beneath the portico too, lending it a warm glow. One that did nothing to ease the chill in Grave's blood.

"I still can't believe you mated with a phantom," Snow said and Grave shot him a glare.

His cousin had spewed the same line at least two dozen times during their long journey, and each time Grave had only answered him with a scowl. It seemed Snow was intent on getting a real answer out of him, and if it would shut him up and stop him from constantly mentioning Isla, dragging Grave's treacherous thoughts to her, he would give it to him.

Because he was finding it hard enough to keep his mind off her, his heart away from thoughts of her that didn't belong in it after what she had done, without his cousin bringing her up every fifteen minutes.

"I did not realise she was a phantom at the time. She had substance... flesh, bone and blood." And he couldn't get over the taste of her.

Everyone else he bit tasted like ashes, but she tasted like Heaven.

Like everything he could ever want or need.

Grave ventured a step forwards and paused again, struggling to muster the courage to reach the dark wooden door and rouse the inhabitants.

He looked back at Snow and scowled at him when Snow gave him a soft look, one that sympathised with him and made it clear he knew Grave was having trouble overcoming his fear of this place.

His fear of the one who lived in it.

Grave cursed him in his head. If his cousin could see his weakness, then the one he had come to speak with would see it too. He schooled his features and systematically shut down his feelings, one by one, pushing them back into place and then extinguishing them, until he felt nothing.

He stepped up onto the porch and rapped his knuckles against the door.

A slender petite mortal female answered it, her caramel-coloured eyes so large that she appeared doll-like.

"I must speak with my brother," Grave said, and it felt as if he had never spoken words more difficult to voice than those.

She bowed her head, stepped back to allow them to enter and then closed the door quietly behind them. He studied her as she hurried away, her head still bent, her dark chocolate hair brushing across the back of her short black dress in soft glossy waves.

Bastian had always had a thing for embracing the aristocrat way of life to the full, taking everything he believed was his right as a pureblood from a noble line of vampires, including mortal servants. A simple bite was enough to enslave them. While it had once been acceptable to force a mortal into servitude, it was now required by vampire law that the mortal chose to serve. Becoming a servant of a vampire offered perks that many mortals found impossible to resist. The lure of a longer life, one free of disease, was often enough to get a mortal to agree to becoming a vampire's servant, but on top of that many of the aristocrats paid their servants well and gave them a roof over their heads.

Grave wasn't sure Bastian paid his servants well, but he knew his older brother allowed them to live in his house, kept them fed and took good care of them.

The sound of footsteps on the Italian marble floor drew his focus back to the room and a shadow emerged from the corridor to the left of the double-height grand entrance hall, taking form as the male stepped out of the darkness, dressed in a fine black tailored suit, his dark shirt opened at the collar.

Night.

Grave frowned at his younger brother. "Where is Bastian?"

"Away." Night rubbed a hand around the back of his neck, giving away his nerves.

His younger brother never had been very good at hiding his feelings, was a sharp contrast to his own nature and that of Bastian. Sometimes Grave wondered why Night had chosen to serve in the Preux Chevaliers when only one son from an aristocrat family was required to serve at any time, and even then only for four centuries.

Night had been serving for close to six, although Grave had assigned him to duties in the mortal world to keep him away from Hell.

His brother could fight, had proven himself in battle, and Asher had questioned him when he had decided to reassign Night from the Second Legion to overseeing their covert missions in the mortal realm.

Grave had told his second in command that Night was more suited to the role of an assassin than a mercenary.

Asher had bought it, but Grave hadn't.

In reality, it had been a moment of weakness on Grave's part.

He had wanted his younger brother away from the constant wars of Hell.

He had wanted to protect him and he had known that Night would have refused if he had issued him an order to leave the Preux Chevaliers, but that he wouldn't refuse the order to head a team of vampires responsible for missions of a more secret nature. So he had created a black ops type group, selecting the vampires most suited to the task from among his legions, and had placed Night in command of them.

It turned out his younger brother was terrifyingly good at it, a tactical genius and one who had been born to move in the shadows, silently eliminating his prey without leaving a trace of evidence behind.

Night glanced at the young mortal female as she re-entered the room.

Grave arched an eyebrow at the way Night's blue eyes followed her as she walked up to them and lingered on her as she bowed.

The female lifted her head and Grave frowned as he saw her neck was unmarked.

Bastian hadn't claimed her as his property yet.

He looked from the mortal to Night, who still hadn't taken his eyes off her.

Perhaps he had been wrong and his younger brother was an idiot after all, because it looked as if he was on the verge of doing something foolish, something that might see his own flesh and blood killing him before the demon prince could even track him down.

"The room is ready," she said in a quiet voice, one that trembled with nerves.

Not born of fear.

Grave slid his gaze back to her and caught the hint of colour on her cheeks before she turned away, leading them towards the room she had prepared. She was courting his brother's attention and was enjoying it when she should have been aware of her position in the household and should have been acting accordingly, behaving like the servant she was.

Night obediently followed her. Grave lingered and looked to Snow.

"He will get himself into trouble," Snow said, confirming he had seen what Grave had.

Grave huffed and stormed across the vestibule, following Night as he disappeared into the room beneath the twin wooden staircases opposite the entrance. He caught up with his younger brother just as he reached the trio of antique gilt-framed red chairs that formed a horseshoe around the black marble fireplace in the deep-red-walled reception room.

Night gestured to the couch that faced the fireplace as he took the armchair to the left of it, a position that would allow him to easily watch the mortal female. She had set up her tray of crystal goblets and steel canisters on the mahogany side table near the right corner of the room, beside one of the four tall French doors that lined the same wall as the fireplace, two on either side of it.

Grave shot his brother a warning look that Night failed to notice as he watched the female pouring blood for them.

Snow lingered at the door and his wariness was the only thing that stopped Grave from saying something to Night. He looked back at his cousin instead. Snow's pale blue eyes were locked on the blood as it flowed into the glasses and red began to ring his irises.

"No blood," Grave said and the female snapped her head up, looked directly at him and then swiftly dropped her eyes back to her feet.

Either Bastian had a long way to go in training her on the correct way to behave around an aristocrat vampire, or Night's overfamiliarity with her had made her forget her place.

Grave waved her away.

She bowed her head, gathered her things and left.

Night's gaze followed her but stopped when it reached him. It narrowed and Grave gave his younger sibling a look he hoped conveyed how little he cared that Night was threatening him over a mortal female of all things.

And how insane he thought his brother was.

He took a seat on the couch at the end nearest Night. Snow chose the other armchair and eased his big frame into it, but still looked uncomfortable and severely out of place. Grave wasn't sure he could ever remember a time when Snow had looked to be in the right place for him.

Perhaps back where they had grown up, surrounded by a wild white mountainous world.

"I need you to leave this place," Grave said and Night frowned at him. He spoke before his brother could dare to question him. "There is a demon, one who declares himself a prince of that kind... belonging to the Devil."

Night's eyes showed a flicker of fear for a moment, a brief second of weakness before his expression hardened again.

"A mission for the Preux Chevaliers that myself and Snow led should have eliminated all of his bloodline but somehow he survived, and now he is bent on killing us all in the name of revenge. So you have to leave." Grave reached for Night's hand and his brother didn't move it, instead allowing him to place his hand over it and squeeze it.

How differently this night would have gone had Bastian been home.

Bastian had never allowed him to get this close, had always held him at a distance even when they were young. The bastard acted like the father they had lost, was bent on making him and Night live up to a standard that he deemed worthy of their family name, uncaring about how they felt or whether they killed themselves to reach the dizzying heights where Bastian believed they were meant to stand.

Grave didn't give a damn about what Bastian thought he should or shouldn't do, but over the years he had begun to realise that it had shaped him as a youth, had driven him to succeed and surpass him, to scrub out his brother's hallowed name in the history of the Preux Chevaliers and carve his own in its place.

When he had succeeded in that, Bastian hadn't been pleased, not as a male so bent on forcing his brothers to raise their family name to the highest it could go, so high that all other vampires had to look up to them, should have been.

No. Bastian had turned on him, had been angry and cold, and vicious.

Bastian had grown to despise him, not love him for his achievements as he had promised.

So Bastian didn't give a damn about him now, and Grave didn't give a damn what Bastian thought of him.

He really didn't.

"Disappear, Night." Grave tightened his grip on his younger brother's hand and Night looked down at it and then up into his eyes.

Pale blue ones. Short dark hair. Looking at Night was often like looking at a reflection of himself.

But one thing was different.

His eyes dropped to the scar around Night's throat, a silvery line that stretched from below one ear to the other.

Night snatched his hand away and lifted it, bringing it up towards his throat. He stopped before he touched it and looked away, cleared his throat and lowered his hand. Grave silently apologised. He knew Night hated it whenever someone looked at the reminder of the wound he had somehow survived.

"Listen to me," Grave said and Night's red-ringed blue eyes slid his way. "You must disappear."

"I cannot. I have to remain here and keep my promise to Bastian."

Grave frowned at that. "What promise?"

What on Earth could possibly keep Night here when he had just told him that a demon from the Devil's ranks was after his head?

The scar around his neck should have been enough to remind Night just how easily a vampire could die and have him leaving right that moment.

Something was making him stay, and Grave had the feeling it was more than just a promise to Bastian. It was something to do with the female.

"I told Bastian I would take care of the house while he was away on business." Night refused to look at him, even when he growled a warning at him.

"This is not a game, Night."

His younger brother rolled his shoulders beneath his black suit jacket. "I can see that from your escort. How is business, Snow?"

Snow leaned back in his armchair and eyed Night, his voice as cold as the lands they all hailed from. "Going well. You should listen to your brother. This is no time to joke and be foolish."

Where Grave had failed, Snow succeeded in pulling a reaction from Night, another brief flash of worry that his younger brother didn't mask this time.

"When Bastian returns, we will all head north."

Grave's eyebrows dipped low. "All?"

"Myself and Bastian." Night said it a little too quickly and Grave sensed a hint of fear in him, worry that his instincts said wasn't for himself or Bastian.

He meant to take the mortal female with them.

Grave opened his mouth to protest and drive some sense into his younger brother's thick skull.

Another blast of pain came, blazing like an inferno across the mark on his back, and he grimaced and growled as he breathed through it. When the sensation eased, he looked down at his right hand.

It pressed against his chest, clutching the pendant hidden beneath his black shirt.

"What's wrong?" Snow and Night said in unison.

Grave continued to stare down at his hand.

He didn't have an answer to that question. He wasn't sure. It was the same sensation as he'd had outside the house, a sharp burst of pain and then the feeling that something was wrong.

Very wrong.

Pain pulsed across his mating mark.

Was it Isla's pain?

How strong must it be for him to feel it?

He had never felt pain from her before, even though she must have hurt herself sometimes. Was it even possible he could feel it in the first place? He sensed when she was watching him through the mark, but he never felt her feelings. He knew other bonds between species, between mates, allowed one to feel the emotions of the other. The ancestors of the vampire race, the elves, included.

He gritted his teeth as the burning came again, so fierce it felt as if his heart was on fire.

The second he closed his eyes, he saw Isla.

Saw her reaching for him, tears staining her ashen face.

And then she was gone.

He launched to his feet. "Where is the nearest portal?"

Snow stared at him through wide eyes. Night looked equally as astonished by his outburst, but recovered quickly, concern filling his ice blue eyes as he looked up at Grave.

"Brother... what is wrong?"

Grave answered without considering the consequences, without giving a damn about what Night would make of what he was about to reveal.

All that mattered was Isla.

"I think the demon prince might have my mate."

CHAPTER 11

Light filtered in. Slowly at first, but then it gained speed, driving back the darkness and the dream, memories of a world filled with warmth. With love.

Isla clung to it and the feel of Grave's arms around her, holding her tucked close to his bare chest. She clung to the sound of his heart beating steadily against her ear, powerful and strong.

A heart that was hers.

He slipped from her arms into the light no matter how fiercely she tried to hold on to him though and she blinked rapidly as the world she had left behind faded, replaced with one that seemed cold and desolate to her, the source of nothing but pain and suffering.

She stared at the ceiling of her white room, the four carved white posts of her bed the only other thing in her field of vision. White. Never had that colourless shade seemed so cold to her before, but now it made her think of snow and ice. Desolation. Loneliness.

Death.

Death was white.

Not black.

Silence was white. It stretched around her. Shrouded her. Death was white. It stole all colour from the world. All life. It left everything in its wake as pale as snow, as cold as ice.

Light danced across the ceiling, and she was vaguely aware a fire was burning in the grate beyond the foot of her bed, but she saw no beauty in it today and felt no warmth.

She wasn't sure she could see beauty in anything anymore.

Her sister was gone.

Her nephew with her.

Because of her.

Because she had hunted a vampire and bonded with him, and now that vampire's enemies had become her own. She was paying for what she had done to Grave, and she deserved it.

The door to her left opened but she didn't take her eyes from the ceiling as the demon male entered, his scent telling her who it was. She wasn't sure she could look at him and see the pain in his eyes.

He had lost his sister-in-law because of her.

His nephew.

Isla rolled onto her side, facing away from him, and curled up into a ball on the covers of her bed.

His deep sigh spoke volumes. He was still hurting her even now.

"Do not push me away." The warm baritone of his voice didn't soothe her today. It only brought fresh pain with it as she heard the fatigue in it, mingled with hurt and hope. With affection she didn't deserve. "We are still family."

Isla screwed her eyes shut.

"If you know what is good for you, you would not say such a thing. You heard what Melia said… because of the things I have done, a demon prince killed Tarwyn when he could not find me." Her throat tightened and she had to squeeze the rest of what she needed to say out. "I should have been here."

"I should have been here too." Frey closed the door and she heard him step closer, felt him more clearly on her senses, and a flicker of light pierced the darkness clouding her heart. "We can both blame ourselves as much as we want, but in the end there is only one responsible for our shared pain and that is the demon who took Melia and Tarwyn from us."

She hated that he was so understanding. She wanted him to be angry with her, needed someone to blame her as she blamed herself. Even Melia had forgiven her in the end, hadn't gone to her death hating her for what she had done. In her final words, her sister had spoken only of her being happy, of forgiving and living.

Loving.

Isla clenched her jaw and refused to think of Grave.

The bed behind her depressed and she rolled back towards Frey. He placed a hand on her left arm.

"You have been sleeping for three days now," he said in a low soft voice.

Her eyes opened. Wide. Three days? It surprised her but it didn't at the same time. She had been so tired, had worn herself out hunting for the phantom mage.

Trying to save herself.

Trying to live.

She couldn't give up on that desire now.

Melia had wanted her to live too. She had wanted her to love and be happy.

Isla wasn't sure the last two things were possible. Her heart hurt so much, felt cold and black inside her chest, dying without the light her sister and nephew had brought into her world.

She dashed away the tears that wanted to fall and shuddered as she drew in a breath, and vowed that she would try.

"I heard Melia's words to you."

Isla tensed.

Frey had heard them?

He smoothed his hand along her bare arm, his voice calm and low, gentle. "I will not push to know… but is it true you did something to the vampire as payment for what he did to Valador?"

"I did," she whispered, expecting him to be happy about it.

He sighed again.

"I know of the Preux Chevaliers… they fought for us once, and they fought against us more times than that." He lifted his hand from her arm and cold went through her, as if he had taken away his affection rather than merely his comforting touch. "I fought beside Valador in the battle that claimed his life. The vampire you entwined yourself with is one of noble stature, a male with dark hair and eyes like frozen seas, yes?"

She considered not doing it, but then she nodded, and rolled towards him, needing to see his face to see if he really knew Grave. The solemn edge to his pale blue eyes had her rolling away again and casting her gaze down to the cerulean sheets of her bed.

"They are mercenaries, Isla." He leaned over and tenderly brushed away a strand of hair that had fallen down across her face and tucked it behind her ear. "They fight for coin. Valador might have hired them for himself if he had been willing to pay more than the other side… but he was always tight with his coin and he paid for it."

"And I made the vampire pay for it too," she snapped.

Frey caught her arm and tugged her to face him, pinning her left shoulder to the bed when she tried to roll away again. "Did you tell the vampire he is paying for killing Valador?"

She slowly shook her head and tried to move again, but Frey held her firm, his blue eyes glowing with fire as he leaned over her, golden horns beginning to curl forwards through his long blond hair. That hair swayed away from his bare chest as he leaned over her more, bringing their faces closer together.

"So how would the vampire know?"

She blinked.

"Grave Van der Garde is a mercenary, Isla. He was paid to kill a demon king and that is what he did. He receives only necessary information." His tone softened, some of the hardness leaving it as he eased back and lifted some of the weight off her shoulder. "It is unlikely he even knew he would leave a widow behind or would hurt your sister as he did."

The cold in Isla's veins became ice as she thought about that. Grave might not even know why she had done what she had to him.

She had never thought to spell it out for him, had presumed that he would know that Melia had been Valador's wife and that his actions would have wounded her sister deeply.

What if he didn't know?

What if all these decades he hadn't known why she had gone to him, why she had tricked him into becoming a phantom, and why she had left him?

She stared up into Frey's blue eyes, lost in a sea of thoughts, an ocean of pain.

"Will you come with me to the tomb?" Frey softly said, his words barely piercing the buzzing in her mind.

But they did pierce it and thoughts of Grave became ones of Tarwyn and what Frey wouldn't say.

They had buried him while she had been asleep.

She didn't want to go there. It was too soon, but she could see in Frey's eyes that he wouldn't take no as an answer and she couldn't bring herself to refuse him when she also saw that he needed company.

He needed comfort and support too.

The kingdom rested on his shoulders now.

He had never spoken of ruling, seemed content with life as a warrior, and now he was the king and she couldn't imagine how he felt, knowing he would rule when the kingdom should have been Tarwyn's.

Frey had to bear that for centuries or longer, until death released him.

He had joked once that he lived in fear of becoming like the Second King, hurled into a role he had no interest in playing because of the death of an elder brother, and that Tarwyn had saved him from that life.

Now that fear had become all too real for him.

Isla took hold of his hand, rubbed her thumb across the calluses on his palm and stared at his rough battle-worn fingers. The hands of a warrior. She looked up into his eyes. He would make a good king, even though the circumstances of his ascension would always pain him. He would harness that pain, would strive to remember how he had come to be king, and from it he would become a leader who would ensure those in his land didn't have to go through what he had endured. He would keep them safe and lead them well.

He was kind and gentle, as brave as Valador had been, but with it he was intelligent and strong, able to make tough decisions and a skilled tactician. She had fought beside him in battle once, and the First Realm could wish for no better male to lead them now.

She nodded. "I will go with you, Frey."

He managed a smile and turned his back on her, sitting on the edge of the bed facing the wall and the door to the corridor.

"Put some clothes on though. We do not wish to frighten the guards." His rich baritone held a warm note, and she smiled for a moment at the sound of it and the promise of better days, but then what he had said sank in.

Isla looked down at herself and realised she was only wearing a small red satin nightgown.

She shot up in bed and quickly gathered the blue sheets over her. "Who undressed me?"

Frey chuckled.

Isla slapped him on his bare back, sending him jerking forwards, and he scowled over his shoulder at her. She pulled the sheets higher, covering more of herself even though he had already seen her in the ridiculous excuse for sleepwear.

"It was not me. I swear it. I only removed your boots and your holster." He turned away again. "I last checked on you a day ago and you were wearing your leathers then. You must have woken at some point and been uncomfortable."

She didn't remember it. She looked around her white room and spotted her cerulean leather trousers and corset strewn across the floor, while her boots were set neatly near an armchair beside the fireplace and her holster with her two blades rested on the blue seat. Two of the three drawers in her white wooden dressing table to the right of the room were open, with clothes spilling out of them.

Isla peered down at herself under the covers, at the red satin slip she hadn't worn in a very long time.

One Grave had given to her and she had meant to throw away, thought that she had but obviously she had failed in that task and had pretended to herself that it was gone.

Grave.

The mark on her back tingled and warmed. Did he know the reason she had hurt him?

Or was he oblivious and had spent close to a century bound to her, hurt by her, without ever knowing what he had done to deserve it?

Had it all been for nothing?

All of his pain. All of hers.

She didn't want to think about it, couldn't right now when her heart ached for Tarwyn and Melia and she was weak. She was afraid of what she might do. It would be too easy to fall into Grave's arms and beg him to forgive her, and hope that he was unaware of why she had broken from him. It would be a foolish move. Even if he didn't know, and he did forgive her, one day he would find out and then the hurt she would feel would be soul-destroying because she wouldn't just love him, she would be in love with him again.

"Turn away," she said and Frey's powerful bare shoulders shifted in a deep sigh.

"As if I want to look at you naked. It is like looking at my sister."

That was rich. Frey had looked upon her very differently from the way a brother would look at a sister when she had first arrived. His interest had quickly waned though, his love of war more powerful than any emotion he could feel for a female who wasn't his fated one.

Isla slipped from the bed and gathered her clothes, and returned to the spot directly behind Frey where he couldn't see her. She faced him as she dressed, pulling her blue worn leathers on under her slip and fastening them before she removed it. She quickly slipped her corset on over her head and yanked on the two laces dangling from the back of it, tugging them until the top tightened, hugging her torso. She tied the strings at the base of the corset and strapped on the holster so it fit snugly against her back.

"There." She fastened the final silver buckle over her stomach.

Frey stood and came to face her, his blue eyes running down the length of her. "As formidable as ever."

She shook her head at his teasing and scowled at him even while silently thanking him for trying to act normal in some vain attempt to lessen the aches in their hearts. They couldn't pretend nothing had happened. Neither of them were capable of such a thing.

A hunger for vengeance burned in her heart like an eternal flame, and it shone in Frey's eyes too, blazed in his soul.

He wanted the demon to pay for taking Melia and Tarwyn from them.

She wanted that too, with every drop of her phantom blood.

He preened his blond hair back and fastened it at the nape of his neck before extending his hand to her.

Isla looked at the long braided length of leather in it, gold and black twined together. She couldn't wear a torc as the demon males who lost their mates did, but she could wear this smaller token of mourning for her sister and nephew. She took it from Frey, pulled her white hair up into a ponytail, and wrapped the leather thong around it and tied it tightly, allowing two long strands of it to fall down the back of her hair for all to see.

She sat on the edge of the bed, put her boots on and fastened them, and then stood again and pulled down a deep breath to settle her nerves. She had to pay her respects, even when she hated the tomb and its reminder of death, a shadow that felt as if it was looming over her as the seconds ticked by.

Frey opened the door and Isla followed him out of it.

She kept her eyes on her feet as she walked, unable to look at the corridors around her or the grand rooms they passed through. Everything reminded her of Melia. Everything brought her fresh pain.

Everything made the hunger for revenge burn hotter in her blood.

By the time they reached the tomb deep in the bowels of the castle, that hunger pounded fiercely inside her, driving back the cold, filling her with fire.

Frey entered the candlelit chamber before her. It was little more than a cave dug into the rock that the castle stood upon, but it was so much more than that at the same time.

The sound of metal striking stone filled the chamber, a song of sorrow that had her eyes lifting from the smooth white flagstones to the statue of noble Valador and the demon males dressed in black tunics and trousers beside it, working tirelessly on another block of white marble.

Already her sister's face was emerging from the stone, her beauty captured perfectly by the skilled hands of the sculptors in a pose so like Melia. She gazed upon her demon love, and he looked down at her in a way Isla had never noticed before now. She had been to the tomb before, and at the time she had thought Melia had asked the demons to sculpt her fallen mate in a fashion that he would be looking at her when she visited, but now Isla realised Melia had asked them to sculpt him in a way that he would be looking at her statue when she joined him in eternity.

Isla lowered her eyes and closed them, sending hot tears rushing down her cheeks.

Frey placed his arm around her and she sank against him.

Sank *into* him.

He sharply turned towards her. "Leave us."

The sculptors hurried from the room, leaving her alone in the silence with Frey. She lowered her eyes to the floor between them and waited for him to say something, aware that he had seen her fade, her shoulders shimmering for a moment before she had become solid again.

"I understand Melia's words now," he murmured and took a step towards her. "Seek the help you need, Isla... do it now."

"I tried." She looked up at him and then away, her eyes falling on the block of marble. Her sister's words echoed in her mind. "I tried and look where it got me. Nowhere. Grave will not help me and when I tried to fix this alone by finding a mage... Tarwyn... Melia—"

She couldn't bring herself to finish.

Frey placed his hands on her shoulders and hunkered down in front of her, bringing his face level with hers. "Try the vampire again."

"It is hopeless. He will not help me, Frey." She met his gaze and held it this time, needing him to see that Grave was a lost cause. He hated her too deeply and had made it clear he would sooner die than help her live.

Frey's handsome face darkened and his pale horns curled, flaring forwards as his pointed ears flared back. Fangs flashed between his lips as he growled.

"Then find the mage... because you are the only family I have now and I will not lose you too." His grip on her shoulders tightened. "I will send men. However many it takes."

Isla pressed a finger to his lips. "Thank you, but I will go alone. I will not drag anyone else into this. The demon prince is looking for me and I cannot stomach the thought that more of your people might die."

Frey closed his eyes and nodded, took her wrist gently in his hand and drew it away from his mouth.

His eyes opened again, meeting hers, determination flashing in them. "I will help you in any way I can then. Whatever you need. Supplies. Coin. Even me. I am not my people."

"No. You are their king."

He looked off to his left and sighed, and she lifted the hand he held and pressed it to his cheek, hoping to comfort him and reassure him at the same time that staying here in the castle was the right thing to do and that she would be fine.

She would do as Melia had asked. She would not fade. She would find a mage to make her solid once more, powerful again, and then she would hunt the demon who had taken everything from her and Frey and would bring vengeance down upon him.

For both of them.

"I appreciate your offer, brother dearest... and there is something I can use from you."

His gaze sought hers. "Name it, Sister."

"Teleport me somewhere."

CHAPTER 12

Four days.

It had been four days since he had experienced what he was now certain had been Isla's pain. Four days since his walls had crumbled, his hatred of her not strong enough to withstand the force of the love that still lived in his heart for her, and he had been driven to find a portal and go to her.

Four maddening days since his younger brother had destroyed all of his plans to save Isla mere seconds after he had formed them.

Night had asked where he intended to go.

Grave hadn't been able to give him an answer.

He didn't know where Isla lived, where to begin looking for her. It had taken him wasted hours at Bastian's mansion to decide to scout the demon castle in the Devil's domain, and then he had wasted days reaching it only to discover it lay in ruin. The only sign of life in the area had been him and Snow.

When he had suffered another attack, his hands fading as they descended the mountain on which the black fortress stood, Snow had taken command.

Since then, his cousin had been more than insistent that they find a phantom mage to fix his problem before he weakened further, and Grave could hardly argue with him when he made a valid point. He needed to be strong if they were going to find the demon and stop him.

But the longer he traversed the lands of Hell in search of a phantom mage, the deeper the ache within his heart grew, and now he could think of nothing other than Isla. She haunted his every waking and sleeping second, filling his mind with thoughts of her, and clouding his heart with emotions that he could no longer contain nor deny.

Gods.

His gloved fingers were on the pendant beneath his black combat shirt before he was even aware of what he was doing, tracing the pattern of the silver Celtic knot, and his thoughts turned to Isla again, going from light to dark as they ran the course they always did.

Something had happened to her. Something terrible.

His breaths came faster, shifting the strip of black cloth that covered the bottom half of his face, and his heart accelerated as panic sank its claws into him.

He clutched the pendant and focused on the mark on his back, and it warmed and tingles spread along the lines of it, so he could see it easily in his mind. His heart settled as the connection to her opened, the familiar sensation comforting him for once.

She was alive, out there somewhere. His bond to her told him that much. It gave him hope.

Hope that he kept to himself, together with his need to see her again and discover what had happened to her.

Snow's steady gaze landed on him as they trekked across another featureless black valley, heading towards an imposing spire that rose from the centre of it to tower almost one hundred metres high. Grave kept his eyes on that castle, refusing to look at his cousin, afraid that if he did Snow would see the fear in his heart, and everything else he hid there.

Saving himself wasn't the real reason he had hunted down three phantom mages so far.

If he had been mistaken and she was free of the demon, Isla would be looking for one too.

He was trying to find her.

Needed to find her.

Gods, he needed to see her again, needed to reassure the darker part of himself that she was fine. He hadn't felt any pain from her since that day, but it wasn't enough to reassure him that she was well. He had to see it with his own eyes in order to make his wretched softer side believe it.

He felt Snow's gaze leave him and mentally breathed a sigh of relief.

He wasn't sure Snow would understand if he allowed him to see beyond the walls, but then he wasn't sure his cousin wouldn't understand either. Snow had been through countless ordeals, had suffered tremendously in his years, and seemed stronger for it. Grave still didn't feel like putting himself out there, risking everything to share something with his cousin that was private.

If Snow didn't understand, if he said something wrong in response to discovering that Grave still harboured love for Isla, despite the things she had done to him and everything he had told Snow about hating her, then Grave wouldn't be able to stop himself from attacking his cousin.

His bloodlust was a deadly beast liable to rage if anyone said a word against Isla, more than ever now that he hadn't fed in days and his dark thoughts of her being in danger kept it constantly close to the surface, on the verge of emerging and seizing control of him. He had given up trying to subdue it, because it was impossible when the warrior in him knew he would need it if he found her and she was in trouble.

He would need it in order to save her.

"Hopefully this one will be home." Snow's hushed voice broke the silence, muffled by the cloth over his face, drawing him back to the black world around them as they hunkered down behind an outcrop of rocks just a few hundred metres from the eastern side of the tower.

Grave nodded as he shifted the angle of the blade hanging at his waist to make it more comfortable and grasped a boulder, peering over it to scout the high black wall that encircled the base of the tower. No sign of guards. Or a gate. He would have assumed it was on the western side he couldn't see from this vantage point, one that was close to a forest of gnarled bare black trees, but there was a path worn into the dark earth that led to the wall on this side.

Maybe there was a gate or something he couldn't see from this distance, even with his heightened sight.

Maybe someone had shored up the entrance and the castle was empty.

Grave's heart did a strange kick in his chest at that thought, a brief surge of adrenaline rushing into his blood, shaking his hope but not enough that he lost hold of it.

This one had to be alive.

He was growing weaker, running out of time. If the demon chose to attack his family now, he wouldn't be strong enough to protect them.

He wouldn't be strong enough to protect her.

He glared at the castle, willing a mage to live in it still. He was Grave's last hope.

The previous two mages they had tracked across Hell had been dead ends, literally, and it had left him with only this one to pursue. He scanned the dark grey sky, heart beating steadily against his chest despite the trickle of fear that began to run through his blood, a sensation he had been fighting from the moment they had neared the valley.

Snow leaned against the boulder beside him and he glanced at his cousin. Blue eyes shifted to him, the only thing visible between the black face mask and skull cap. Their clothing was a necessary precaution.

Not because of the phantom mage.

It was the fallen angels he was worried about.

They were the reason he and Snow were now dressed head to toe in black, as much of them covered as possible so they could slip into the valley unnoticed. The last thing he wanted to do was alert a fallen angel to their presence. He was no match for them in his current condition, and he wasn't sure even his cousin could take one down. Any passing fallen angel would view them as easy prey.

An easy meal.

The plan was to get into the castle, and back out, without being spotted.

Although, he hadn't seen any fallen in the vicinity since they had arrived. There had been one in the distance then, beyond the tower, lazily circling something on the western side of the valley. It had disappeared from view a moment later and he hadn't seen it since. He didn't like not knowing where it had gone. If he had seen it fly into another valley, or teleport, he would have felt more at ease, and more in control.

Darkness bubbled just below the surface of his skin, a black hunger for violence that he struggled with as he scouted the tower, fighting to keep it under his control. His stomach rumbled, loud enough that Snow looked at him.

He glared at his cousin, warning him not to say anything.

They had agreed they would feed once they had followed this lead to its conclusion, and that was still the plan. It wasn't as if there was anything to feed on in this godsforsaken valley anyway.

A scent swept past him, carried on a warm breeze that rolled across the valley.

One that made his gut clench and heart ache.

Isla.

He scoured the lands for her, gaze tracking fast over everything, half of him sure he was imagining her.

His eyes darted back to the edge of the forest.

She stood out like a sore thumb against the backdrop of black, her blue leathers and white hair making it easy for him to see her even though there was at least six hundred metres between them and very little light in the valley.

"Fuck," he muttered and Snow frowned at him. Grave pointed her out to his cousin. He knew the moment Snow had spotted her, because his cousin threw him a confused look. He sighed. "My mate."

Snow jerked his chin towards the castle. "She will get herself killed."

Grave's eyes shot there and widened as they landed on a pack of three Hell beasts patrolling the perimeter of the wall, huge black hairless animals that were taller than he was, a cross between a bull and a big cat, complete with obsidian horns.

How the fuck hadn't he scented them before?

He didn't hesitate.

He kicked off, crossing the black lands with all the preternatural speed he could muster in his weakened state, little more than a blur in the darkness. Isla zoomed towards him, his single point of focus.

She stepped out from the cover of the forest.

Grave slammed into her and dragged her back into the gnarled black excuse for trees. She was still for a moment and then she began thrashing against him, kicking at his legs as he pinned her back against his chest and clawing at his arms. His skin chilled where she touched him, the warmth draining from it and leaving him ice cold, and his muscles stiffened as he tried to keep hold of her.

"Let me go," she snarled in the demon tongue and he covered her mouth with his hand, his heart slamming against his chest as he focused to sharpen his hearing, afraid that the Hell beasts would have heard her.

Foolish female.

A hot sting shot through his palm and he grunted.

Isla stilled as warmth bloomed where she had bitten him.

"Grave."

His hand muffled her, but not enough that the sound of his name whispered in her voice didn't reach his ears and sink into his blood, heating him from the inside.

Blood that she had tasted, and recognised as his.

She settled against him, her back against his chest and her head on his shoulder, seemed to lean into him as she went limp in his arms.

She shoved out of them before he could hold her closer and whirled on him, her eyes glowing blue in the low light. "What the hell are you doing here?"

Grave couldn't answer. He could only stare into her eyes as tears began to fill them.

"Leave me alone. Just go away." Her voice faltered, losing its strength and growing increasingly quiet as her fight visibly left her.

She sank to her knees on the black ground and tears left glittering trails down her cheeks.

"What's wrong?" Snow said from beside him and she seemed surprised when she lifted her head and looked at him, as if she had only just realised Grave wasn't alone. His cousin pulled the black scarf covering the bottom half of his face down and pushed his black skullcap back, so tufts of his white hair sprang free.

Isla blinked slowly, her eyes going wide as she gazed up at Snow.

The darkness that had been riding Grave for the past four days pushed for freedom and he slid his cousin a look meant to order him to back off, but Snow played a dangerous game by refusing to look at him, by keeping his eyes on Isla.

On his mate.

He tore his own hat and scarf away and took a step towards his cousin, unable to contain the black need to drive Snow away from her by force and make it clear that he wasn't to look at her like that—as if he cared about her.

She was his.

He grasped the hilt of his blade.

Isla shook her head and swallowed hard.

The pain that had gone through him in Bastian's mansion returned, arresting his steps as it blazed inside him like cold fire, burning away all of his anger towards his cousin and dragging every drop of his focus back to Isla.

She wrapped her arms around herself, pale fingers digging into her bare arms, and lowered her head. Her white ponytail fell forwards and for the first time he noticed the braids that hung from her temples, and the crystals at their ends. Blue. Red. For her?

For him?

Her lips peeled back off her teeth and her white eyebrows furrowed as she squeezed her eyes shut, and the pain that beat within his heart and across the mark on his back grew stronger, stealing his breath.

He was only feeling an echo of what she experienced. How fierce was her pain? What had happened to her to make her suffer so greatly?

He couldn't bear it when more tears came, running freely down her ashen cheeks.

He crouched in front of her and reached for her shoulders, but hesitated and drew his hands back a few inches as his courage faltered, fear of what would happen if he gave in to his need to comfort her making him wary.

A sob broke free of her lips.

He placed his hands on her arms, uncaring about what might happen to him. She was hurting, and that was all that mattered.

Her hand came up fast and he grunted as it slammed into his chest, knocking him away from her and onto his backside. She scrambled backwards across the loose earth, until her back hit the rough trunk of one of the trees, and glared at him.

Denied him.

He picked himself up off the dirt and brushed his fatigues down, cursing himself in his head as his hands shook. Fool. He shouldn't have tried to comfort her. He should have known she would reject him. Hurt him.

Grave looked at her and every drop of anger he had managed to muster evaporated again as he saw her backed against the tree, a wild look in her tear-filled blue eyes. His beautiful Isla. He needed to comfort her. A stupid need, but one that was both powerful and commanding, and impossible to deny even when he knew she would only lash out at him and he would provoke her phantom powers into manifesting again.

She stopped him in his tracks when he advanced a step towards her, willing to risk her wrath.

"It is your fault," she whispered, the pain in her voice turning it dark and malicious, warning him to keep his distance from her. His senses issued a warning of their own, telling him that she meant to attack even when she looked so frail, a broken little thing as she shook and began to curl into a ball. "You are the reason I lost..."

Her demeanour changed in an instant and she flew at him, her eyes brightening again as she slammed into him and knocked him back. He placed his right foot behind him, bracing himself as she hurled punches at him, each blow that managed to strike him before he could block it leaving him cold where it had hit. Her skin paled further and her eyes glowed as she battered him with her fists, her anger flowing through him via their bond, together with her agony.

Grave refused to fight her.

If lashing out at him would help ease her pain, he wouldn't try to stop her. He would take every blow, everything she needed to throw at him, if only it would make her feel better.

He probably deserved it.

That noble thought and desire shattered when she managed to knock him over and landed on top of him, pinning him to the earth, and struck him so hard across his left cheek that she knocked a molar loose and the taste of blood filled his mouth.

Blood.

His fangs punched long from his gums and he snarled through them as a black hunger rose, a terrible need to fight her. He wrestled with it, refusing to succumb to his bloodlust, but each blow Isla landed only stoked the fire hotter, until it burned away the cage he kept it in and began to seize hold of him.

"It is your fault," Isla bit out and cocked her right fist.

Snow's forearm banded around her stomach and his cousin hauled her off him. She tried to get back to him when Snow set her down but his cousin snagged her wrist, holding her back.

Grave breathed hard, pushing back against the darkness, determined to subdue it as he rose back onto his feet. He would not hurt Isla. He would not. He could not.

Isla didn't seem to share the same feelings towards him.

She broke free of Snow's grip and her palm struck Grave's left cheek so hard his head snapped to his right and the sound of her slap echoed through the trees.

Grave closed his eyes and stood there in the thick silence that followed, breathing to steady his bloodlust and bring it back under control, his cheek stinging fiercely. He had probably deserved the slap too, for countless reasons, but he wanted to know which one had her so bent on attacking him.

He could only think of one.

He slowly opened his eyes and turned to face her, determined to discover why she was so upset with him. "Is this because I would not help you?"

Her chest heaved against her blue corset as she struggled to breathe, heart hammering out a tempting rhythm on her neck, a neck that he had marked with his fangs more than once.

A neck she usually kept hidden for that reason, her long white hair down to conceal the scars.

He frowned at that and reached out without thinking, his eyes glued to one set of marks—the one from the first time he had bitten her.

Isla slapped his hand away and hot lightning zinged through his bones and up his arm from the force of the blow, even as his skin turned to ice where hers had touched.

Her bright blue eyes narrowed into glowing slits in the low light and her voice dropped to a deadly whisper that seemed to suck the warmth from the air around him. "They are dead... my sister... my nephew. They are gone because of you... because of me."

"Because of me?" He didn't understand.

What little light there had been disappeared, swallowed by an inky shadow that stretched outwards from Isla, and he shivered as the air around him grew colder, the temperature dropping rapidly.

Her eyes shone in the darkness, as cold but as beautiful as the moon and the stars. "A demon killed my nephew and my sister... my sister faded... went to join her love Valador in eternity."

Grave's blood grew colder, and not because of her power manifesting itself this time. "Valador?"

Isla snarled, the unholy sound sending an icy shiver down his spine, and he felt her malice wrap around him like sharp tendrils, cutting into his skin, freezing him but burning him at the same time.

Her voice gained an echo in his mind, a disjointed repeat of every word she said.

"The First King of the demons."

He had killed her sister's mate.

His ears rang as that sank in and he forced himself to believe it, to see her with new eyes, and everything began to make sense. A sick sort. One that had his strength draining from him as he pieced it all together and came to one terrible conclusion.

One that tore him apart inside.

Ripped him to shreds.

She advanced on him but Snow grabbed her arm again and she turned ice cold eyes on his cousin. She fought his hold, but Snow only tightened his grip, until his fingers burned white and Grave was on the verge of demanding he unhand her because it was clear he was hurting her.

A fool.

What did he care if Snow hurt her? She certainly didn't extend the same feelings towards him. She didn't care that she had hurt him.

It had all been a lie.

But it had been real for him.

She wrestled with his cousin, the darkness lifting and the air warming as her focus was diverted from him and the agony of losing her family, replaced with a more immediate pain.

"Settle down, because I will not let you harm my cousin," Snow barked, his fangs flashing between his teeth and his eyes flaring crimson and pupils turning elliptical. "If the demon prince killed your nephew and sister, then I am as much responsible for that as Grave, because I was joint leader on that mission."

Isla stilled.

Grave stared at her, numbness sweeping outwards from the centre of his chest, slowly engulfing him as he waited for her to attack his cousin, to turn her anger on Snow.

That numbness swallowed him entirely when she merely looked away from Snow and pinned her glare back on him, making it clear she blamed him alone for what had happened.

He tried to muster some anger of his own, some shred of feeling, even a drop of hatred or rage. When that failed, he called on his bloodlust that had been so eager to seize control just minutes ago, needing it so he could lash out at Isla in return. Now it was nowhere to be found. Gone.

Faded from existence.

He looked down at himself and then up into Isla's eyes, the numbness becoming a cold that sank deep into his bones, and his voice was distant to his ears as he whispered the words he had wanted to scream at her.

"Are Valador and your sister the reason you did this to me?"

He held his hands out between them.

The air shimmered where they should have been.

CHAPTER 13

Isla stared at Grave's hands as they shimmered in and out of existence between them, able to see the dirt through them one moment and then his strong fingers the next. When they finally became solid again and stayed that way, he curled them into fists and lowered them to his sides, his gaze boring into her, demanding an answer to his question.

The male at her back seemed equally as intent on knowing it.

She closed her eyes and then forced them open again, made herself look into Grave's pale blue ones and see what she had done to him, and witness his reaction when she answered him.

"It was."

Those two words fell hard between them and the feeling that had been growing within her from the moment she had left him reached a new pinnacle as his eyes narrowed on her, red ringing his pale irises, and he ground his teeth.

Anger sparked in the depths of his eyes and skittered across the mark on her back, and she wanted to look away but held his gaze instead. She had lashed out at him, blaming him for what had happened to her family, and he deserved to do the same to her in return, taking out his pain on her, the suffering she had put him through.

His hands went slack beside his black-clad thighs and the anger she had anticipated, the rage she had expected, didn't come.

Grave stared at her, red battling blue in his eyes.

"I did not know," he whispered.

She cursed him in her mind, begged him to rail at her and be furious about what she had done, anything to alleviate the guilt that was crushing her inside. She deserved his wrath. She needed it to make the hollow feeling that squirmed inside her go away, because she couldn't bear it.

She couldn't bear knowing that he had suffered for almost a century without knowing why.

She could see in his eyes that he was telling the truth. He hadn't known, which meant that he had spent the past decades believing that she had left him for no reason, and that made something else hit home.

He hadn't lashed out at her through their connection, making her witness things he did to spite her, to hurt her, because he knew she had used him and had tricked him into becoming a phantom as an act of revenge.

He had done it because she had wounded him.

Gods, he *had* loved her.

"I am sorry your family was dragged into this."

Isla turned her cheek to him and closed her eyes, but she couldn't shut out what he had said as easily. It rang in her mind, resonated in her heart, touched that deepest part of herself that she tried to keep hidden and protected, shielded from him even when he was already on the inside, buried so deep inside her heart that it was impossible to keep him out.

He went to walk past her and she shot her hand out and grabbed his left wrist, stopping him. She felt his eyes on her hand, and then on her face, and she pulled down a breath to find some courage in her weak timid heart and turned her face towards him.

"Why are you here?" Because it was the last place she had expected to cross paths with him again, but at the same time she was glad he was standing before her, here when she needed him most.

"Why are you?" he countered and shirked free of her grip, and her hand fell to her side as the red in his eyes began to win against the blue, and his pupils stretched in their centres, turning elliptical.

He didn't need to show his rage to her like that, not when she could feel it burning on her back, blazing in their bond.

"It took me a long time to track down this mage. Too long." She looked over her shoulder, through the trees at the black tower. The key to her vengeance was in there, locked away but finally within her reach. She could feel it like insects crawling under her skin, the same sensation she'd had when she had found the phantom mage who had cast the spell on her in the first place. Once she had a stable form again, she would turn all of her focus towards the demon and hunting him down. "Do you know how rare they are now?"

She wished she hadn't looked back at Grave when she saw the darkness in his eyes as he stared at her, the cold that she had created in him, one that she feared would never leave his heart.

"I know," he said, his tone dangerously casual and calm. "Because I killed most of them. In fact, I thought I had killed them all."

A hot rush of anger went through her and she grabbed his shoulder before she could consider what she was doing and spun him to face her. "What possessed you to do such a thing?"

She knew the answer to that question as he glared at her, malice and fury beyond what she could ever muster even in her true phantom form burning in his eyes, and her hand shook against his muscular shoulder.

"I was a little upset." He rolled his shoulder free of her grip and turned his focus back to the mage's fortress.

Isla wasn't sure what to say.

It was obvious he had been more than a little upset.

In the wake of her leaving him, he had gone to war. He had blamed the phantom mages for what had happened to him and had gone after them with all the fires of Hell burning in his heart, bent on revenge.

His bloodlust must have seized him.

Isla covered her mouth with her hand and tried not to imagine what he had been like as he had hunted down every mage he could find, obsessed with destroying them. There had been a period when he had held the connection between them closed, years in which he had shut her out.

Was this what he had been doing?

The mages had been spread far and wide across Hell.

But he had hunted them down.

She studied his noble profile as he stared at the tower, assessing it with red eyes that seemed to burn in the low light.

It hit her hard that she really had hurt him, and her stomach squirmed again and her heart reproached her as she stood before him, responsible for all his pain and suffering, and now the deaths of innocent mages.

Was he here to kill this mage too?

She couldn't let him do such a thing.

She reached for him but he flashed fangs at her hand, and she pulled it back towards her. "Grave."

He growled at her and she refused to look away, would no longer be cowed by him. She would keep her promise to her sister. She would make things right somehow.

"I cannot allow you to kill this mage." She stepped in front of him, blocking his view of the tower, so close that she could feel the warmth he radiated.

Gods, she wanted to move closer, yearned to feel his hard body pressed against hers and his arms around her, giving her the comfort she craved as her cold heart warmed and the hunger for revenge gave way to a hunger to be near him.

The dark edge to his eyes kept her at a distance though.

"I do not intend to kill him," Grave said and looked beyond her shoulder, his eyes sharpening as he stared at the black tower. "I intend to fix this problem and then I intend to hunt down the demon who hurt you and see to it he will never do it again."

Shock rippled through her, stealing her voice, and she could only stare at him as his eyes briefly met hers and then darted away. That split second was all she had needed to catch a glimpse of something that seemed impossible.

Affection.

"I am sorry for your loss, Isla." He moved past her and the big white-haired vampire who had announced himself as Grave's cousin followed.

She stood there for a moment, lost and adrift, shaken by Grave's contradictory behaviour and uncertain of herself and the path to choose.

Melia's words echoed in her mind, telling her again not to let him go.

She wanted to be strong enough to do such a thing, but while there had been a glimmer of affection in his eyes and in his words, there was still so much anger and pain. So much hate.

Isla looked back over her shoulder at Grave and whispered an apology to Melia, her heart aching as she considered what she was about to do.

She didn't think it was possible to fulfil all of Melia's dying wishes after all.

She would carry out her original plan as intended.

"I am going with you," Isla said and Grave slowed to a halt.

"No."

Stubborn vampire. She would give him no choice. He had come here to make himself stronger, and her plan would do just that if it was a success. He was a strategist, a born leader, and she was going to play on it.

"I was not asking your permission. I have wronged you, but in this I will not fail you." She walked towards him and the white-haired male moved aside, allowing her to reach his cousin.

Grave refused to look at her, and she refused to let that deter her and stepped in front of him again.

"I can give you the strength you need to protect your family, Grave." And to avenge hers.

"And how will you do this?" He still didn't look at her.

Isla wished that he would, because fear began to creep into her heart and the tower in the distance behind her seemed to become a living thing that loomed over her, a shadow of doom, and she wanted to see in Grave's eyes that he knew why she was doing this.

She wanted to see that he knew the feelings she kept hidden in her heart and hear him speak out against her plan, admitting the feelings that still beat in his.

"Phantom mages are obsessed with my kind."

She studied his eyes, watching closely for a spark, a hint of his feelings, anything that might reveal he truly had loved her and still did.

Anything that would give her a reason to fight for him.

"I will offer myself to him in exchange for setting you free from the phantom world."

Grave was silent for a long time, seconds that stretched into hours as the shadow of doom she could feel against her back grew stronger and slowly settled over her, driving all the light of hope from her heart.

Cold eyes dropped to meet hers.

Not a glimmer of feeling in them.

"Very well."

CHAPTER 14

Snow had reluctantly left them at the edge of the forest once the coast had been clear of a local Hell beast pack and Grave had made him swear to go back to the nearest town and wait for him there. The big vampire had clearly wanted to come with his cousin, and she envied the bond they shared.

One that had stolen her voice and cast her adrift on sombre thoughts.

She hadn't spoken a word since setting out for the mage's tower, couldn't find anything to say, not even when Grave looked at her. Whenever he did, she felt his gaze on her like a hot bolt of lightning that coursed through her veins and lit her up inside, even as it ripped her apart.

Her gaze remained rooted on the path worn into the black earth at her feet, the pain in her heart weighing her down as she thought about Melia and Tarwyn, and the promise she had made to Frey. She would keep it. She would find a way to stop herself from fading, even if it was only for long enough to end the demon and have their revenge.

Melia.

Gods, she needed to speak with her sister now more than ever.

She needed to talk with her about the fact that Grave hadn't known why she had cursed him to a phantom life, and admit that what had started out as a lie had quickly become a truth. One that burned in her heart still.

The heart that still loved him.

Grave glanced at her again, but this time the effect he had on her was weaker, stirring less heat in her veins. That heat quickly gave way to cold, ice that was growing outwards from her heart. She had been a fool to hope he would try to stop her, and now she felt as if she was marching to her doom and he was going to throw her to the lion that prowled in the black tower ahead of her.

She didn't understand.

Grave had said that he wanted to protect her and that he wouldn't allow anything to hurt her again, but here he was escorting her into the epitome of phantom Hell, seemingly intent on personally handing her over to the mage.

Had she heard him wrong? Had she misunderstood?

His eyes landed on her again, and this time she wanted to look at him, but the weight on her heart was too heavy and she couldn't bear the thought of finding his eyes as cold as they had been back in the forest, when he had made it clear he wanted the bond between them broken and her out of his life forever.

She didn't understand.

She really didn't.

She deserved his anger for allowing him to suffer with a bond to her when he had never known why she had done it, but still a part of her had dared to hope there might be some feeling left in his heart for her, some compassion. Some love.

His steps slowed and she looked ahead of them, and a sudden need to run bolted through her. Great black gates towered over her, set flush into the wall, and they creaked as they slowly opened.

Isla swallowed hard.

She had to run.

She took a step back and Grave looked at her, and the feel of his eyes on her was enough to have her staying where she was. She clenched her fists, tipped her chin up and held her head high as she watched the gates opening. She had done enough running in her life, from him and from herself, and it was time that she stopped. She would pay her debt to Grave here.

Her family were gone, but his were not, and if placing herself at the mercy of a phantom mage would save them, then she was glad to do it.

She was.

She tensed as the doors jerked to a halt, slamming against the walls with a loud boom that sounded like a death knell.

Grave walked forwards, his left hand casually resting on the hilt of his blade.

Isla hesitated.

The sensation of insects crawling and writhing beneath her skin grew more intense and she rubbed at her bare arms, trying to scrub them away.

The mage.

He stood on the other side of the gate, his green eyes fixed on her, a twisted sparkle to them that she didn't like. He raked his gaze over her, from head to toe and back again, over and over until she wanted to scream at him to stop.

His calm and curious demeanour shattered when he finally noticed Grave.

His slim face darkened and a faint golden glow lit his eyes as a breeze tousled his long black hair and toyed with the tails of his black ankle-length coat, causing them to flap against his tight trousers and boots.

The mage snarled and inky ribbons swirled around his hands as he raised them before him, all of his focus locked on Grave. White-blue threads of magic entwined with the black and Isla fought the pull of them, but they tugged at her phantom side, luring it to the surface with the promise of power and retribution.

Isla staggered a step towards him.

Grave snapped his gaze to her and then back to the mage, and surprised her by placing himself between them. The pull of the mage's magic weakened enough that she could move back a step and she gathered herself, steeling her heart and mind against the male's power.

"You're not welcome here." The mage advanced on Grave, a sharp clip to his step as he emerged from the tower, his eyes glowing gold as the magic swirled up his arms and caressed his neck. "Leave."

"I thought you might say that." Grave's calm tone gave none of his feelings away and he had closed the connection between them, shutting her out so she couldn't detect his emotions through their bond. Why did the phantom mage want to turn him away? Was it because he knew Grave had killed other mages in the past? Grave jerked his thumb over his shoulder and icy cold seeped into her blood. "It is why I brought her."

The male looked past him, and now that he was closer to her, she realised something. Something that had her reconsidering her plan to run.

He looked like the mage who had cast the original spell on her.

He was too young to be that male, appearing barely in his thirties in mortal terms which placed him around the century mark in mage years, but she recalled sensing others in the castle at the time. Was it possible this male was the son of the mage who had helped her?

She shifted her gaze from him to the back of Grave's head. If that was the case, then the reason he wanted Grave out of his sight was perfectly clear to her.

Grave had killed his father.

"Is there anyone in Hell you have not angered?" she hissed at Grave's back, not caring if he heard her.

If she was being honest, she wanted him to hear. She wanted him to know that she was angry with him for what he had done, because now the mage would be less inclined to help them and that meant it was going to be harder for her to convince him. She had started to hope that perhaps offering herself in exchange for Grave's freedom wouldn't be necessary. Gods, she was a fool.

Grave shrugged.

Isla considered smacking him around the back of his head but the mage's eyes landed on her again just as she was on the verge of raising her hand and going through with it, and cold stole through her, freezing her in place.

She stared back at him. Insects. Crawling. She didn't like that look in his eyes.

Males had looked at her like that before and she had used it back then, luring them to their doom so she could feast on their souls. She wished she could do the same with him, but mages took precautions, learned at an early age how to protect their soul from phantoms.

"We have a problem, and I need it fixed," Grave said and the mage didn't take his eyes off her, merely acknowledged him with a regal bow of his head. "You can stop us from fading?"

Us?

Her eyes shot to Grave. He was going to find a way to save them both?

He kept his back to her, his eyes locked on the mage and their connection shut.

She couldn't believe it.

"I can… but you will need to offer me something worth my services." The mage slid his green eyes her way again and she shuddered as they met hers. "I am sure we can come to some arrangement."

He turned away from them and swept back into the huge base of the black tower, disappearing from view. Grave followed him, leaving her standing alone outside the walls.

Isla couldn't move.

She stared at Grave's back, taking in the broad line of his shoulders and the way his torso tapered down into a narrow waist, and how good his backside looked in mortal combat clothing, cupped by the close-fitting black material.

She still wasn't sure what his intentions were, or the mage's ones, but when Grave paused at the threshold of the tower and looked back at her, she moved towards him, closing the gap between them.

Power hummed in the air around her as she entered the tower, the dark of Hell giving way to a weird greenish light that emanated from clusters of crystals growing from the polished black walls.

Insects.

She supressed a shudder and looked straight at the source of that sensation. The mage waited at the foot of a twisting black staircase that spiralled upwards in jagged sections. When she reached the middle of the huge vestibule, he ascended the steps, and she bravely followed him, aware of Grave close behind her.

The sensation that he was marching her to her doom returned but she managed to crush the urge to run the moment it went through her this time and kept walking forwards, her blue boots silent on the black stone steps. Her gaze leaped ahead of her, up beyond the mage to the next floor, trying to catch a glimpse of it.

The same green light filled the space above her and she frowned as she reached the next floor. It was nothing like she had expected. Rather than one large open room, she stood in a curving corridor. The angular staircase continued upwards at her back, but to her left and right the corridor encircled a central room. A huge archway cut into the smooth black stone in front of her revealed that room. The only furniture in it was a throne at the other end of it, made of the same green crystals as the lights, but mingled with black ones.

It looked uncomfortable.

She glanced left and right, and spotted arched doors on the other side of the corridor from the wall of the central room.

Isla looked up at the ceiling, picturing the height of the tower.

How many rooms did it have?

She looked down too.

She hadn't noticed an entrance for a dungeon, but it wouldn't surprise her if the mage had one. His father had been rather proud of his. She suppressed another shudder.

"Come," the mage said, his voice unnervingly soft and gentle, and she couldn't hide the shiver that went through her when she lifted her gaze and found him standing close to her, one pale hand extended to her.

As if she would take it.

Isla swept past him into the central room, feeling his eyes on her, lingering on her backside for a few seconds before he moved to follow her. His heeled boots were loud on the black floor, followed by the softer thud of Grave's rubber-soled leather ones.

The sensation of power grew stronger as she neared the crystal throne and she slowed to a halt metres from it, unwilling to get any closer to it. Whatever spell the mage had used to create the crystals, it did something to her, pulled at her and made her feel a little hazy.

A little compliant.

She didn't like it.

The sensation eased and she looked across at Grave as he stopped beside her, his left hand still resting on the hilt of the blade that hung from his waist. The mark on her back pulsed with warmth that flowed along the lines, heat that seemed to give her some protection from the mage's spells.

The black-haired male seated himself on his throne and crossed his legs, causing the two long tails of his black coat to fall away from them. He settled his arms along the rests and his fingers curled over the ends, dark nails blending into the near-black crystal that formed them.

His green eyes raked over her again, sending another shudder through her.

Isla kept her chin up and didn't shy away from his perusal, refusing to allow him to fluster her as he so clearly wanted. She was strong, even in her weakened state. If they fought, there was a chance she would win.

But she couldn't fight him.

She needed him to fix their problem.

She needed vengeance.

Needed to give Grave back the life she had stolen from him.

"One night in exchange for one century of corporeal life." The mage's words fell heavily around her.

Isla opened her mouth to refuse him, unwilling to give him what he desired.

Power over her.

Grave wasn't so kind.

"You can have her ten nights," he said, tone cold and devoid of feeling, and she snapped her head towards him, unable to believe what she was hearing even as each word struck her heart like a white-hot spear, burning it to ashes and leaving her dead inside. He was throwing her to the lion after all. "In a row. I intend to live a long life."

Isla swallowed hard and fought to find her voice. She could understand that he was angry with her, bitter about what she had done to him, but he was condemning her to a nightmare. Phantom Hell.

She tried to speak to give them both a piece of her mind but no words left her lips, and her gaze whipped back to the mage. He smiled coldly at her. Bastard. Her eyes darted around at all the crystals in the room and finally settled on the throne. It glowed around him.

He was using the crystals to enhance his power, to strengthen it enough to give him a sliver of control over her without him having to do anything that might rouse suspicion in Grave.

Grave stared at the male. Waiting?

When the mage nodded, Grave looked over at her.

Isla tried to shake her head, tried to plead him with her eyes, but all she could do was stare at him. Mute. Unmoving.

No.

"I will have rooms prepared for you."

No.

Isla struggled again, fighting the hold of the mage's power as her heart thundered, spreading fear through her veins. Despair. She kept trying to shake her head, to speak, to do something to give Grave a sign that she was far from fine with the mage's proposal, but nothing she did worked.

Two females entered, dressed in long green robes, their heads bowed and long black hair streaming over their shoulders to conceal their faces.

"Go with them." The mage stood.

Grave lingered, his pale eyes slowly moving between the mage and her, and Isla gave one last desperate attempt to reach him and tell him that she didn't want to do it.

She focused on their mark.

It warmed against her back.

Then went ice cold.

No.

Grave's face darkened, and she cursed him in her head. She hadn't shut him out. It was the mage.

Her vampire pivoted on his heel and followed one of the females and all Isla could do was watch him walk out the door, her heart sinking as her hope left with him.

"Do not despair, my beautiful phantom." The mage's voice curled around her and she closed her eyes, trying to shut him out. "I will be gentle and tender with you."

It became impossible when he stopped beside her, his coldness washing over her, and cupped her cheek in his palm. Insects. She shivered and tried to escape his touch, but he grasped her jaw and held her tightly, his fingertips pressing in between her teeth, forcing her mouth open.

She whimpered and flinched away.

He leaned in, his breath washing over her face, and fury rose inside her, a frigid cold that turned her blood to ice. He chastised her with a cluck of his tongue.

"None of that now." His grip on her softened and she cringed as he stroked her jaw and down her neck. Her skin crawled in the lines his fingers left in their wake and she shuddered when he reached the swell of her breasts and hooked them into the top of her blue leather corset. He sighed and his voice was distant, nothing more than a dreamy whisper when he spoke. "We must see to dressing you more appropriately."

He snapped his fingers and the other female grabbed her arm and pulled her away from him, dragging her from the room.

Isla went willingly with her, relieved for the temporary reprieve. If she could get far away enough from him, she might be able to shatter whatever silencing spell he had placed on her.

The female led her up the staircase, floor after floor, until Isla's legs burned and she wondered whether they were heading for the top of the tower. Surely there the spell would be weaker and she would be able to communicate with Grave?

She kept trying their mating mark, but it remained cold, even when she sensed him nearby as they passed another floor and kept heading upwards.

Isla looked back down at the floor they had left, aching to be there, to find Grave and make him see that she didn't want this. She had told him in the forest that she would offer herself to the mage though, so he probably thought she was fine with what he had proposed.

Gods, what must Grave think of her?

He already thought her a liar, a treacherous female who had used and betrayed him for the sake of revenge. Was he thinking she was a whore now too, willing to give herself to any male in exchange for something she wanted?

She was far from it.

Her heart and her body belonged to one male, and they had from the moment she had fallen in love with him.

Isla tried to force their connection open, desperate to reach him.

Nothing.

The female caught her arm again and pulled her in another direction, and Isla's eyes widened as she focused back on the world around her.

A huge room surrounded her, tall arched windows lining the curved walls, with green crystals growing from the narrow black stone supports between them. Hell stretched in all directions beyond those windows and she turned in a slow circle, stunned by the sight of it.

It wasn't black, grim and cragged.

Through the windows, the valley was green, the mountains snow-capped, and the sky was blue.

What magic was this?

The female tugged her forwards and Isla stumbled along behind her, unable to tear her eyes away from the beautiful vista.

Until her servant halted and spoke.

"Dress." She pushed Isla forward.

Isla's knees hit something soft and she almost fell onto it. Her stomach dropped when she saw what it was.

A massive circular bed draped in green silk in the centre of the room.

On it, a pale blue dress had been laid out.

Isla turned to tell the female she wouldn't be wearing it.

She was alone.

She decided to say it anyway.

Her mouth moved, but only a squeak left her lips. Damn. She eyed the crystals on the wall. They weren't strong enough to give the mage's power a boost, allowing him to control her.

Isla frowned down at the bed and slowly backed away from it, and her stomach did more than drop, it plummeted into her boots.

The entire floor had threads of green crystal running through it.

She reached for Grave through their bond but it still remained closed to her.

She looked over her shoulder at the steps that led downwards, tempted to try them, but resisted that urge when she sensed that the servant hadn't gone far and was waiting on the level below. If she attempted to leave, the female would stop her, and would probably tell the mage what had happened. He would be furious, liable to use his magic on her, and the gods only knew how it would end. It would be easy for him to kill her in her current state.

Her eyes drifted to the dress on the bed.

Could she do this?

One night in exchange for one century of life.

It seemed like such a small sacrifice.

One single night and she would be strong again, able to hunt the demon and have her revenge.

But Grave had promised the mage ten nights.

Isla pushed that thought away. She would convince the mage to settle for one night. Somehow.

She was a phantom after all.

The phantom mages viewed her kind as something fascinating and elusive, something they wanted to obtain and keep like a treasure. It was their weakness and she would exploit it to bend the mage to her will, pulling him under her seductive spell. Once he was bewitched by her, she would use all of her wiles to force him to allow her to go after one night, promising that she would return to him.

It would work.

Isla picked up the dress and held it before her, and her nerve faltered when she saw straight through the sheer blue fabric that matched her eyes.

She steeled herself, drawing down a deep breath. It was all an act, and hadn't she performed it so well a thousand times over in her years, luring men to their doom and using their desire against them to get what she wanted?

That was all this was too.

She was going to act like a phantom for the first time in one hundred years.

She drew on that side of herself as she stripped off her leathers. The air was cool in the room, like ice kissing her skin, and she delighted in the feel of it as she set her clothes aside. She couldn't remember the last time she had felt so free. Odd considering she was essentially in a cage at the top of a tower. Power hummed in her veins, running over her cold skin, and she drifted around the room, savouring it. It had been too long since she had given her phantom nature free rein, allowing it to rise to the surface without fighting it.

Gods, part of her had missed this sensation.

This absolute power.

Her white hair tickled her back as it shifted against her skin and she reached over her head and pulled the thong from it, allowing it to drop from her ponytail, and wrapped the twisted strands of leather around her wrist, securing them there. Her hair touched her back and then floated upwards, dancing in the air around her as she turned in a circle. She ran the fingers of her right hand through the strands, teasing them into floating higher.

Her eyes widened.

Her skin was white.

Isla drew her hand towards her and frowned at it.

She had almost forgotten how pale she was in her phantom form. Colourless.

Like death.

Melia flashed across her mind, crimson splattered across her, Tarwyn resting in her arms.

Death.

Isla swayed on the spot as hunger to bring that end to the demon who had stolen her family from her swept through her.

Yes. She would bring him death. She would become the terrifying manifestation of his doom and he would quake on his knees before her, would beg her for mercy.

She would have none.

Her nails began to turn pale blue and then jagged black at their tips.

Isla snapped herself back to the room, shattering the hold her need for vengeance had over her, and breathed hard as she looked down at her bare body. Her white skin turned a soft shade of cream and she staggered towards the bed and sank onto it.

She had to be careful.

She couldn't allow herself to get swept up in her hunger for revenge when the mage came to her. There was a chance she would do something to him, might even kill him when the need overwhelmed her. As much as she wanted him dead, she needed him alive more.

She needed him to perform the spell to give her a solid form again.

Isla pulled the dress on over her head and smoothed it down with trembling fingers, and reached for the connection to Grave again.

Still nothing.

She paced the room, bare feet silent on the stone floor, working off some of her tension. What was keeping the mage? She wanted this over with, and he had seemed eager before. Now he was keeping her waiting?

Isla frowned at the outside world.

The sun was setting over the mountains.

Impossible.

But incredible.

She got caught up in watching the bright golden orb as it descended, turning the scattered fingers of cloud in the sky pink.

"You are beautiful."

Isla tensed and her gaze shot towards the owner of that voice.

The mage.

He stood at the top of the steps, dressed in nothing but loose black trousers, his long black hair tied back at the nape of his neck.

His green eyes perused her and she forced herself to keep still and allow it. It was all an act. A trick. She was a phantom after all.

None of it was real.

Her heart began a slow drumming against her chest.

Her hands started to shake.

Isla clenched them and breathed through her fear. Vengeance. She needed it. One night was a small price to pay in order to avenge her family.

The mage crossed the room to her, his eyes never leaving her body, lingering on her breasts and her hips, and then lifting to her face as he reached her.

She played her part, slowly raking her eyes over him, giving him the impression that she wanted him as much as he desired her. He had a good body, slender yet honed, and he was handsome, but she didn't desire him.

It was an act.

An act.

Isla stepped towards him and bent her head, lowering it to one side, playing on what she had learned about him so far. He liked to feel powerful, and he thought himself handsome and attractive. Perfect, probably. The females he kept in the tower were no doubt responsible for that high opinion of himself. They probably fawned over him.

Now Isla had to do the same disgusting thing because of them.

Revenge.

It would be hers. It was all that mattered.

His hands came down on her hips and she managed not to tense, kept relaxed beneath his touch as he slid them around to the small of her back and drew her towards him.

"You seemed upset before... defiant," he murmured as he leaned closer, lowering his head to her shoulder. He pressed a soft kiss to it and shuddered. "Gods, you taste like Heaven."

He lifted his right hand and fisted her hair, tugging her head back, and she resisted him this time, aware that he had enjoyed her defiance and wanting to banish any suspicions that might be growing in his mind. If she was too compliant, he might go back on their agreement.

He groaned and pulled harder, and she gave in to him this time. Her eyes fixed on the black ceiling as he tongued her neck and she drifted there, suspended away from her body, parting herself from what he was doing to her. He could touch her body, but he wouldn't touch her soul and her heart, her mind. She would lock everything else away from him.

He scooped her up into his arms and kissed down her chest, and she forced a soft moan to leave her lips when all she wanted to do was growl and shove him away.

Revenge.

The hunger sent cold through her.

The mage moaned against her neck and lowered her onto the bed. "I did not imagine a phantom would feel so..."

She smiled as he drew back, luring him deeper under her spell. His green eyes turned hazy.

Sharpened.

He grabbed her jaw and glared down at her. "Do not think to use your powers on me."

Isla fought the urge to flinch away and managed to relax into the bed beneath him. "I would not... you are more powerful than I."

A smug smile of male satisfaction curved his lips and he trailed his eyes over her, leaned on his right elbow and skimmed his fingers down her body in their wake. His pupils dilated as his fingertips traversed her breasts and she clenched her teeth when he stroked them over her nipple.

"Far more powerful," he murmured, falling back under her spell as she loosed another false whimper of pleasure and arched into his wretched touch.

Revenge.

Life.

Just one night.

His hand closed over her right breast.

Gods, she couldn't do it.

She struggled against him, managing to knock his hand away, and he snarled as he gripped her throat and shoved her down against the mattress.

"I am more powerful... do not fight me, Phantom." He pressed harder against her throat and then his mouth was on hers, and she whimpered as he kissed her, forcing his tongue between her lips.

His left hand squeezed her breast and tears stung her eyes.

She tried to fight him, but he was right. In her corporeal form, she didn't have the power to overwhelm him, her phantom side held beneath her skin by both the spell his father had cast on her and the one he was funnelling through the crystals around her, rendering her even weaker still.

He shoved his left knee between her thighs.

Isla squeezed her eyes shut, her heart thundering, and pushed her hands against his bare chest. He grabbed her wrists and pinned them to the bed, and loomed over her. Her eyes slowly opened and she stared up at him, trembling from head to toe, fearing what was to come.

Gods, what had she done?

Grave.

Her heart called for him, even when she knew he wouldn't answer, wouldn't hear her because of the mage's spell.

Even when she knew it was hopeless.

"I changed my mind."

Relief poured through her as that rough baritone shattered the tense silence in the room and the mage looked over his shoulder at the source of it.

She gasped as a hand appeared on his shoulder and then he was gone, ripped away from her and sent flying across the room. He hit the wall between two windows hard and fell to the floor, landing in a heap, and the spell over her lifted a little more.

Her eyes shifted to Grave. He stood between her and the mage again, his back to her, but she didn't need to see his face to know how it would look, drawn tight with anger that she could feel flowing through their bond.

She had never been so relieved to feel that he was furious.

"The female is bound to me and should service only my needs. I do not like sharing." Grave turned away from the mage as he picked himself up off the black floor and gathered her clothes, bundling them under one arm.

He walked over to her where she sat in the middle of the bed and held his hand out to her.

She stared at it, too shaken to reach out for him as she wanted and seize hold of him only to never let him go again.

He hesitated, a look on his face she couldn't decipher, not even with their bond finally relaying his feelings to her again, and then he grabbed her wrist and dragged her off the bed and towards the stairs.

Isla looked down at his hand where it circled her wrist, strong fingers closed tightly around her, far fiercer than the mage or Snow had held her.

He was being rough with her, but she couldn't hate him for it.

Because he was saving her.

But he was damning them at the same time. She looked back at the mage, torn between remaining silent and pleading the bastard to help her. Without another spell, she wouldn't be strong enough to fight the demon and avenge her family, and without it both her and Grave would fade.

She frowned down at his hand as he hit the stairs and stormed down them, pulling her along with him, and then up at the back of his head, and focused on the mark on her back. On their bond. There was anger in it, but there was something else too, and it reminded her of something Melia had said.

Something that might give them the time they needed.

She had been trying to seduce the wrong male.

Grave still desired her. His hunger was there for her to read in their connection, had sparked to life the moment he had set eyes on her sitting in the middle of the bed, revealing his desire to her. If Melia was right, then she could strengthen their weakened bond by being intimate with him, as her sister had with Valador.

She had seduced Grave once to pull him into their bond.

Could she seduce him again to save him from its effects?

CHAPTER 15

A knock at his door halted Grave in his tracks as he paced across his small dreary room in the inn. He continued to mull over what had happened back at the tower and how he had fucked everything up in a stupid fit of anger and jealousy, a slave to a fierce possessive need.

He opened the door.

A possessive need that overcame him again as he stared into Isla's blue eyes.

He had avoided talking about what he had done during their journey from the tower to the nearest town, and she had been mercifully quiet throughout it, barely looking at him and not uttering a single word other than to thank him.

Thank him.

Gods, he had realised in that moment that she had been terrified, and he had been the one to throw her at the mage.

What kind of bastard was he?

The worst sort, one who could sacrifice even the woman he loved in order to get what he wanted.

No. He hadn't been able to do it, even when it had been her suggestion and she had looked ready to go through with it when they had met with the mage. He had gone mad trapped in his room in the tower, aware that male was with her.

Touching her.

Touching what was his and always would be.

He knew the moment his eyes transformed, blazing red with his fury, with his need to erase the mage's scent from her and mark her with his own.

Isla's eyes widened slightly, a ripple of shock running through their bond.

Grave went to lower his head so she didn't have to see the hunger in his eyes, a reflection of the darker need rising inside him again, one he had been battling since dragging her from that castle.

Isla's palms captured his cheeks.

He blinked at the sudden soft press of her against him and then her mouth was on his, cool but warm at the same time. His hands flexed at his sides, his breath coming quicker as he fought to convince himself this was real and to not push her away out of spite or bitterness.

He needed her too much to deny himself.

He seized her hips and drew her up against him, moaned low in his throat as she sank into him, her breasts squashed against his bare chest and leather corset cool against his flesh. Her hands skimmed along his jaw and she pulled him closer, wrapping her arms around his neck. Her sweet whimper almost did him in, pushing at his control, and he growled as he grabbed her backside and lifted her, bringing her mouth up level with his so he could kiss her harder.

He stepped back, kicked the door closed so hard she gasped, and pinned her against it.

Gods.

The hunger for her that had always simmered in his blood boiled to the surface, stripping away his control, and Isla only gave it a firmer hold over him as she wrapped her leather-clad legs around his waist. Her heat pressed against his hard cock through his black combat trousers, pinning it between them, and he grunted as he rubbed against her, breathing hard into her mouth as he kissed her.

She tasted too good.

Warm. Sweet. Wonderful.

He groaned and deepened the kiss, tangling his tongue with hers, driving her into submission. She went willingly, stoking his need for her. His little phantom. He loved the way she was with him when she was fire and ice to everyone else in this world. He loved the way she didn't have to be strong around him, and he didn't need to be strong around her either.

He clutched her closer to him and shuddered as she licked his fang, stroking it from root to tip, something she had always done to tease him and make him think about her doing that somewhere else. Somewhere that ached for her attention.

He leaned in to kiss her harder and show her just how crazy she made him.

His fang nicked her tongue.

The taste of blood flooded his senses.

Hunger roared to the fore and saliva pooled in his mouth, and he snarled as he grasped her jaw to hold her in place as he kissed her deeper, desperate for more.

He shoved away from her a second later and paced across the room, heart pounding and blood thundering, his strides clipped as he tried to work off some energy. Enough that he wouldn't hurt her.

One look at her undid all his hard work, and his bloodlust boiled back to the surface.

"Out," he snapped.

Her eyes widened.

When she didn't move, he stormed across the room to her, roughly grabbed her by her arm and yanked her away from the grotty wooden door. He opened it, shoved her out into the corridor, and slammed it in her face.

His hands shook as he ran them over his short hair, his whole body trembling as he battled his bloodlust, struggling to get it back under control. He couldn't remember the last time it had been this strong, too powerful for him to harness it.

He tunnelled his fingers into his dark hair and clawed it back, breathing hard and trying to settle his mind. Impossible with the taste of Isla on his tongue.

Where the hell was Snow?

His cousin had decided to go on a mission to find some blood for them the moment he had set eyes on Grave when he had arrived at the inn with Isla. He had tried to stop Snow, aware that it was dangerous for him to be around blood, but his cousin had been right about a few things.

He needed to feed, because the bloodlust was riding him too hard, stirred to a frenzy by the thought of Isla with another male and his growing hunger for her.

Gods, just one drop of her blood had sent him hurtling over the edge.

His fangs ached, saliva filling his mouth as he remembered its sweet taste of life. Of her. Everything he needed.

He looked over his shoulder at the door and then forced himself away from it. She would stay away from him. He knew that and was glad of it. Her pain radiated through the mark on his back. She probably thought he had rejected her to hurt her, to make her suffer in a new way for what she had done to him.

He had done it to protect her.

His bloodlust was growing stronger as he grew weaker, and she triggered it too easily, her scent too sweet and alluring for him to ignore. It roused the thirst he had always had for her, an endless need to drink of her blood in order to pull her down into him, to ensure she was always with him.

Grave breathed slowly and cleared his mind, focusing on his heartbeat and his blood, and the darkness swimming in it. Control came and went, slipping through his fingers each time he thought he had it.

He closed his eyes and focused harder, afraid Snow would return and witness how weak he really was.

His iron self-control was the crux of his pride and his reputation, an unbreakable will that had all vampires whispering his name in awe and fear because he used it to master his bloodlust, allowing him to use its savageness to his advantage.

But it was also his ultimate weakness.

He looked back at the door and focused on the mark on his back and the female linked to him through it, needing to feel her.

He was beginning to believe his self-control was the reason he had lost her. His iron grip on his emotions, keeping them in check so no one knew what he was thinking and therefore no one had any power over him because he revealed no weaknesses to them, might have been his undoing after all.

If he had shown her how he really felt about her, how deeply he loved her, she might not have shattered the heart that beat for her alone.

She might not have left him.

She had confessed that a need for revenge had brought her to him, and he had been furious with her and crushed at the same time when he had heard that, but during the long hours he had been alone in his room in the tower, he'd had time to contemplate it and the things she had told him without words, through her eyes and their bond.

Revenge had brought her to him, but something else had made her stay.

If she had wanted to merely curse him to life as a phantom, a single kiss would have sufficed, and she had managed that victory bare minutes after they had met.

No. Isla had wanted more than that. She had cursed him, but she had stayed with him. Not for days, nor weeks. She had stayed months with him, rarely apart from him, and she had been happy. The woman she was now was a sharp contrast to the one he had held in his arms, had spent long lazy days with in his apartment. Something inside him had broken when she had left him, and now he believed that same something had broken inside her too.

She had loved him.

They were alike in so many respects.

More than just their feelings.

In that tower, shut away in that room, he had paced himself into an epiphany and that dawning of realisation had given him the strength to go to her, to show her that he wasn't as cruel as this world thought he was and there were softer feelings inside him, ones that made him burn for her.

He had put himself in Isla's place.

If someone had killed Aurora, leaving Snow alone in the world with their offspring, a constant reminder of the love he had lost, and Grave had witnessed her death, he would have done the same thing.

He would have hunted down the one responsible and taken revenge on them.

While his method would have been swift and brutal justice befitting of a vampire, Isla had chosen a phantom way. She had wanted him to suffer as her sister did, drawing out his pain.

But what she had wanted had changed when she had met him, when she had grown to love him. He truly believed that.

So as much as he wanted to hate her for what she had done, he couldn't because he knew that if he had been a phantom in her position, he probably would have done the same thing.

For almost a century he had taken out his pain on her, and on everyone else in this world, and he had believed he hated her, that anything he had felt for her had died that night she had left him, but his love for her had never died.

It never would.

He would love her forever.

Did she regret the things she had done as fiercely as he regretted his actions?

The part of his heart that he normally tried to ignore answered that question and he listened to it this time.

Of course she did.

She had shown it to him countless ways since walking back into his life. Just as she had shown him that she still had feelings for him.

So what the hell did they do now?

The decisiveness he relied on as a leader, the ability to form a plan of action that was both perfect and infallible, was nowhere to be found when it came to Isla. He wasn't sure how to proceed with her.

No matter how fiercely he wanted that knowledge.

He turned towards the door and sank onto the foot of the bed, the musty grey bedclothes creasing as the soft mattress depressed beneath his weight.

The mark on his back tingled.

Grave reached for her too, aching to have her here with him, no longer strong enough to deny her or his feelings for her. He wanted her back with him, craved the feel of her in his arms and the taste of her on his tongue, and her sweet cries of pleasure in his ears, but he couldn't risk it.

He wasn't strong enough to control his hunger for her blood, not as he was now.

He needed to feed, and then maybe he would find the courage to speak with her.

His body refused to get the message that they had to wait though. That single taste of her had him primed, rock hard in his black trousers despite his mind being elsewhere, aching for her. He palmed his length, groaned low in his throat as pleasure shot through him, and imagined it was Isla touching him.

She would see it through their connection, but this time he didn't care.

He might be a cruel bastard, but he wasn't that evil. He wanted her to know that he did still desire her, even after everything that had happened.

The door burst open.

His hand shot away from his cock and his eyes darted to the person standing there, expecting to find his cousin with a canister of blood.

Isla.

She slammed the door behind her and strode towards him, resolve etched on her beautiful face.

"Get out," he barked but she paid him no heed as she stopped in front of him, a steely look in her blue eyes.

Gods, he had forgotten how breathtaking she was when she was determined.

"Leave." He pushed her blue leather-clad hip, a weak attempt at turning her away when all he really wanted to do was gather her to him and drown in her.

Isla shoved him in return, with a little more force than he had managed, sending him slamming flat onto his back on the bed.

She pressed one knee onto the mattress beside his hip and then the other, so she kneeled astride him, and he swallowed hard as she leaned over him, her palms hitting the bed above his shoulders and her long white hair falling down to brush across his bare chest.

"Isla," he whispered, voice thick with the emotions he still wanted to hide from her, afraid she would use them against him again.

"Grave," she murmured. "Quit fighting me, Idiot."

Her mouth was on his, her kiss blinding him as she sent him soaring, and all of the fight she had spoken of left him and he sagged against the bed beneath her, at her mercy.

He groaned as she sank into him, her leather corset cool against his bare chest but soon absorbing his heat and warming. Her mouth mastered his, tongue teasing and stroking, sending him up to new heights where he could barely breathe. He groaned and surrendered to her and the need running thick in his blood.

She came down onto her elbows and ran her fingers through his hair, and gods, now he couldn't breathe. Her touch felt too good, overloading him with sensations he couldn't handle after so many long years alone.

Her sweet murmur of pleasure rolled through him, heating his blood as she kissed him, the tip of her tongue teasing his fangs, playing a dangerous game with him when he was hungry. He fought to master his bloodlust, letting her do as she pleased with him as his focus locked onto it.

He hadn't even noticed she had broken away from his mouth until he felt the electric jolt of her tongue stroking a hard line up his neck from the notch between his collarbones. Another moan escaped him and he couldn't stop himself from tipping his head back, allowing her to trace her tongue over his Adam's apple and up the underside of his chin. He shuddered when she nipped his jaw with her blunt teeth.

Too much.

He wanted to tell her that, to warn her that he was barely retaining control, but the sweet hazy pleasure ebbing and flowing through him stole his voice and all he could do was wrap his arms around her and hold her to him, determined to never let her go again.

He skimmed his hands down the back of her corset and she breathed harder against his jaw as she kissed along it, her soft breath cool against his damp skin, sending shivers tripping along his nerves.

When he reached her backside, he pulled her down into contact with him. She groaned in unison with him, and he had never heard a sweeter sound. It drove him on, giving his hunger more control until the roar of it drowned out the quiet voice of reason that warned him to be gentle with her.

He wasn't sure that was possible even if he somehow kept his wits about him enough to retain control.

He needed her too much.

He had gone too long without her, had been half-mad with need of her for a century already and had lost his mind completely in the last few days.

He raised his hips and ground against her, shuddered and moaned as the feel of her pressing against him threatened to undo him. He needed to be inside her. Not because he needed release at last, but because of the mage.

The sight of that vile bastard touching her had given birth to a deep and consuming need, a powerful urge to stake his claim on Isla. He needed her to know that she was his.

He needed to know it too.

She rocked against him and her mouth found his again, tongue plunging between his lips to tease and torture him as she worked him into a frenzy. Her hands pressed against his shoulders when he tried to get closer to her, pinning him to the bed beneath her, her touch chilling his skin in a way that he had missed.

One that felt like Heaven to him.

He kissed her back, fought her for control and seized it, and she trembled in his arms as he surged between her thighs, imagining taking her body as he took her mouth.

Took her neck between his fangs.

He wanted that. Needed it. Would have it.

He growled low in his throat as that powerful need overwhelmed him again and his fangs lengthened, his mind already leaping ahead to picture the exact place he would sink them into her flesh.

He broke away from her mouth and grasped her shoulders when she tried to kiss him again.

"Leave." He pushed against her.

She didn't budge. Her eyes softened as she looked down into his.

"Do not do that," she whispered and he closed his eyes and turned his face away from her. She gently caught his right cheek and smoothed her palm over it, her touch soft and tender, unravelling more of his control. Her thumb brushed his cheekbone and she slowly drew him back to face her. He refused to open his eyes. She sighed. "Do not push me away… I can handle your hunger. I can help you with it."

His eyes snapped open, locking with hers, and he couldn't hide the disbelief that ran through him, forcing him to seek the truth in her eyes.

Isla reached her right hand behind her head, caught her fall of white hair and drew it away from the left side of her neck, revealing it to him. The braid that hung from her left temple swayed against her throat and his eyes followed it down to the silver wire and the red crystal.

Red for him. He knew that now.

His gaze drifted across to the pale scars on the curve of her throat. The only set she bore on that side, made the first time he had bitten her, when they had sealed their bond.

He groaned and wanted to be the better male, a gentleman, and reject her offer in order to protect her, but he wasn't that male. He never would be.

When faced with her neck, the only thing he could do was obey his hunger for her.

His fangs ached and he edged towards her, head coming up off the bed, but then sank back against it.

It turned out he was more of a gentleman than he had thought possible.

The thought of biting her after everything he had done to her and all he had done in their time apart. He couldn't sully her like that.

"I'm not worth it," he whispered and he had never wished so hard that he was worthy of someone. Gods, he had always thought himself above everyone and that they weren't worthy of him, but looking into Isla's eyes he realised he couldn't have been more wrong. He wasn't worthy of her and he wasn't sure he ever had been. He had done nothing in his life to deserve someone like her, someone to truly love him. "I've bitten so many females... all to—"

Isla pressed two fingers to his lips, squashing them against his throbbing fangs, her touch too much for him to bear. He frowned up at her, torn between two hungers—one for her blood and one for her body.

No.

He was torn between two cravings—one for her blood and one for her love.

He needed this soft touch and that look in her blue eyes that warmed even the coldest reaches of his heart.

He needed it more than blood.

Now he understood why Snow loved Aurora so damned much.

He thought he had loved others, but Isla had made him see that he had never loved someone, not the way he loved her. He loved her like crazy, a man gone mad when he was with her and insane when they were apart for even a second. She was everything to him, filling his world with light that had given way to a terrible darkness when she had left him, a black void that had given his bloodlust a fiercer hold over him, for one reason.

She was the only one he had ever given enough of himself to, who had ever had enough of him to break his heart.

"I know," she murmured softly. "You do not need to say anything... but I know you also showed me those things to punish me... and I deserved it."

He caught her wrist and drew her hand away from his mouth, and whispered, "Isla."

She shook her head. "Let me finish. I deserved it. I never should have turned my back on you... and I do not expect you to forgive me... but I need you to know it hurt me as much as it hurt you... I wish..."

She lowered her eyes to his chest and he hovered on the brink of demanding to know what she wished, because he wasn't sure he could bear her silence and not knowing.

Her eyes slipped shut.

"I wish I had not done it... I wish I had not left you, Grave."

The moment her blue eyes opened, seeking his, he tugged her back down to him and kissed her, unable to deny the need for her that had always burned so brightly in his heart but now blazed like an inferno, given new life by her words and the feelings that had been in her eyes, emotions that flowed through their mating mark too and echoed his own.

He couldn't play their vicious game anymore either.

Life seemed too short to waste it taking pot shots at each other's heart when all they really wanted was to erase the years they had been apart and forget they had ever happened.

She moaned and sank against him, and he kissed along her jaw, teased her left earlobe with the tip of his tongue and shivered as her breath skated over his neck and her hands shook against his shoulders.

"Grave," she whispered, the tremble in her voice his undoing, shattering his control.

He would take them back to the start, to where it had all began, and this time they would do it right.

He brushed his lips across her neck.

Opened his mouth.

Sank his fangs in deep.

CHAPTER 16

Sweet gods.

Isla's cry of pleasure was almost too much for Grave. Combined with the way she trembled in his arms, the bliss he could feel in her through their bond and the taste of her on his tongue, he was on the verge of release already and they were only just getting started. He was damned if his first time with her in close to a century was going to end with him climaxing in his trousers.

But the taste of her.

Sweet gods, the taste of her.

He thought he had remembered it clearly, but the reality was far more intoxicating than his memory of it. Her blood had a taste like the fragrance of honeysuckle and night dew, with a rich undernote of smokiness like morning mist that curled through his senses as he fed from her vein. He couldn't get enough of her or the way she writhed against him, rubbing his aching cock through his trousers. It strained against his fly, even the slightest brush too much for him to bear, sending hot shivers tripping through his entire body.

Isla moaned into his ear.

Too much.

He tore his fangs from her throat and kissed her, pouring the need coursing through him into it, needing her to feel what she did to him. What only she did to him. No other female had made him feel the way she did, had made him lose control with only a press of her body against his or even a single sultry bloody glance in his direction.

Isla had total power over him, and he was a willing slave to her, a male who couldn't get enough of her.

Would never get enough of her.

They could have a thousand years and he would still crave a thousand more with her.

He swallowed her gasp as he rolled her over, ending up wedged between her leather-clad thighs. The material was soft and smooth beneath his fingers as he palmed her backside with his left hand, his thoughts leaping ahead to touching her in the same place when she was naked and he was inside her, holding her backside off the bed so he could drive deep into her just the way she loved it.

"Grave," she murmured against his lips, a husky plea for more.

He growled and kissed her harder, silencing her with his tongue. She fought him with hers, battled him for control in a way that had always stoked his need to startling heights. Her hands pressed against his shoulders and he snarled again, grabbed her shoulders with both of his hands and then her arms.

He pinned them to the dirty grey bedclothes above her head and she moaned and writhed beneath him, her chest lifting to press her breasts against his chest.

Gods.

Grave gathered both of her wrists into one hand, leaned away from her and yanked hard on the bottom of her blue leather corset. Her breasts sprang free of the top and he groaned at the sight of them and the way her dusky nipples puckered in the cool air.

Isla moaned again and arched her back, raising her breasts towards him.

As if he would refuse such an invitation.

He snarled as he swooped on her left breast, pulling the taut bead into his mouth, and groaned as she cried out, the sound of her pleasure filling the room. He drank every whispered moan and sweet cry, teased her nipple with his teeth to elicit more for him to devour and savour.

His sweet Isla.

She responded to him so beautifully, her pleasure mastering him even as he mastered her body.

Her moans only grew louder as he skimmed his hand down the flat of her belly to the waist of her trousers. She raised her hips, rocking against his touch as he pulled at the leather laces to undo them and then tugged at them, loosening them enough for him to slip his hand inside.

His fingers found her moist core and slipped between her plush petals to tease the tight bud of nerves there as his teeth teased her left nipple.

Isla jacked off the bed and shuddered, and her keening cry drove him over the edge of control, deep into the fierce desire that had always ruled them both, a wicked hunger that was never sated and never controlled. Both of them could only hold it at bay for a short time, neither ever able to master it. It was consuming, powerful and intoxicating.

It was love.

Love in its deepest, purest and wildest form.

It blazed inside him, burned so ferociously he could only hope to leash it enough to retain some sense of self, so he didn't become a complete slave to sensation and need, to the hunger that raged so beautifully within him, a tempest of love and passion.

He squeezed the sensitive bud between his fingers and Isla tried to wrestle free of his grip, arched her hips and moaned for more. She didn't need to rush. He would see to it that she found release, the most powerful one he could give to her.

She stilled when he released her nipple and kissed across to her other one, teased it with a flick of his tongue, and then eased down her body. Her hands slipped free of his grip and he skimmed his fingers down one arm and under the curve of her breast as he stepped off the bed.

Gods, she was beautiful like that, her arms held above her head, white hair spilling across the sheets, and her rosy lips swollen from his kisses and her breasts on show. He growled, caught her hips and shoved her up the bed, so her head hit the pillow. Her little gasp was music to his ears, driving him on together with the way her eyes darkened a full shade, her pupils devouring the blue as they dilated.

He stroked his hands over her waist and slowly lowered them to her hips again, and her eyes dropped to follow them, her lips parting as he slipped his fingers into the waist of her blue leather trousers.

Her breath hitched.

Grave eased her leathers down, torn between looking at her face and watching the beautiful way desire flared across her delicate features, and watching as he revealed her body to his hungry eyes.

When she lifted her bottom from the bed and he pulled her leathers past it, he couldn't stop himself from looking.

He groaned as his eyes found Heaven at the apex of her thighs, a soft neat thatch of white curls that glistened with the evidence of her desire, need for him.

Need he would fulfil for her.

He yanked at her trousers until they hit her boots, and growled at the cursed obstruction.

Isla was on them immediately, sitting up and tearing into her left boot. Grave smiled at her enthusiasm and then attacked her right boot. He tossed it away a second after she threw her one across the room. She shoved at her trousers and he pulled them free of her legs and turned slightly to throw them onto the chair.

When he turned back, he stilled, his heart hammering against his chest and cock going painfully hard in his trousers.

Isla crawled up the bed away from him, her pert backside on show.

A feral snarl escaped him as his control snapped and she gasped as he grabbed her ankle and pulled her back to him, dragging her to the edge of the bed. She tried to turn but he snagged her around the waist and pulled her up to him, pinning her back to his chest. She stilled and pressed back against him, and he kissed her shoulder as he caressed her stomach and then down her hips.

A moan trembled on her lips.

He shifted his hands forwards and she shook as he eased one between her thighs and tugged them apart. Her breath came quicker as he lowered his other hand between them and found her bundle of nerves again, starting a slow teasing stroke that took his fingers from there to her core and back again.

"Grave," Isla murmured, need echoing in her voice and his veins.

He lifted his free hand and tugged her hair away from her back, twisting it into his fist. The intricate mark on her back shimmered, pulsing with faint light. A mark that matched his. He groaned and kissed it, ran his tongue over it to trace each line, and savoured the way Isla reacted, little breathless moans escaping her as she spiralled towards her climax.

She never had been able to handle him doing this.

Her mark was more sensitive than his, especially when she was aroused.

Her moans deepened and she rocked her hips into his hand.

He stilled.

Growled as need went through him, a hunger he could no longer deny.

He tore at his trousers, shoved them down and groaned when his cock sprang free. He had it wedged between her buttocks before she could even gasp and rubbed between them, his moans joining hers as he held her in place, one fist in her hair and the other between her thighs. Gods. She was cool against him, but the touch of her flesh against his still seemed to warm him. He shuddered, need wracking him, riding him harder.

Isla shoved him back over the edge.

She pressed her hips back against his.

Grave snarled, grabbed his cock and the back of her neck and pushed her forwards. He dipped his body, rubbed the blunt head of his length down the seam of her backside and found her hot core. He groaned and shook as he felt how wet she was for him and smelled the scent of her need. Isla trembled, body quivering around his as he eased into her, too lost in the feel of her gloving him to rush when he had wanted to drive hard and deep before.

He grunted as he hit as deep as he could go and pulled her back up to him, so her back was flush against his front.

Sweet gods.

It had been a long time since he had been with her, but he hadn't been prepared for this. She was so tight around him, clutching his cock, her juices seeping down his rigid length to his balls.

"Grave," she moaned and rotated her hips.

Too much.

He snarled against her shoulder, grabbed her thighs with both hands and pulled them apart, so he could go deeper again, so she would feel all of him and know what she did to him.

She cried out as he thrust hard into her, making her take every inch.

She trembled, body flexing around his when he stilled, goading him into giving her more. Oh, he would give it to her and it wasn't going to be gentle. They never had been very good at tender or sweet. Never. Their passion and need always slipped the leash and overwhelmed them.

Right now, he had no control, not even a fraction of it to hold himself back. A century. A century of waiting for her. A century of needing her. It all rolled into this one moment.

He twisted her hair into his left fist and held her hip with his right hand, and drove into her, lifting her knees off the bed each time he filled her. She moaned and sagged against him, her hands coming up to skim over her breasts as they bounced with each hard plunge of his cock into her core. He yanked her head back and sucked on her neck as he thrust into her, losing himself in the feel of her and the connection that sparked to life between them, growing stronger and running deeper in his veins, until he could feel every drop of her pleasure as it rolled through her, slowly building towards a crescendo.

Her right hand dropped between her thighs and he grunted as she arched forwards, pulled her hair to keep her in place as he took her, sliding deeper still with each long hard stroke of his cock. She moaned and whimpered, and he almost joined her when her fingers teased his length as he pumped into her, dropped to his balls and tugged them.

Sweet mercy.

He grunted again, little more than a snarl in his throat as she fondled him and his balls tightened, release rising as he soared higher.

Grave grabbed her right breast and pulled her shoulders back to him, lost himself in devouring her shoulder with wet kisses and blunt teeth as he drove into her and she played with his sac, rolling and tugging, stroking and teasing. Damn.

His fangs ached and he sank them deep into her shoulder.

Isla cried out and quivered, her body pulsing around his cock and hot release scalding him. Bliss flowed through their link, a fire that swept through his blood like an inferno, and he snarled into her shoulder as he pulled on her blood, drawing more of her into him. She cried out again, jerking in his arms, shaking so fiercely he could barely keep hold of her as she shattered, consumed by the release he had silently promised her.

One that had her going boneless in his arms.

He shuddered and managed a few more thrusts into her quivering core before stars exploded across his eyes and detonated in his blood, wildfire heat shooting through him. He trembled as fiercely as his cock as he spilled inside her, his entire body quaking and his knees becoming rubber beneath him.

They hit the edge of the mattress, his cock slipping from her body, still pulsing with release, and he barely managed to land on the bed and not the floor.

Grave stared at the ceiling, breathing hard, his whole being shaking from the force of his release—body and soul.

Isla slumped onto the bed and rolled towards him, her soft breath teasing his bare skin. When she shuffled closer, her breasts pressing against his chest and her right leg coming to rest over his, heat stirred in his blood, born of the hunger for her that he could never sate.

He groaned as his length twitched, already eager for more.

Her soft hand dropped to it, fingers stroking upwards from his balls to the tip, and he shuddered and moaned as his eyes slipped shut and pleasure rolled through him.

Gods, she would be the death of him.

But that was a risk he was more than happy to take.

He pulled her on top of him and claimed her mouth in a fierce kiss.

CHAPTER 17

Isla found it difficult to concentrate on the conversation between Grave and Snow as they stood in the cobbled street outside the small inn. Her body still buzzed from being with Grave, tingled in all the best places, and she couldn't keep her eyes off him or her thoughts away from tempting him into another encore, even when she knew she should be listening to the information Snow had gathered during his outing.

Apparently he had gone to fetch blood for Grave. The immense white-haired male hadn't seemed surprised when he had returned to find Grave fed though. He had simply slid a knowing look at her, even though she had bathed and her hair had been down, concealing the fresh sets of marks on her skin. Her cheeks heated again as his pale blue eyes settled on her briefly before shifting back to his cousin.

Grave frowned and looked her way too. The second his eyes met hers, that frown melted away, his dark eyebrows smoothing and his pupils dilating as he stared at her. Her blush burned hotter and she looked away from him, casting her eyes down to her boots. The blue leather was a rich contrast against the black cobbles. Fascinating.

Her mate's eyes left her and he began talking with Snow again, and Isla tried to find her voice to participate in their conversation about the demon and where to look next.

This was her mission too now. She wanted vengeance, and nothing would stop her from having it. She would make the demon pay for taking her family from her.

Family.

Her fingers traced the twined leather around her right wrist.

She needed to report back to Frey and check on him. He was going to be disappointed when he discovered that she hadn't been able to get the mage to cast a new spell on her to stop her from fading, but hopefully her new plan to save herself might give him some relief in a difficult time. She didn't want him worrying about her when he had the weight of a kingdom on his shoulders.

She was sure her plan would succeed.

Melia had given her everything she needed to save herself but she had been too stubborn, and too afraid of getting her feelings for Grave trampled on, to walk that route. Now, she bravely trod it, determined to make it happen.

Her sister had told her that the bond she had created needed periodic strengthening, a renewal of sorts, and that was exactly what she was going to do.

Well, it was exactly what she was doing.

Last night with Grave had only been the start, and she already felt stronger. Did Grave feel it too?

She cast a glance up at him and he looked her way, his scowl easing again as his eyes found her face and she moved a step closer to him.

"Grave," she started.

A slender male with spiky sandy hair and steel grey eyes appeared on the other side of him and she grabbed Grave's arm and pulled him behind her at the same time as she drew one of her blades from the leather holster against her lower back.

Snow's large hand snapped around her wrist before her blade could reach the intruder's throat, staying her hand.

"This is Payne," he said, voice a deep rumble that held a warning note as his near-crimson eyes locked with hers.

The one called Payne backed off a step, his eyes blazing with cerulean sparks as he glared at her. He folded his arms across his chest, the rolled up sleeves of his grey pinstripe shirt stretching tight over his muscles as he gripped his right biceps.

Isla frowned as markings caught her eye and she tracked the lines of elaborate patterns along the undersides of his forearms.

Her senses switched back and forth as she tried to detect what he was, flipping between labelling him a vampire and an incubus.

Perhaps he was both, although she had never heard of such a thing.

It would explain the fact he could teleport, and also the fangs she spotted as he curled his lip in her direction.

Isla realised she still held her blade in the air, aimed for his throat.

She lowered her arm and Snow released it. She slipped her blade back into the holster with the other one and backed off a step.

"Fucking phantoms," Payne muttered, his accent as unmistakably English as Grave and Snow's, and the look he gave her said he had met her kind before and he hadn't enjoyed it. In fact, he looked as if he hated all of her kind because of it.

That didn't surprise her, but the fact he could tell she was a phantom when she was flesh and blood did.

How acute were his senses?

Incubi were predators of the highest order. Did his heightened senses give him the ability to learn a species base scent or something about them that allowed him to easily distinguish them from others?

Most mistook her for a fae, sometimes a siren but often a succubus. Since becoming corporeal, she hadn't met one person who had been able to tell just by looking at her what she was. Even Grave hadn't realised she was a phantom until she had told him. Until it was too late to save himself.

Gods, he had been angry with her, but looking back she had the feeling that his fury hadn't been because she was a phantom and had condemned him to an incorporeal fate, but because she had wounded him by turning on him.

The stolen glances he had given her during their past few meetings left her feeling that if she hadn't been out for vengeance that night, if she had gone to him purely to confess she was a phantom and not to hurt him, he would have reacted in a way that would have melted her heart. She felt sure of it. He would have drawn her to him and kissed her instead of pushing her away, just as he had drawn her to him and kissed her last night.

She smiled to herself about that.

Payne and Snow arched eyebrows at her. Her smile fell and she scowled at them, and the amused looks fled their faces, scoring a victory for her. Or at least she had thought it her victory.

Grave stepped past her, his face a mask of darkness as he glared at his cousin and Payne, his eyes bright crimson and pupils stretched into thin vertical lines in their centres.

Now that she was aware of his anger on her behalf, she could feel it too, flowing through their mating mark. She lowered her gaze to his right hand, edged hers towards it and brushed her knuckles across his.

His frown instantly faltered and he looked down at their hands, and then up into her eyes, a beautiful lost look in his.

"He knows she's a phantom, right?" Payne said and Snow grumbled something in response.

"Of course I know," Grave snapped and his face darkened again, his eyes locking back on the newcomer. "I would warn you to keep your eyes off my mate, Incubus."

So she had been right and he was part incubus at least. Grave's words seemed to provoke the vampire in Payne though, turning his eyes crimson and his teeth sharp as he took a firm step towards her mate.

"I have a mate… and I am getting pretty fucking tired of everyone thinking I want their bird. I'm not interested. My incubus blood doesn't make me a whore."

"Payne," Snow said and the male looked at him, some of the darkness fading from his eyes as they settled on him. Possibly because it couldn't beat the darkness of Snow's expression, a stormy look that warned of danger. "Did you come for a reason?"

Snow's dark mood faltered, a glimmer of light breaking through the clouds as he searched Payne's red eyes.

"Is Aurora well?"

Payne nodded and Isla bit back a sigh over the beautiful expression of relief that flitted across Snow's face, a reflection of his love for the one called Aurora. She hadn't heard of the female before, but it was clear the big vampire adored her. Was she another vampire?

"She wanted to come, but… well… we all know Hell is no place for an angel… so here I am… a devil in disguise." Payne casually lifted his shoulders, but there was nothing casual about his eyes. He honestly thought himself a devil. Poor soul.

He was no more evil than she was.

Isla frowned.

Aurora was an angel?

Before she could pursue an answer to that question, Grave moved a step closer to Payne, capturing all of their attentions.

"Why did you come?" The cold note to his voice echoed in their bond as a strange sort of emptiness.

Fear.

Isla blinked and looked to Payne, suddenly desperate for an answer to her mate's question, because she feared she knew it.

Payne looked down at his boots, hesitated and then lifted his gaze back to meet Grave's. "We had word from your brother... Night. He apparently returned to his home in London to grab some shit before he went into hiding and found his flat torn apart."

"But he is safe?" Grave surged another step forwards and his hands clenched and unclenched at his sides, and she could feel his need to take hold of Payne and rattle the answer out of him.

Payne nodded. "He went back to the mansion and said they would leave it tonight, but he asked me to tell you about what happened in case you went looking for him at his apartment and found it wrecked."

Grave blew out his breath, his relief palpable, but it soon faded, replaced by a rising cold that flowed through her, chilling her blood too.

"The mansion," Grave muttered and slowly shifted his gaze to Snow, and she looked there too, found his cousin wearing the same mask of fear that he did.

"We have to go now." Snow grabbed Payne's arm and jerked the male to face him, earning a black look. "Can you teleport three?"

"Four," Isla interjected.

Grave shook his head. "No. It is too dangerous. Wait here."

She planted her hands on her hips.

"I do not do as you say, obeying orders like your men." She ignored the scowl that drew his dark eyebrows down over blazing red eyes and pushed on, and his demeanour changed as she spoke, his look softening again and warmth filling his eyes. "This demon took my family from me and I will not stand idly by while he attempts to take yours. Vengeance burns in my blood... and I must answer its call."

"Isla." He lifted his hand and sighed as he carefully brushed a strand of her white hair behind her left ear. He caught the braid that hung from her temple on that side and raised it towards him, his eyes on it as it slipped over his fingers. When the bead at the end reached them, he brushed his thumb across it. His eyes lingered on it, their crimson colour matching it. Another sigh escaped him and he let the braid fall, raised his eyes to hers and nodded. "Very well. I cannot deny you your vengeance. We will make sure the demon pays for what he did to your family... to you."

The fight she had been mustering inside her, everything she had been practicing in her head in order to convince him to listen to her, faded away and she wanted to frown at him. She had been expecting more resistance. In the past, he had fought her whenever she had wanted to participate in a battle, and had usually won.

But that was the past.

She could see in his eyes that he wanted a different future for them, and he was trying to make it happen.

Starting with allowing her to fight at his side, where she felt she belonged. She had hated it whenever he had gone to war alone, even when he had promised to only be gone a day or two. She had hated not knowing whether he would return and spending the long hours monitoring their mating mark, convinced that every tiny twinge that skittered across it was a sign someone had taken him from her.

This time, she wouldn't have to worry. She would be there to protect him and keep him safe from harm.

"So four to teleport. Should be able to do it," Payne muttered but he didn't look confident. "I don't know where the mansion is."

"I will tell you everything nearby and we can see if you know any of them." Snow pulled the vampire away from them and Isla made a mental note to thank him later, because she needed to speak with Grave before they left.

He needed to know everything, but honesty wasn't the only reason she was going to tell him about their bond and her plan. She wanted to ease the fear building steadily in his eyes, hidden from most but clearly visible to her. She wanted him to be confident again, certain that he was strong enough to fight the demon.

"Grave," she whispered and then cleared her throat as his eyes landed on her, burning into her face, heating her right down to her bones.

Gods. She had forgotten the feel of his eyes on her, the intensity of his gaze and the way it stirred fire in her veins, her body seeming to come alive in response to just an innocent glance from him. She drew down a deep breath to calm herself and claw back some control, because if all went to plan she could have more of Grave later, when they were alone again.

"There is something I must tell you." She resisted the temptation to fidget and held her chin up when it wanted to dip. She couldn't stop her cheeks from heating under his scrutiny though, and she didn't like the dark edge his eyes had gained. "It is nothing bad... in fact... it is something good. I think."

He arched his right eyebrow. "You think?"

She scowled at him. "You always fluster me."

A slow smile curved his lips, a wicked spark lighting his eyes as they faded from crimson to pale blue. She held her frown, refusing to give in to him even when she wanted to melt into his arms and kiss him. Damned vampire. He always had exuded an alluring sort of confidence. Not cockiness. Just a quiet confidence that radiated from everything he did, from his body language to his way of speaking. It added a whole new level of masculinity to him, one that tugged at her feminine side and made it difficult to resist him, especially when he turned on the charm as he was now.

"I like to fluster you," he whispered as he edged closer, one slow step that made him look like a predator, a powerful male and one who took what he wanted, and gods, she wanted him to take her.

She cleared her throat again, gathered all her strength and shored up her defences. She should have considered how dangerous it was for her to seduce him, should have factored in that she would unleash the same irresistible male he had been a century ago, when he had stolen her heart.

Gods, he was stealing it all over again.

"Since you enjoy it so, you may perhaps not be averse to what I intend to suggest as a way of slowing the effect our bond is having on us… it might even go some way towards reversing it." Now he looked rather interested in more than just getting her back into bed, his eyes shining with a strange light, curiosity mingled with hope. She had never seen that look in his eyes before and she took it as a good sign, one that gave her the courage to continue. "Melia believed our fading was because our bond was weakening… she said it required a periodic renewal… so if we strengthen our bond, there is a chance it will stop us from fading."

The right corner of his mouth curled and the light in his eyes turned wicked again. "If you want to sleep with me again, you only have to ask, Isla."

She was tempted to punch him in the chest, but his expression turned serious, saving him from a beating.

"You really believe that our being close will stop us from fading… it will make us stronger?"

She nodded. "I do."

He lifted his right hand and cupped her cheek in his palm. It was cool but warm against her, and she fought the urge to lean into it and seek more from him.

Gods, he made her weak.

Had Melia felt like this when Valador had touched her? Had her strength been stripped from her? It was frightening when she was used to being strong, one of the most powerful creatures to roam the Earth.

Frightening but exciting.

Exhilarating.

"Then I will not leave your side," he whispered and she pressed her hands to his chest as he leaned towards her, felt his heart drumming strong and steady against her palms, and the pendant he still wore.

A token of her love for him. A love that had never died. A love that would never die.

She closed her eyes and tipped her chin up, aching for his kiss.

"So, we ready?" Payne's voice shattered the intense silence.

Followed closely by Grave's growl of frustration.

Isla silently echoed him as he pulled away from her.

The sudden rise in nerves she could feel through her bond with Grave stopped her from cutting down Payne where he stood, serving as a reminder that now wasn't the time to lose herself in her mate. Anger swiftly followed on the heels of his nerves, and she knew it was partly directed at himself, with a slice reserved for her. He was upset that he had so easily forgotten that his family were in danger, had been caught up in her again, and she echoed those feelings.

She had vowed to avenge her family.

Nothing could stand between her and achieving that.

She stepped back, intending to distance herself to gain some control over herself in order to focus on her mission.

Grave's fingers closed over her right hand, obliterating what little focus she had mustered, so all of it fell to his large hand were it encompassed hers. She could only stare at their joined hands as he led her towards Payne and Snow, at the way he shifted his and laced his fingers with hers. Another first. He had taken her hand before, but never like this.

Never in a way that looked so unbreakable.

She was on dangerous ground.

She couldn't focus on Payne, Snow and Grave as they talked. She didn't notice Snow taking hold of her other arm, linking all four of them together. She didn't see the darkness as it swallowed her.

There was only Grave.

Holding her hand in a way that shook her, because it made her aware of a fear that had slowly wormed its way into her heart, deep enough that she couldn't shake it.

Fear that the feelings she sensed in him, the ones he showed her in his eyes and in his actions, were born of a need to be strong enough to protect his family and a need to punish her for the things she had done. Was he making her fall in love with him all over again so he could break her heart this time?

Isla pushed back against that fear, but she couldn't destroy it. It lived within her, festering inside her heart, whispering poisonous words to her.

She raised her eyes to his chest, to the sliver of silver visible through the open top of his black shirt. The pendant.

Did he really wear it to remind him of the things she had done?

She forced her eyes up to his and found him looking down at her, a soft but steady look in his eyes, one that boosted her courage and confidence, and quietened the insidious voice.

He wore it because it meant something to him. *She* meant something to him. She believed in that and in him, and she wouldn't allow her faith to be shaken again.

Grave wasn't intent on breaking her heart.

He was intent on mending it.

He wanted to fix things and she wanted that too, and she wouldn't allow anything to stand between them.

Dark power rolled over her and Grave's hand tensed against hers.

Isla looked off to her left, to the source of that incredible power, and reached for one of her blades.

Vengeance would be hers.

CHAPTER 18

An orange glow lit the night sky in the distance, silhouetting the sharp tips of the pine forest ahead of her.

Isla locked her eyes on that glow, racing towards it, bone-deep aware that the demon was there. So close. The smell of smoke hit her nose as she entered the forest, darting between the thick rough trunks of the trees, leaf litter dancing around her feet as she sped past.

She could feel Grave and the others hot on her heels, pursuing her as she pursued her prey, but she refused to slow and let him take the lead, even when she knew he wanted to be ahead of her, burned to reach the demon first and deal with him. She silently apologised to him and redoubled her effort, pushing past her limit.

If she had been incorporeal, she could have simply willed her form to materialise at a point in the distance she could see, and then willed herself to the next one. She couldn't teleport like many species, but she could move quicker than most.

The forest disappeared around her and she stumbled a few steps, managing to stop just short of hitting the broad trunk of a pine.

Isla looked back over her shoulder, her eyes widening as she saw the huge gap between her and Grave.

No.

She looked down at her hands and breathed a sigh of relief when she saw they were solid. She had lost one of her blades, but not her form. She glanced back at Grave as he closed in on her again and then in the direction of the fire. She had willed herself to travel a great distance though, and something deep inside her warned that wasn't a good thing at all.

The hold the phantom world had over her was growing stronger despite the time she had spent with Grave.

She vowed that once they had dealt with the demon, she would spend every waking and sleeping minute close to him until their bond was strong enough to stop them both from fading.

Right now, she had a demon to fight though.

She kicked off, twisting around at the same time, her right boot skidding on the thick gathering of pine needles at the base of the tree, and darted towards the blaze.

The forest began to thin as she caught up with Grave and her eyes darted around to take in the scene.

It was a mansion. The one she had seen through Grave's eyes.

The entire pale stone building was ablaze, the inferno so intense that it heated her skin even though she was still more than four hundred metres from the house.

Grave skidded to a halt on the dewy grass as the right wing of the mansion collapsed, hurling a tempest of sparks high into the dark sky and showering the land around it with dust and rubble.

"Night!" Grave yelled and launched himself forwards, little more than a blur as he shot towards the house, the blade he wore strapped to his waist bouncing with each long stride.

Isla knew that Night was apparently his brother, a fact that was new to her together with the discovery that he had cousins, but she was damned if she was going to allow Grave to get himself killed by rushing into the building in search of him. Pain beat fiercely in his heart, echoing in hers, telling her how desperately he needed to find him though, warning he was liable to do something stupid if she didn't stop him.

She sprinted after him and managed to catch him close to a hundred metres from the house, snagging his arm and dragging him to a halt. He snarled and lashed out at her, his right hand slamming hard into her forearm, knocking it away from him. Fire and lightning zinged along her bones and she grunted as she staggered backwards.

His crimson eyes shot to her face and the darkness in them lifted for a heartbeat, replaced by a tender light that bore an apology.

She rubbed her arm, easing the pain, and looked towards the house. He could apologise for striking her later, once they were alone.

Snow ground to a halt on the other side of her, his blue eyes darting over the mansion.

"There's no one inside. No trace of vampire blood in the air either." His voice was little more than a deep growl in the night, laced with the anger etched on his face, slowly turning his eyes scarlet. Those eyes leaped off to the right, to a point beyond Grave, and he grunted, "Company."

Grave was moving before Isla had even spotted the five demons emerging from the shadows, slowly walking into the sphere of golden light surrounding the blazing house. That light shone along their black ram-like horns as they advanced on her group, long muscular black-metal-clad legs eating up the distance between them.

Which was the leader?

She scanned each of them from head to toe as she ran towards them, her right hand reaching for her remaining blade. As she looked them over, something dawned on her, something that made her blood burn as fiercely as the building to her left.

The sensation of dark power she had felt when they had arrived in the area was gone.

The demon prince had left, leaving them with five of his minions.

Grave clashed with the one furthest to the right of the group, a male with only one black horn curling from his shorn head, slamming hard into him and driving him back as he began to attack, slashing at the demon with his claws.

Isla targeted the one next to him, a bare-chested male with wild black hair and blazing gold elliptical pupils.

She had met demons from the Devil's domain before, and had quickly learned it was best to avoid them. They were taller than she was, easily seven foot in height, and all muscle, power that was beyond what she could tackle and hope to defeat in her corporeal form, and every single one of them had been trained for combat, honed in the art of war. Warriors. Powerful, dangerous, and deadly. Befitting of the Devil.

And here she was rushing one.

He smirked and a black broadsword appeared in his left hand. His black eyes narrowed on her, their gold pupils seeming to glow brighter as he hefted his sword and swung it at her.

Isla hurled herself forwards feet first, sliding across the golden gravel beneath his blade as it sliced through the air where her body would have been. She snarled and lashed out with her small curved blade, catching the brute across his shin, leaving a long groove in the metal plate of his armour. She huffed. It seemed she needed to attack somewhere a little softer if she was going to take him down.

He roared, twisted at the waist and stabbed at her.

She let out a gasp as she rolled swiftly out of the way, narrowly avoiding being skewered, and came to her feet behind him.

Snow and Payne reached the fight, taking on two of the demons together, working as a team to battle them.

She had never experienced that sort of solidarity in battle. It was beautiful to her. A phantom led a lonely existence, even if they had family as she had. It was a solitary life, but she had never thought she was missing anything, not until she had become corporeal and had been accepted into that world by her brother-in-law and Frey, and then by Grave.

Her senses blared a warning and she turned on a pinhead towards the source of it. A blade zoomed towards her, a dark blur as it cut through the air. Another blade struck it before she could get her head together and find the will to move, the silver katana knocking it off course, sending it swinging back the way it had come.

"Pay attention," Grave snapped and then roared as he grasped his blade in both hands and slashed upwards, attacking the demon who had come close to cutting her down.

The male staggered backwards, blocking each fierce strike of Grave's blade with his own, on the defensive.

The demon Grave had been fighting snarled and picked himself up off the floor, and Isla ran at him. She swept her leg around, slammed the heel of her boot into his face and knocked him back down onto the gravel. He grunted and flashed fangs as he shook his head, but she didn't give him a chance to recover.

She lunged at him with her blade.

Someone grabbed her from behind, hauling her up into the air. Her legs flailed for a moment as she got her bearings and then she lashed out at the bastard with her elbow, driving it hard into the side of his head. The other demon finally found his feet and grinned as he advanced on her.

Isla gritted her teeth and narrowed her eyes on him as she kicked with both feet, pummelling him as he attempted to get to her. He tried to grab her legs and she fought harder, a wild thing as she battled both the male who held her and the one trying to get hold of her.

That male managed to snag one of her legs and pain shot up it as he twisted it hard. She bit down on her tongue to stop herself from crying out and narrowed her eyes on him, fury pouring through her veins as he fought to catch hold of her other ankle. She kicked him hard in the face, knocking him back, but he kept hold of her leg.

The male behind her chuckled into her ear.

It was the last straw.

She cursed her corporeal form. Weak. Pathetic. It inhibited her phantom powers too much.

Cold crawled through her, slowly at first, creeping up from her feet and her hands. It travelled faster as the demon finally grabbed her other leg, engulfing her and wiping the smirk off his face as the iciness reached the surface of her skin, chilling his hands. The male behind her grunted and she called on more of her power, let it wash over her and through her, coaxed it until it built inside her and destroyed the last of the warmth, leaving only frigid cold behind.

Hunger rose within her, a fierce craving that consumed her.

With an unholy snarl, she locked her feet around the second demon's neck and dragged him up to her. His wide eyes met hers as they came face to face, a split second of him staring at her as if she was his worst nightmare, and then he screamed as she clutched both sides of his head and pulled him closer still, until their mouths were only inches apart.

Light and heat rushed through her, energy that crackled and burned, flooded her tired body and renewed her strength. She moaned as she devoured it, sought more of it and found it as she pressed her lips to his, and devoured that too, savouring every drop she could get as it filled the space that had been inside her, satisfying the gnawing hunger.

The male slumped and she pressed her feet into his body as he fell and kicked off, using the momentum to flip over the head of the other demon. She looped her arms around his neck and whipped around from his back to his front, coming to face him. He didn't have a chance to block her.

He didn't have a chance to even blink.

No sound left his lips as hers pressed against them and more light and heat flowed into her, making her head spin and body tingle. Gods, she had never felt such a rush. She wanted to laugh as her entire being came alive, seemed filled to the brim with so much power that she couldn't contain it.

She needed more.

She turned cold eyes on another male, one whose white hair and blue eyes matched hers. Powerful. Strong. She wanted to devour him too.

"Isla!"

That name, spoken in a familiar male voice, snapped her back to the world and she looked over her shoulder at the owner of it.

His pale blue eyes held hers, his dark hair and sculpted face splattered with the glistening blood of his foes, and the sight of him stole her breath away.

Her mate.

Her fierce, beautiful mate.

She reached for him and stilled when her hand came into view, not the one she had grown to love seeing, but a ghostly white form that shimmered in the golden light from the blaze. The cold inside her increased, a chill skating over her body as she swallowed hard and looked down at it.

Looked through it.

No.

She floated above the floor, the ragged hem of her corseted white dress ending almost two foot from the gravel. She shook her head, tears burning her eyes even though none could fall when she was like this.

A true phantom.

Her eyes sought Grave again.

She screamed as he shimmered right before her and she could see through his entire body for a moment, no sound leaving her lips as she poured out her fear and her pain.

It was her fault.

He turned solid again, but his skin seemed paler, his complexion drawn and gaunt as he stared at his hands and then at her.

It was her fault.

She had allowed her phantom nature to consume her and it had given it more power over her, and in turn over Grave, accelerating his demise.

The secret tears in her eyes burned hotter as she tried to shed her phantom form but found she couldn't, no matter how hard she fought it. Her limbs tingled each time, felt as if they would go solid again, but then the cold returned, driving back the warmth.

She fought her rising panic but fear that she would never turn back ran through her, too fierce to deny or control.

"Isla," Grave whispered and advanced a step towards her, and then another.

As he drew closer, the tingling in her limbs returned, stronger this time, and she focused on them, willing her body to shift back from the phantom world and into the mortal one. Warmth teased her fingers and she felt her toes as she wriggled them, and the tears that burned in her eyes fell onto her cheeks as she looked down and saw her blue leathers and boots.

Grave reached for her.

She backed off a step.

He lowered his hand to his side and she wanted to say something to explain her actions, but she wasn't sure what to say. She was afraid that if he touched her, it would sway her from the path she knew she needed to take, one that was going to hurt but that was necessary.

She had to save him.

It was clear to her now that she couldn't fight the demon prince. Her phantom nature would devour her again, the drive to have her revenge allowing it to consume her as she sought enough power to defeat him.

In turn, the phantom world would devour Grave, and she wasn't sure he would come back from it next time.

Gods. She looked into his blue eyes and fought to hold his gaze, to put the love that showed in his to memory so she could cherish it and would have the strength to do the right thing.

She loved him, with every drop of her blood, and that meant she had to do what she could to save him and give him the strength to protect his family from the demon prince. She would do that for him, and entrust him with her own vengeance, allowing him to carry it out for her.

She would stop them both from fading.

She had wanted to do things her sister's way, but there wasn't time. They had been close, intimate recently, but it hadn't stopped her from turning phantom or Grave from turning incorporeal. Restoring their bond through intimacy was going to take too long.

The demon prince was closing in on his family, might have captured the one who had lived in the mansion already. She had to act now. No matter how much it hurt her.

"Isla," Grave whispered, half plea and half warning.

She drifted to him, cupped both of his cheeks in her palms and pressed a soft kiss to his lips.

He wrapped his arms around her and pulled back when they slipped straight through her, a frown marring his handsome face as he looked at her ghostly form and then into her eyes.

"Do not," he snapped but it was too late.

She glanced off into the forest and disappeared, reappearing in a clearing in the trees. Pain spread across her back, so fierce she couldn't breathe, and the sound of his roar tore apart the night, sending birds from their roosts above her.

Isla looked back towards the house, towards Grave, aching to go to him.

He had to know she wanted nothing more than being with him, that she loved him, and so he had to know why she was doing this and that it wasn't goodbye forever.

It was only goodbye for now.

She would return to him.

Once she had made things right.
Once she had saved him.

CHAPTER 19

Gods, Isla hoped she was doing the right thing.

She was still over two hundred metres from the black tower where it reached high into the dark grey sky of Hell and already her skin was crawling with insects. The thought of placing herself at the mercy of the mage turned her stomach. It had been churning since she had chosen this path, and she had been close to throwing up more than once.

The mage wanted one night with her.

She had been close to going through with it before. Her nerve wouldn't fail her this time. One moment with the mage was a price she could pay in exchange for giving Grave the strength he needed to defeat the demon prince, and stop them both from fading. Once it was over, maybe they could find a way to move past what she had done. She hoped.

The thought of sleeping with any male other than Grave repulsed her, but she had spent her entire journey to the tower thinking of alternatives and nothing had come to her. They didn't have time to strengthen their bond, so the only way of fixing their problem was the mage, and he had already set the price for his services.

It was only one night.

She blew out her breath as she neared the tower.

The gates creaked and began to ease open ahead of her.

Isla bravely walked forwards, her eyes fixed on the arched doorway of the tower as it was revealed to her. She could do this. Grave would forgive her.

She marched into the black tower and followed the twisted staircase upwards to the next floor. The sensation of insects under her skin grew stronger but she didn't allow it to frighten her or shatter her resolve. She turned at the top of the steps and strode across the curving corridor and into the central circular room, her eyes never straying from the mage where he lounged on his throne, his pale skin a sickly hue under the light of the green crystals growing from the black stone walls.

"You have returned," he drawled, the left corner of his mouth curving into a wicked smile and his green eyes raking over her. He sighed and skimmed the palm of his right hand down his bare chest. "As beautiful as ever. What do you want with me this time?"

"We had a deal," she said, not allowing her rising nerves to show in her voice. He would detect them in her, and she was damned if she would give him any power over her.

She was a warrior.

A phantom.

If anything, he should be frightened of her.

His smile stretched wider but darkness shimmered in his eyes. "We did, but I recall someone breaking that deal."

"It was not my choice to leave." Hopefully he would buy that, because she hadn't exactly fought Grave when he had saved her from the mage's bedroom.

She sidled closer to the wretch as he perused her, his gaze lingering on her chest and then her hips before slowly returning to her face.

"I want to remain corporeal." She dropped her voice to a whisper, ran her eyes over him in return and played up to his ego by teasing her lower lip with her teeth, as if she felt attracted to him. Wanted him. She wanted to retch. That was what she wanted.

He leaned back a little more, looked down at himself and then back at her, his green eyes gaining an interested edge. "We can work something out."

"So the deal is still on?" Hope soared, despite what she would have to do to fulfil her side of it. "One night for one century?"

He shot that hope out of the sky with a slow shake of his head.

"I want more… you… bound to me."

Her first instinct was to step back and tell him where to go, but she somehow managed to remain rooted to the spot, her face a mask of pleasantness as her insides churned with a dark need to lash out at him and shove him away.

"You want me bound to you?" She couldn't quite bring herself to believe she had heard him right. "But I am bound to the vampire… so I cannot bind myself to you."

The way he smiled at her again made her skin crawl and the look in his eyes said he didn't view her bond with Grave as a problem.

He was going to break it to forge one of his own with her.

The thought of shattering her bond to Grave left her feeling as if it was shattering her heart right that minute, tearing it to pieces inside her chest. The mark on her back shimmered with heat and she clung to it, afraid of losing it and her connection to Grave.

She couldn't do it.

"If I break the bond to the vampire, he will be free of you."

Free of her?

"He will no longer be affected by our bond?" She couldn't believe that, but gods, she wanted to and she needed to hear him tell her that she had heard him right.

He nodded.

Her heart tore her in two directions and she wavered between them, fighting to find the right path to take. If she left now, Grave would still be in danger of turning incorporeal when he fought the demon prince, or might fade before he could even slay the bastard to protect his family, leaving them in danger.

If she took the mage's offer, she would no longer be bound to Grave and would instead be bound to the wretch in front of her, a slimy excuse for a male, but once she was bound to him and Grave was safe, she could take another path.

She could kill the mage.

It would kill her too, but she would gladly pay that price for Grave's freedom.

Isla stared at the mage, dread pooling in her stomach, weighing her down. Gods, he repulsed her, and the thought of being bound to him was too much for her to bear. She couldn't do it. She would find another way, another mage, one who would ask less of her in return for his services.

There had to be one somewhere in Hell or in the mortal realm.

But it would take too long, and Grave needed his strength now, needed the power to fight the demon prince, protecting his family and avenging hers.

Her heart leaped into her throat as the mage was suddenly right in front of her, filling her field of vision, and she didn't have time to react before his hand was against her forehead. Fogginess streamed through every inch of her, gathering heaviest in her mind, and she blinked slowly as she wavered on her feet.

"I fear I must take the decision out of your hands, my sweet." Those words wobbled in her mind, slippery elusive things that she struggled to grasp as darkness encroached.

Decision?

She slumped but strong arms caught her, lifted and cradled her.

She slipped into the black abyss.

Green light shimmered around her, whispered words chanted in a foreign tongue, and a strange sense of lightness ran through her body, as if she was floating.

Floating.

In the darkness of her mind, she saw ghostly transparent hands stretched outwards from her and lowered her gaze to find a flowing white dress dancing gently in a breeze she couldn't feel.

"Isla," a male voice whispered softly into her ear and tears stung her eyes but she wasn't sure why she wanted to cry.

Cold swirled around her and she sighed as it caressed her skin, a comforting embrace that she had missed.

"Isla," another male said and she frowned this time, a sense of danger and sickness running through her. Disgust. Hatred.

She flicked her eyes open and the owner of that voice loomed above her, his tousled long dark hair falling down around his cheeks and green eyes bright with desire.

"You are awake." He smiled but she felt only cold, shards of ice that cut away at her insides, cleaving open the empty space behind her chest. "Good."

He eased back. A wise move. Hunger rose inside her, fierce and demanding, and she wasn't above using the mage to sate it. Mage.

She frowned and fought to remember what had been happening and where she was. Her eyes shifted from him and slowly took in the room, and as they ran over the tall rectangular windows that lined the curving black wall, revealing a strange fantasy world of sunshine and snow-capped mountains, the cold that had been spreading through her dropped ten degrees.

Mage. Tower. It was all coming back to her now.

Isla shot up into a sitting position and the mage practically leaped from the bed. Afraid of her?

The answer to that question became apparent when she looked down at herself. White dress. Pale limbs. She could see the green silk bedclothes through her body.

A phantom again.

Grave.

A sharp rush of tingles shot through her limbs and she reached for the connection to him, fearing her current phantom state would be affecting him too.

Nothing.

Those tingles became a thousand shards of ice that pricked her skin.

She looked to the mage on her right for the answer. He stood abruptly and moved back a step, distancing himself from her. He feared her now. With good reason. In this form, she was more powerful than he was, able to battle and overcome the damned spells and enchantments he had used on her before, even with the green crystals that grew from the walls between the windows and threaded through the black floor enhancing his powers.

Sickness brewed in her stomach. What had she done?

She tried the connection again, reaching for the mark on her back, but nothing happened.

Isla glared at the mage as he dared to move a step closer to her again and reached for her. She ducked away from his touch and drifted to the other side of the bed, keeping enough distance between them that he couldn't touch her.

He sighed. "We had a deal... but I will give you some time to grow accustomed to it. There is no rush now you are no longer bound to the vampire."

Hope sparked in her chest again and another path opened to her.

The mage had broken her bond to Grave, but hadn't forced her into one with him while she had been unconscious and at his mercy. He had waited, no doubt wanting her awake so she could participate in whatever twisted ritual he had devised as their mating ceremony, but it had been a bad move on his part.

If she could escape now, she would escape a bond with him and she could go after the demon prince, could unleash Hell on the bastard without fear of affecting Grave.

Relief beat through her, so strong she felt giddy. Everything had fallen into place so perfectly. She was stronger as a phantom, and Grave would be stronger without his bond to her affecting him. Together they could fight the demon prince and defeat him.

"Of course," the mage drawled and rocked on his heels, and she didn't like the look on his face, the smug one that rankled her and made her feel she had missed something. Something terrible. Something he was going to take pleasure in revealing. He smiled slowly. "The vampire being free of your bond means that right about now he should be turning incorporeal."

Her stomach dropped and cold swept through her. "No."

It wasn't possible. He had said that Grave would be free of her and no longer affected by their bond.

Her stomach dropped faster, plummeting deep into the core of the Earth, and numbness spread along her limbs and settled in her chest and her mind. Gods, she had been a fool again.

The mage had only said that Grave would be free of her, and that he would no longer be affected by their bond. It wasn't their bond that had cursed him to a phantom life. She had done that with a single kiss long before she had bound herself to him, tying their lives together. He was free of their bond, free of her, but he wasn't free of the phantom world.

The mage clucked his tongue. "You know what you did to him is irreversible. Once a phantom, always a phantom."

"He cannot die," she whispered, nurturing the tiny shred of hope in her heart, cradling it gently inside her so it would live and grow.

Grave was free of her, of their bond, and perhaps that meant he was also free of the danger of fading. He might be a phantom now, but her beautiful, savage and clever vampire would find a way to use that to his advantage, just as he had learned to harness his bloodlust.

He would find a way.

He would survive.

And she would find him.

What if they were still in danger though? If she made a new bond with him, would that be enough to save them from fading? Would it make Grave corporeal again?

A problem presented itself as she looked down at herself, watching the green silk sheets shimmer beneath her, distorted by her ghostly appearance. She didn't have a solid form, which meant even if she bound herself to Grave, they wouldn't become corporeal. They would remain phantoms.

She edged her eyes up to meet the mage's.

"How do you expect me to bind myself to you when I am incorporeal?"

He smiled and slowly walked around the circular bed, and she didn't move away from him this time. She waited for him and managed not to flinch when he stopped behind her and placed his hands on her shoulders. She could feel him even though she wasn't solid, and she could feel the insects as they burrowed and crawled through her.

He lowered his head, bringing his mouth to her ear.

"I will use the same spell my father did to give you a solid form."

And she would kill him the moment he had finished uttering the words. There had been a gap between the completion of the spell and her becoming corporeal when his father had helped her, a space in which she would have enough time to battle the mage and destroy him.

Once she had a solid form again, she would find Grave.

She would keep with the plan he had set in motion, taking the next step for him.

They would do everything over and get it right this time.

They would have forever.

CHAPTER 20

Grave had tried, and failed, close to one hundred times to put into words how phenomenally pissed he was that Isla had run away from him, no doubt to do something both noble, and stupid.

The last time had been a tirade of curse words loosely strung together with ones about how very annoyed he was that he had rather abruptly turned into a damned ghost.

That tirade ran on repeat in his head as he mentally trudged across the black lands of Hell. Mentally, because now he floated everywhere. *Floated.* How the fuck was he meant to intimidate anyone when his patented permanently angry clip to his stride was now a sort of wispy drift?

He huffed.

Snow smirked.

"I do not see how this is funny." Those words left his head more than his lips, and Snow shuddered as he received them directly in his mind. "For all I know this is a very temporary step between life and death and I will fade at any moment."

Although he didn't feel as if he was fading. This felt different to how it had before whenever his hands had turned translucent, and when he had gone completely ghostly back at the mansion after Isla had lost it when killing and feeding from two demons.

He didn't feel tingly. He felt weirdly solid considering he could see through himself, was little more than a white echo of the male he had once been.

Although Snow had reassured him that his eyes were still blue.

A phantom blue.

Snow's smile slowly returned as Grave launched into another rant to himself, one that was supposed to be private and stay in his head, but apparently his cousin could hear. He wasn't sure how Isla had lived all those years as a phantom, with everyone being able to hear whatever she thought.

Maybe there was a trick to it, one he needed to learn, something that would allow him to turn the broadcast of his thoughts on and off.

Snow was taking his new form rather well. He had expected his cousin to lose it when he had gone incorporeal, becoming a phantom, but Snow had remained quietly confident that everything would be well and nothing bad was happening.

That confidence kept Grave's ticking over too, kept him believing that he was a phantom now, and not about to fade, and maybe that was the only reason his cousin had kept his head. Snow wanted him to keep his.

At least Night and Bastian hadn't witnessed him turning into a phantom. Much to his relief, Bastian had called in from a safe house in the far north of Norway, and Payne had returned from gathering medical supplies at the theatre with word that Night had arrived there and was safe. The demon prince's attempts to take out his brothers had failed, but Grave doubted they had seen the last of the bastard.

Payne had returned to the theatre to get everyone moving on evacuating it.

Snow had looked as if he wanted to go with him until Grave had announced his intention to stop Isla from doing something stupid, something they would both regret. His cousin had insisted on going with him, and Grave was glad of his company now that he was a damned phantom.

He had the feeling Isla had already done something very foolish, and he could only hope that he found her in time to stop her from making things worse.

His back felt cold, his chest empty without the connection he couldn't open between them for some godsforsaken reason. Because he had gone fully phantom?

He wanted that connection back.

He wanted her back.

The thought of the mage touching her made his blood boil. If he still had blood. He wasn't sure. Whatever life force ran through him now, it boiled. He was going to rip the mage to shreds when he reached the tower.

Although, that did mean figuring out how to attack anyone while in a phantom form.

He knew phantoms could turn solid long enough to lure men to their doom with a kiss, and then everything the female did with him afterwards was done in their ghostly forms. Could he make himself solid long enough to kill a mage?

If it was a matter of willpower, then it wouldn't be a problem. Willpower was something he had in spades and used to control his bloodlust. He was sure he could use it to control his phantom form.

As he drifted down the sloping side of the black valley, his eyes fixed on the tower that rose high in the centre of it, he focused on his body, on being solid. Mind over matter. His fingers tingled and his toes followed them, and then he suddenly dropped the distance between his boots and the ground, and stumbled forwards a few steps before he was floating again.

"Did you see that?" Grave snapped his head towards Snow, a surge of excitement blasting through him.

Snow nodded, something glimmering in his blue eyes that looked a lot like relief to Grave. Relief and hope. Those two emotions pounded inside him too, lifted his spirits and put a new swagger in his drift.

He would kill the mage.

His claws and fangs extended at the thought, both aching to sink into him and rip him to shreds, making him pay for taking Isla from him.

His left hand shifted to the hilt of the blade strapped to his waist, a weapon that had come with him into the phantom realm. He wasn't sure whether it could harm anyone not on the same plane of existence as him, but he was going to find out. He was going to sink it to the hilt in the bastard's black heart.

It would either kill him or it wouldn't, but gods, it would go a long way towards appeasing the black hunger to destroy the mage that had been building inside him from the moment he had set eyes on him. No one looked at Isla the way he had and lived.

Grave swept down the side of the mountain, picking up speed as the need to find the mage rolled towards a crescendo inside him, becoming an urge that was impossible to deny, one that pained him, sank claws deep into him and began to burn away his control.

He growled through his clenched fangs and Snow glanced across at him as he broke into a run, the black look in his crimson-to-blue eyes echoing the rising hunger inside him, the need for violence and bloodshed.

Snow's lips peeled back off his fangs as the crimson won against the blue in his eyes, transforming them. They blazed in the dim light of Hell, and Grave felt his eyes do the same, burning with the bloodlust that demanded an offering to assuage it.

One he would gladly give to it.

He would paint the black walls of the tower scarlet with the blood of the mage. He would slowly break him apart, would devour his cries for mercy and then his bellows of pain. He would make the bastard intimately acquainted with the reason he bore the title of King of Death.

He would uphold the motto of the Preux Chevaliers.

Nulla Misericordia.

No Mercy.

They reached the defensive wall of the tower and Snow growled as the gate ahead of them remained closed. Grave tipped his head back, eyes scanning up the height of the tower, until they stopped on the very top where black spikes speared the sky. Green light shone from the windows below, a beacon that called to him.

Made his skin crawl.

Gods, was this how Isla felt around the mage?

He scrubbed his right hand down his left arm.

Was this how she was feeling right now, up there with the mage? He could sense her presence, was drawn to it as fiercely as he was drawn to the mage's power. Did it affect her too, leaving her feeling hazy and as if control was slipping through her fingers, stolen from her by the mage?

He had to reach her.

He rushed forwards, raised his fist and brought it down hard on the black gate. It went straight through it. He looked back at Snow, caught the shock as it rippled across his face, and then the slow smile that curled his lips.

A smile of victory.

The mage could keep out the corporeal with his defences, but he couldn't keep out death himself.

Grave grinned as he pushed forwards, ignoring the unsettling cold that went through him wherever he was in the solid black rock. He kept drifting forwards, forcing himself through the wall as he met with resistance, willing his body to become nothing more than air and focusing on the room at the base of the tower on the other side.

On where he needed to be.

His head emerged from the wall and then green light burst to life around him, driving the darkness back, and he frowned and turned in a fast circle, heart drumming quicker as he found himself in the lowest level of the tower.

Could he teleport?

He willed himself to appear in the bedroom at the top of the tower and nothing happened.

A huff escaped him. It turned to a gasp when he looked at the top of the twisted staircase and was suddenly standing there. His smile returned and he looked upwards, to the next level, and the world rushed past him in a white blur. When it settled, he was standing at the top of the steps. He could teleport, in a manner of speaking, one good enough for him because he needed all the speed he could muster. He needed to reach Isla.

He made the leap from one floor to the next, but each one had his head spinning a little quicker, his limbs feeling a little weaker. He stopped at the floor below the top level and rested against the wall in the curving corridor there, catching his breath and waiting for his body to stop trembling. It appeared there was a toll for using such power, but it had gotten him to his destination faster, and his body was already feeling stronger again, the energy he had consumed to leap each floor swift to return.

He was starting to like being a phantom, but he was damned if he was going to remain one.

His way of fixing this problem was above him, so close now that he could smell her sweet fragrance and his body ached to feel her pressed against it, his heart burning with a need to have her back in his arms. Safe again.

Grave pushed away from the wall and silently glided up the steps that curved and led him upwards. The chamber at the top came into view, the huge windows in the walls revealing a sunset he knew wasn't real, and his right hand came to rest on the hilt of his blade. He slowly drew the katana as he neared the top step and his eyes settled on the male in the centre of the room, standing with his back to him, dressed in nothing more than black trousers.

Beyond him, Isla sat in the middle of the circular bed, her hands tucked against her chest, her fear a palpable thing that drummed in his veins and stirred the darker side of his nature.

Grave clutched his blade, stared at the bastard she feared, and drew down a deep breath, mentally and physically preparing for the battle ahead of him. His strength wavered and he eyed the green crystals that sprouted from the black walls between each window. No spell would stop him.

He gritted his teeth, narrowed his eyes on the mage's back, and snarled. The male's shoulders tensed.

Grave was right behind him before he could turn, thrusting his sword forwards, aimed straight for the bastard's heart.

It struck thin air and he growled as he pivoted on his heel, his phantom senses screaming the mage's location to him. The mage threw his hand forwards as he came to face him and ribbons of black shot towards him, twisting and leaping through the air.

Magic.

Grave focused on a point on the other side of the bed in the huge circular room and white streamed past him, swallowing the world for a heartbeat before it came back again.

The mage let out a low snarl of frustration and hurled another blast of magic at him, this one holding twisted ribbons of green and white-blue light.

"No." Isla was between them before the spell could reach him, her ghostly form turning solid just as the magic struck her.

She cried out, the sound echoing in his mind and setting his blood back on fire, and then slumped to the black floor. Grave shot to her side and crouched beside her as she breathed hard, pale fingers clutching the polished obsidian tiles and her knee.

"I am fine," she whispered and pulled down one last breath, and slowly exhaled it. Her blue eyes sought his, filled with so much affection that the hollow space in his chest finally felt warm again. "Run."

As if.

She knew him better than that, and the look that slowly crossed her beautiful ashen face confirmed that she did, that she had been a fool to hope he would listen to her.

He rose back to his feet and faced the mage.

"Leave her out of this." He swept his blade down at his side.

The mage smirked. "I do not think so… is she not the reason we fight after all? How can we possibly leave her out of it?"

Grave should have killed the bastard the first time they had been here.

With a roar, he hurled himself directly at the mage. The male threw his right hand forwards, followed by his left, unleashing two blasts of magic this time. Grave dodged them both, the speed of his movements shocking him as he pirouetted around one twisting black and white-blue orb and then the other and they both smashed into the wall behind him.

He grinned at the mage's startled expression, feeling for the first time that he had the upper hand, that he was no normal phantom in this form. He was faster. Stronger. His vampire abilities enhanced his phantom ones.

Including his bloodlust.

It rose within him, a dark and terrible power that he was quick to harness as it consumed him, pulling it back under his control. He felt his eyes shift, the room growing brighter, until the green crystals blazed white, and his fangs lengthened, and he snarled through them as he dodged another two blasts of magic and closed the distance between him and the mage.

He thrust his blade forwards as he kicked off.

The mage's eyes widened and he ducked left, but not quickly enough.

Grave's ghostly blade plunged deep into his side.

And straight through him without leaving a damned mark on the bastard.

It seemed he needed to be solid in order to harm him.

He rushed forwards, ghosting through the mage rather than going around, and shuddered as a sickly cold feeling spread over him, the sensation of his skin crawling growing to an unbearable degree.

He swept around behind the mage, resisting the temptation to make a gagging noise in his throat as he shook off the horrible sensation, and calculated his next move.

The male let out a low laugh unfitting of the occasion and stalked towards Isla.

As if his victory was assured simply because he was closest to her now.

A mighty roar shattered the silence and Grave grinned as Snow barrelled into the room and into the mage, sending him flying across the room and smashing into the wall. A satisfying pained grunt left the mage's lips as he fell to the polished black floor.

The male lifted his head, his long black hair hanging in tangled threads around his slim face, and pinned him with a glare.

"I did not say I would fight alone." Grave shrugged off the male's anger and slowly drifted towards him, Snow falling into step beside him. "I am afraid vampires rarely fight solo."

Snow drew Isla's curved blade from his belt and tossed it onto the circular bed, nodding to her as she pulled herself onto her feet and looked his way. When she reached the blade, his cousin drew the sword sheathed at his waist and together they advanced on the mage.

Dark menace rolled through the room, a sense of danger that jangled warning bells in Grave's head that he didn't bother to heed. His cousin was no threat to him.

He glanced across at Snow. Crimson eyes blazed with a hunger for violence and bloodshed, a powerful need that surged through Grave too, even more so than usual because he couldn't satisfy it as he was.

A fucking ghost.

But he hadn't been one back on the mountainside. For a brief moment, he had been solid, and it had been glorious.

He would be solid again.

"Nulla Misericordia," Snow muttered, the two words raising Grave's spirits and filling him with a fierce need, a pounding desire to live up to those words, to pay them the respect they deserved and carry them out in the name of the Preux Chevaliers.

"Never did have any." Grave tossed a toothy grin at his cousin and then roared as he hurled himself at the mage.

Snow was close on his heels, tearing the mage's focus between the both of them. Weakening him. It would be harder for him to effectively fight against two foes, giving them the advantage now.

The mage raised his hands and a spiralling whirlwind of black formed between them, laced with ribbons of green and white-blue.

As that green and white-blue appeared, the haziness Grave had felt on entering the tower returned and grew stronger, and a swift glance at Isla revealed it affected her too.

"Bad magic," she whispered to him and he nodded to show her that he understood.

While the black magic would probably hurt, it was the white and the green that were the most dangerous to him, and to Isla. Phantom spells?

The mage lowered his hands, his eyes narrowing on Grave. Target acquired.

Snow was beside the male in the blink of an eye and the mage's garbled bellow of agony echoed around the room a split second before Grave saw the male's right hand drop to the floor with a wet thud. Blood sprayed from the severed limb and burst from the stump his cousin's blade had left behind.

Gods, Grave had never admired Snow as much as he did in that moment, as the mage screamed and the spell that had been aimed at him shot towards the wall instead, blasting a hole in it. The warm air of Hell rushed into the room, carrying a slight note of sulphur, and the magic that changed the view in all the windows stuttered, flickering between the real world and the fantasy the mage had created.

Snow snarled and raised his blade again, his eyes locked like a demon on the bastard's neck.

The mage lashed out with his left hand and Snow couldn't dodge the black orb of magic that shot from his palm. It struck him in the stomach, hurling him through the air. Snow grunted as he hit the wall and fell to the floor. Isla rushed over to him and Grave roared and kicked off towards the mage.

He was wide open.

Grave focused all of his will on his body, on his need to fulfil the black desire to cut the bastard down with his blade, and grinned as his hands tingled.

His katana went from white and ghostly to silver and solid before his eyes.

The mage's head slowly turned his way, green eyes widening as they spotted him.

Grave unleashed all of his fury in a feral roar and swung his blade, focusing hard on it and his hands, willing them to remain solid for just a few more seconds.

His hands began to fade.

His sword went straight through the mage's neck.

The bastard's head toppled onto his knees and rolled across the black polished floor towards Grave.

Grave watched it rock to a halt close to his feet where they hovered a foot above the floor. He gritted his teeth, willing himself to become solid again, had to fulfil the desire running rampant through him, a childish but irresistible urge.

His black boots hit the floor.

Grave twisted at the waist and kicked the mage's severed head, sending it flying through the hole in the wall, watching it as it shot through the air until the darkness of Hell swallowed it.

He felt eyes on him.

Isla.

He knew it without looking, because no one's gaze warmed him the way hers did.

He shifted to face her only to find her glaring at him, her hands planted firmly on her hips and her lips a thin mulish line that screamed of disappointment. Because he had kicked the mage's head out of the hole in the wall?

"We needed him," she snapped, the words echoing in his head, and drifted towards him, a decidedly angry edge to her movements that made him want to ask her how she did that because he was a little bit envious.

He clearly had a lot to learn about being a phantom. The look on Isla's pale face said now wasn't the time to ask for pointers. She huffed and threw her hands up, and he noticed for the first time that she was wearing a dress in her phantom form. He had never seen her in a dress. It probably wasn't the time to mention that either, or how beautiful she looked in one.

Sure, he loved the leather look, the way it hugged her wicked curves and long legs, but the sight of her in a corseted dress had him aching for her, filled with a desperate need to draw her into his arms and make love with her again.

She stopped in front of him, barely an inch away, and glared up into his eyes, her blue ones blazing brightly.

"We needed him to make you solid again."

Grave looked past her at the headless mage, slowly realising that she had a point. The bastard had probably been the only phantom mage left in existence thanks to him, and now he was dead, and the look on Isla's face said that his current form of a phantom wasn't temporary this time.

Was he fading?

He felt strong, but what did he know? He would be a fool to assume he was safe now, when Isla had warned he would fade and so would she, and he had been steadily growing less and less solid over the past few months.

He searched Isla's eyes for an explanation but she looked away from him, and he frowned at the way she did that and the sensation that ran through him in response. She was hiding something. What?

She knew something that he didn't, and he hated it when people tried to keep him in the dark.

He moved closer to her, a tactic that normally worked and made her look at him, but this time she remained with her gaze averted, her focus locked on the floor.

"We might have another way." Snow's deep voice rumbled through the room as he crossed it to them, his boots loud on the stone flags.

Grave looked over Isla's head at his cousin and she lifted hers, looking in his direction too. Her curiosity flowed through him, weaker than it usually felt whenever he picked up her feelings.

Because he was a phantom, or because of the something she wouldn't tell him?

He wanted to ask, but Snow caught the whole of his attention when he spoke, his words sounding like the sweetest of promises to Grave, and to Isla too judging by the way her heart leaped in his ears and beat faster.

"I know a witch who can probably help."

CHAPTER 21

It turned out the witch resided at Vampirerotique and was actually the mate of the mixed-blooded vampire Payne.

It also turned out she wasn't the only witch on the premises of the theatre when they finally reached it, exhausted from their long journey from Hell carrying every book they could find in the mage's tower, which was a lot.

Grave stared at the female standing opposite him, her dark chocolate hair tumbling around her shoulders in long glossy waves that blended into her drab black ankle-length dress and her large warm caramel-coloured eyes fixed on him, a nervous edge to them as she struggled to hold his gaze.

Unsurprising considering the male she stood beside.

Night shot him a sheepish smile.

Gods, Grave wanted to roll his eyes and sigh in a way that would let his younger brother know exactly what he thought of what he had done.

It turned out that he had been right to worry about Night and the mortal female, because here they were, and the smooth pale column of her throat bore an unmistakable set of marks on it now.

Not Bastian's, but Night's.

"Does Bastian know?" he bit out and Night dropped his pale gaze to his polished Italian leather shoes before courageously lifting it back to hold his, which was a far better way of dealing with Grave when he was in a mood.

Night turning into a pathetic, spineless and limp male was only going to make him more angry.

It was better he stood his ground, faced him head on and didn't flinch.

"He knows." Night's deep voice was a comfort that caught Grave off guard, but he didn't let his brother see how relieved he was to be standing before him, able to see with his own eyes that he was safe and unharmed. "After the fact."

Grave shook his head and huffed, and then sighed as he admitted, "I probably would have done it the same way."

Taking something from Bastian was dangerous enough, but asking for his forgiveness was always better than asking for his permission. Bastian acted tough and merciless, but he had never refused to forgive him or Night whenever they had done something wrong. He had refused countless times when they had asked for permission first though.

Night shoved his fingers through his dark hair, drawing Grave's gaze to his appearance, and the sense of comfort that had washed through him faded as he noticed how pale he looked, and that his grey shirt and black slacks had clearly been borrowed from someone. Antoine probably. The two were similar in height and build.

What had happened to Night while he had been away?

The growing fearful edge to his brother's pale blue gaze told him not to ask.

He could hardly press Night about it when his brother was being kind enough not to mention that he was standing in front of him looking like a fucking ghost.

He also couldn't tease his brother about the way he glanced at the brunette, Lilian, beside him, looking like a lovesick fool as he gazed down at her and she up at him.

Grave slid a secret glance at Isla and his blood ran a little hotter as he found her watching him, her striking blue eyes warm with what looked like affection. No. He definitely couldn't chastise Night about falling in love, not when he had been in love with Isla for a century, completely bewitched by her.

Her gaze fell to the ghostly white piece of material tied at a diagonal across her chest and her fingers where they gripped it. He studied her a few seconds more, drinking in the sight of her, growing slowly aware of everyone in the room with him as they turned their attention his way.

He dragged his eyes away from Isla and focused on his body, ignoring the way everyone was staring at him and Isla now, their curiosity reaching a crescendo. It wouldn't be long before someone asked what had happened to him.

Snow broke the silence for him. "We have books from a phantom mage… and we need one spell in particular. One that will turn Isla corporeal, and hitting Grave with the same spell probably wouldn't hurt."

He ignored the obvious pleasure Snow took in saying that, slanting him a warning glare, but his cousin just smiled and shrugged his broad black-t-shirt-clad shoulders.

"We'll take a look." The silver-haired female that had been introduced as Elissa, Payne's mate, stepped forwards and took the sack of books from Snow.

She jerked forwards when he released them and the sack hit the floor with a boom that echoed around the double-height room.

Payne chuckled until she shot him a black look. He schooled his features and rushed to help her, easily lifting the heavy sack and swinging it over his right shoulder, flashing the line of markings that tracked down the underside of his forearm.

Grave willed himself to become solid. Isla had explained during the journey that items often became solid before their physical form did, which saved on energy and meant phantoms had to feed less often in order to keep up their strength. The sack of books he carried across his back shot through his body and hit the floor beneath his feet with a thud, and he ground his teeth to suppress the shudder that wracked him in response to the feel of something weighty suddenly going through him.

Isla casually turned completely solid in order to set her own sack of books down at her feet, her blue leathers replacing her white dress for a heartbeat before she turned phantom again.

That stab of envy returned, piercing straight through his heart.

Apparently, he couldn't turn himself fully solid because he was low on energy and needed to feed.

Not on blood, but on a soul.

A single soul would give him enough power to turn solid a handful of times.

The thought of drinking blood had no effect on him, but the thought of consuming someone's soul? Isla had explained how it worked, and what happened to those a phantom fed from.

He curled his lip. It wasn't exactly his style. He killed on the battlefield, and sometimes he killed when feeding, but he had never condemned anyone to life as a ghost or worse, to eternity in a black abyss without any form.

But if Elissa and Lilian couldn't find the right spell, or couldn't perform it in time, he would need to feed to keep himself strong enough to fight the demon prince.

They were making preparations to evacuate the theatre, moving everyone into two separate safe houses, but travel arrangements were proving difficult, slowing the process down. Night had reached out to Bastian to ask for use of his private jet, and Bastian had been nice for once and had agreed, but even that wouldn't have enough seats to transport everyone at once. They had to evacuate in groups, with those with children going first.

Snow, Payne and Night helped Elissa and Lilian with the sacks of books, carrying them over to the small area of couches near the stairs that led up to the staff quarters, and the roof, leaving him alone with Isla.

"I did not realise you had a brother," she whispered, her blue gaze lighting on him for a moment before it returned to Night.

Grave couldn't tell whether she was upset that he had never told her about his family or not. He had his reasons for keeping the existence of his two brothers secret from most.

She slid her focus back to him and smiled softly. "Family is not a weakness, Grave."

He almost smiled at how well she knew him.

"But it is something an enemy can exploit... as proven by the demon who killed yours and is now hunting mine down." He looked away from her, settling his gaze on his younger brother, and sighed as he thought about what had happened to Isla's family, and felt an echo of her pain deep in his heart. His eyes roamed back to her, and that heart ached when he found her watching his brother, a look of longing and hurt in her eyes. "I am truly sorry, Isla."

She forced a smile and dragged her eyes away from Night, settling them back on him. "It was not your fault. Not really. I began this chain of events—"

"No," he interjected. "I began them."

She dropped her gaze to her boots and then lifted her chin and met his again, a flash of something in her eyes, something that had always enchanted him. Strength. Courage. Darkness.

"Melia was right and it was my fault Tarwyn was taken from us by the demon, and I will not hear another word saying differently. I am the reason my sister and nephew are gone, and I will avenge them." She heaved a sigh and stared off into the distance beyond his left shoulder. "I was wrong to attempt to avenge Valador... but my phantom blood demanded it... even now when I can see it was not the right path. It was not personal for you. You are a mercenary and the war against Valador was nothing but a job to you. You are given a target and you take that target down... and you did not even know why I seduced you and turned you phantom. Frey was right about that."

His mood had already been darkening as he listened to her speaking of him as if he had no heart, was as merciless as his reputation and led some sort of twisted existence where he would kill anyone for the right price, but it took a nosedive into a black abyss as he heard the last sentence leave her lips.

He glared at her. "Who is Frey?"

She rolled her shoulders. "No one of interest to you."

That only made his mood take a turn for the worse. She was protecting this one called Frey, this one she spoke of with affection in her eyes and her voice.

"But someone of interest to you," he bit out and regretted it when she scowled at him and planted her hands on her hips.

"If he was of interest to me, why would I be here?"

"For revenge. You said it yourself. You want to avenge your sister and nephew. Your phantom blood demands it... just as it demanded you avenge Valador by turning me into a phantom, by making the heartless mercenary suffer for his sins." He swept away from her and, gods, he felt like a bastard as she muttered a ripe curse behind him and her pain echoed on his senses.

He knew she hadn't meant to make him feel as if he was something low and unworthy of her, a male who led a shallow existence making a living by killing others, skulking around Hell and taking down targets, but she had and he couldn't bear it.

The Preux Chevaliers was everything to him. It was a noble and beautiful institution, whether she could see it or not. It was in his blood, blazed in his soul, and kept his heart beating.

The strongest of vampires coming together to serve a common cause, loyal and courageous, tested in battle and shaped by war into men worthy of leading their bloodlines.

Valiant.

Only the bravest, most powerful survived.

Brave. Powerful.

Not low. Not unworthy.

He wasn't hiding in the shadows, sniping targets from a distance, making an easy living off life as a mercenary. He led the charge, clashed hardest with the enemy, broke bones and tore flesh in close quarters combat, dancing with death each time he took on a job and took down a target.

He growled under his breath, the only way to vent his anger and frustration now that he couldn't pace.

Isla's eyes came to rest on him and for a moment, he thought she would say something, but then she turned away.

"I can help." She drifted over to sit with the others, drawing their focus away from him.

Grave floated around the room, back and forth between the stairs and the end of the corridor that led up to the foyer, but drifting did nothing to work off his tension. Pacing just wasn't pacing when each stride he took didn't echo with the force of his boots striking the floor.

Isla's gaze burned into him again, stoking the fire in his blood, but not with fury this time. She made it blaze with need, with a fierce desire to go to her and apologise, and take her lips with his, and just drown in her.

He drifted across the room to her, drawn towards her as she leafed through a tome, but the words he had wanted to say got stuck on his tongue when she looked up at him and he ended up just staring down at the stacks of books, unsure what to do with himself.

He was used to having a purpose and a direction, but suddenly he had neither. He couldn't help find the spell, because he wasn't a witch and he wasn't familiar with the spell in question as Isla was. Even if he had known it, he didn't have the skill to consistently turn his hands solid in order to leaf through a book.

Snow rose from the couch as Aurora appeared on the stairs, her white dress flowing around her legs as she hurried down them. He met her at the bottom, scooped her up into his arms and kissed her as he carried her up the stairs.

Isla watched them until they disappeared from view, a look of longing on her face that echoed in his heart. Gods, he wanted to do that with her. He wanted to be able to hold her again and take her to a quiet room somewhere and kiss her until she melted in his arms and begged for more.

Until every inch of him was reassured that she was safe now, back with him, and that she wanted only him.

Not this Frey person she had mentioned.

She glanced at him, he had the sensation that she blushed, and then her eyes were back on her work as she flicked through another one of the books.

Night leaned back in his seat beside Lilian and yawned so hard Grave had a superb view of his tonsils. He arched an eyebrow at his brother, who issued an unapologetic look in response and rested his arm along the back of the couch behind Lilian.

She looked across at him. "It's gone dawn. You should get some rest."

Night huffed and looked as if he wanted to refuse her order, but then he pushed onto his feet and dropped a kiss on her brow. "Don't fall asleep on the books... come sleep in my arms... it's way better."

Lilian smiled and leaned her head back. Night took the invitation, pressing his lips to hers in a slow soft kiss that had Grave teetering on the verge of tearing them away from each other in a fit of jealousy when they finally broke apart. His brother placed his hand on her shoulder and gave it a squeeze, and then walked around the couch, trailing his hand off her.

"Don't expect such sweetness from me," Payne murmured against Elissa's neck and she giggled and tensed, her shoulders coming up, lifting the hem of her blue starry halter-top away from her jeans.

He growled and playfully nipped her bare shoulder, and she pushed at his arm.

"Go to bed… Luca is probably still up waiting for his story." Elissa nuzzled Payne's cheek and clearly hadn't been around vampires long enough to know how sensitive their hearing was, because Grave got an earful that he wished he hadn't heard as she whispered to her mate, extremely detailed and explicit promises that turned the ache for Isla into a fierce roar in his veins.

Payne flashed Elissa a wink and disappeared.

Leaving Grave alone with three females and feeling like a fifth wheel as they all stuck their heads back in their books.

Unlike the other vampires in the building, the rising sun hadn't made him tired. Because he was more phantom than vampire right now?

He idly drifted around the double-height room, managing to somehow pass an hour, and then exhaustion finally caught up with him and he couldn't stifle the yawn that hit him.

Isla showed no sign of emerging from her book, and he had the feeling she was hiding in it to avoid him for some reason. Because he had snapped at her? Or was it the same reason she had avoided looking at him back at the tower?

He was too tired to press her for an answer, so he floated up the stairs to the room he had used before. The second level was quieter this time, no sign of life on it other than Night. His brother was still on his senses, and Grave didn't have the heart to wake him just so he could have some company. Lilian was right and his brother needed to rest, to recover from whatever had happened to him. He would find out about that as soon as his brother woke.

For now, he left him alone and ghosted through the wall and into the bedroom, and lay down on the bed. It was odd drifting a foot above it, but sleep soon stole away any concern he had about it, replacing it with strange dreams that slipped through his grasp bare seconds after they had materialised, fading to nothing and being replaced by the next one. He clung hardest to the ones of Isla, but even those escaped him.

He woke more frustrated and lost than when he had gone to bed, and frowned as he focused on his surroundings, trying to pinpoint the hour.

It was still early.

His vampire abilities warned the sun was still out, but lower in the sky now, signalling the approach of evening. Normally, his senses would have told him of danger, but curiously he felt no such sensation this time.

Grave swung his legs over the bed and drifted to his feet. He ghosted through the wall and followed the dimly lit corridor to the staircase. Rather than going down to check on the females, he went up, passing the uppermost floor where his cousins were still sleeping, and heading up to the door that led onto the roof.

He hesitated, facing the plain door, his pulse jacking up as he used his senses again, stretching them far and wide, waiting for his vampire instincts to tell him to back away.

They didn't.

He sensed no danger at all, yet the sun was still shining. He could feel the residual heat of it coming off the door, could smell it even.

It was daylight outside, something he had never stood in before. He had never felt the sun on his skin. He had never witnessed a sunset.

The thought that he might be able to do such a thing, could assuage his curiosity about part of the day that so many other species could experience, gave him the courage to push forwards through the door.

He flinched away as bright light assaulted his eyes and back-peddled towards the door, a sudden spike of fear piercing him. He focused on his body, convinced he was going to burn at any moment.

A pleasing sort of warmth spread over him wherever the light touched, but it didn't hurt him.

He slowly opened his eyes and looked around him at the flat roof of the theatre and then the city beyond, taking it all in as he stood in the sunshine.

Sunshine.

A sudden flash of Isla teasing him about his 'sunny disposition' and the 'sunny colour' of his home in Hell popped into his head and he found himself smiling as he thought about all those times she had mocked him with that word.

And now he was standing in the sunlight.

He couldn't quite believe it.

Even a vampire his age shouldn't be able to withstand such strong sunlight, but here he was, basking in it without any negative consequences. Fascinating.

He drifted around, studying the hotchpotch rooftops around him and the landmarks of London that speared the blue sky. He had seen it all before, but it looked so different drenched in sunshine.

Just as he was.

It was strange, and a little frightening, but it was exhilarating too.

It still stung his eyes, but even they were adjusting to the brightness.

"Have you gone mad?" Isla snapped from behind him and he looked across at her, his smile holding as he caught the thunderous look on her face, a mixture of disbelief, fear and anger. "Go inside."

"I am fine." He turned his gaze back to the distant horizon, tracking the sun as it gradually descended towards it.

The golden light caught the side of the taller modern buildings across the Thames, reflecting off them and dazzling him. He shifted his focus away from them and took in the older buildings that surrounded the theatre. He could just glimpse part of Trafalgar Square. He drifted towards the corner of the rooftop nearest to it so he could get a better look.

In the small part he could see, hundreds of tourists milled around, mingled with the workers as they returned home from their jobs.

Fascinating.

The streets at night were nowhere near as busy as they were at the moment. It was a whole different London below him.

One that made his stomach growl and fangs itch with a need to hunt and feed.

"Go back inside now." Isla came up beside him and pushed at his shoulder, shoving him towards the exit.

Shoving him.

He frowned at her hands on him, and burned with a different sort of hunger as he realised she could touch him. Her phantom form felt solid against his.

She could touch him.

He growled low in his throat and she snatched her hands back, bringing them up to her chest, her heart drumming a wild rhythm in his ears. Not born of fear, but of desire.

Perhaps she had been telling the truth and she wasn't interested in the one called Frey after all.

He wanted to puff his chest out at that, felt an undeniable urge to sweep her up into his arms and kiss her until she knew she belonged to him and him alone. He ached to lose himself in her, but that odd and unsettling look was back in her eyes and he didn't have the heart to press her when she looked so afraid.

"I am pleased you are worried, Isla, but I am not going anywhere." He meant that in two ways—that he wasn't going to leave the roof and he wasn't going to leave her.

If it was their new relationship she feared, he would do all in his power to make her see that it could work and it would be better this time.

He would make it perfect.

He would be the mate she deserved.

His beautiful phantom.

"Why not?" she whispered and her pale eyebrows furrowed, the worry in her blue eyes building to a point where he couldn't resist reaching for her to comfort her.

She didn't move away this time, allowing him to place his hand on her shoulder, and gods, it felt strange to be able to touch her when he had thought he couldn't touch anyone as a phantom. It felt good.

"The sun is due to set soon, and I would like to see it. Just once… will you watch it with me? I would like that." It seemed strange telling her what he wanted, letting her see that he needed her, when he had never shown that side of himself to anyone, not even her. He wasn't accustomed to telling people what he wanted, asking them to do something for him.

He was accustomed to issuing orders and having them followed.

In the past, he would have demanded she stay with him.

Now he was giving her a choice.

She nodded, and a warmth rushed through him, a thrill that surprised him.

"I cannot deny you the pleasure of seeing a sunset, but you must promise that if you feel any sensation that you are in danger that you will go inside."

Gods, that sent a deeper thrill through him. She cared about him. Truly cared.

"I will," he said and then grinned at her. "I like being alive after all."

Her face fell and she looked away from him, her arms coming up to wrap around her white corset. He frowned at her sudden change in demeanour and moved around her, so she was facing him again.

"Isla," he whispered and cupped her cheek with his palm, drew her eyes back up to him. She closed them and he sighed. "Do not shut me out. Something is wrong. I've felt it since the tower… maybe even before then. Speak to me."

"You will not be mad at me?" she murmured but still refused to look at him.

He frowned at her. "Why would I be mad?"

"Just promise you will not be mad at me and I will tell you. Please, Grave?" Her eyes sought his at last and the fear in them hit him hard, had him nodding in agreement because there was hurt in her eyes too, pain that she was holding inside and he wanted to draw it out of her and give her relief.

She sighed, looked away from him and then back up into his eyes.

Gods, she was beautiful. Ethereal. Sunlight made her ghostly form shimmer, almost sparkle, and she stole his breath away just as she had the first time she had walked into his life.

Everything that had happened since she had shown up at the Preux Chevaliers stronghold weeks ago rolled into one fierce barrage of emotion, an onslaught that culminated in the moment she had left him at the mansion. It overwhelmed him and he couldn't stop himself from speaking.

"I thought I had lost you," he whispered, his voice breaking as his throat tightened and he pressed his palm harder against her cheek, filled with a desperate need to reassure himself that she was here with him.

Tears lined her eyes, but she didn't look away this time, and the pain that went through her echoed in him, fainter than it should have been.

The words that fell from her lips answered all the questions that had been building inside him since the mansion.

"The mage… he…" She lowered her eyes to his chest. "He broke the bond between us."

Grave's world felt as if it was crumbling around him as he struggled to take that in and make sense of it. Hurt went through her again, but his own pain eclipsed it as he tried to breathe, tried to hold back the tide of emotions that surged inside him.

His hand shook against her cheek and he let it drop away from her, could only stare at her as he weathered the storm and tried to find solid ground.

She had broken their bond.

He had spent decades wanting to be free of her, and now that he was, all he could think about was that he wanted her back. He needed her back. He didn't want to live without her.

Whatever amount of time he had left in this world, he wanted to spend every second with her. Nothing would give him greater pleasure. Nothing would make him happier.

Gods, he should have listened when his body, heart and soul had screamed at him that something was different, that his sudden shift into the phantom world had been the product of something more than just their bond fading.

He stared at her, unsure what to say.

The reason they were both incorporeal was that their bond was gone, shattered by the mage. Elissa was working on fixing their ghostly state and giving them solid forms again, but the look in Isla's eyes said that she hadn't told the witch what she had done, that this was the first time she had confessed the bond was gone and she had chosen to tell him.

He appreciated that, because for a moment he had thought their problem had turned him incorporeal and he was going to fade, but that wasn't the case at all.

"With the bond broken, I'm simply a phantom, correct?"

She nodded. "I do not think you will fade now, and neither will I. I feel stronger than when we were bound."

That offered some relief.

"I am sorry, Grave." She looked away from him and sighed. "Once we are corporeal again, I will leave."

"No you won't," he snapped and took hold of her wrist and pulled her back to face him. She lifted startled eyes to meet his, her fear a palpable thing as her veins ticked quickly beneath his fingers. "You're not going anywhere. I let you go once, and I do not intend to let you go again. I have spent decades trying to live without you, Isla... I don't intend to spend another second like that."

"But..." she started and he shook his head, silencing her and the doubts filling her eyes.

"I mean every damn word, Isla. You broke our bond, but I want it back."

Her blue eyes widened, beautiful shock flittering across her pretty face, and her lips parted as she searched his eyes. "You really mean that?"

Grave huffed. "I just said that I meant every word. You know I'm not the sort of man to give a damn about pandering to people or lying to appease them. I have always said things straight, haven't I?"

She hesitated and then nodded, and he lifted his hand from her wrist and settled it back against her cheek, and looked deep into her eyes, wanting her to see in his that he did mean every word. He was a man who said things straight, but he was also a man who kept his feelings to himself and it was time he changed that part of himself, because Isla needed to know the love he hid in his heart.

"I want to be your mate, Isla," he whispered and skimmed his hand down to her jaw, shifted it under her chin and kept her head tipped up and her eyes fixed on him. Even in her ghostly form, a touch of colour darkened her cheeks, and she tried to look away but he held her firm. "I feel… empty without our bond."

"Maybe you just want to be whole again," she said, a little too quickly for his liking. She was trying to push him away to protect herself, but it wouldn't work. He had set his sights on her heart and he was a male who always got what he wanted. She sighed. "I want that too."

"I don't give a fuck whether I'm solid or a damned ghost, as long as I have you."

Her eyes widened again, and tears lined them as she stared up at him, her lips parted and a ripple of shock going through her.

He lifted his hand and swept the pad of his thumb under her eyes, brushing away her tears, and whispered, "I really mean that, Isla. I just want you… as my mate… forever."

Gods, he stood on a precipice, a terrifying sort where the land below him plummeted sharply, making him feel dizzy and stirring a need to turn back before it was too late and he got himself hurt.

He sucked down a breath, and rather than stepping backwards, he took the leap, opened himself to someone for the first time in a long time, making himself vulnerable and trusting she wouldn't use it against him, would treat the heart he was placing into her hands more gently this time.

"I loved you back then," he whispered and her eyes went even wider, her heart beating faster in his ears, and she trembled beneath his palm as he caressed her cheek and smiled down at her, thoughts of how he had felt back then and how he felt now warming him and chasing away his fear. "That love never faded. I fooled myself into thinking that it had. I was bitter and angry, but it never faded… because it isn't the sort of love that wanes over time… Isla… it is the sort that lasts forever."

She swallowed hard, her eyes searched his, and then shaky words tumbled from her lips and poured life into his heart. "I never stopped loving you either, Grave. I am sorry for what I did… it started out as a game, a way of getting revenge, but in the end it was real. I fell for you… gods, I really fell for you… there isn't a part of you I did not love… do not love… I love you with all of my heart."

He stepped into her, tipped her head back and pressed his forehead to hers. "Then make things right and mate with me again."

"When Elissa finds the spell—"

He pressed his lips to hers and she tensed and then moaned, leaning into him, tiptoeing and seeking more from him. He broke away from her and breathed hard against her lips.

"Now... Isla. I will not wait another second for you... I need you to be mine again now... or I fear I will go crazy." He kissed her again, deeper this time, and she melted so beautifully in his arms, desperately tangling her tongue with his and trembling against him. He forced himself to pull back.

"But we are phantoms."

"I don't care. I can touch you, Isla... I can feel you." He smiled, held her face in both of his palms, and looked into her eyes so she could see how serious he was. "Mate with me. Be mine."

She blinked and then a slow smile spread across her face and she stole his breath away all over again as she threw her arms around his neck and breathed against his lips.

"Gods, yes."

CHAPTER 22

Isla couldn't hold back the moan that burst from her lips as Grave delved between her thighs, his skilled tongue making her legs quiver and belly flutter. She tipped her head back into the pillow on the double bed in the room she had been given in Vampirerotique, her fingers twined tightly in Grave's dark hair, holding him in place as he drove her wild, teased and tortured her until she felt as if she was going to burst.

She writhed her legs, unable to keep still, and he growled, the rumbling sound sending a tremor through her as it vibrated against her tight bundle of nerves. Another moan escaped her, louder this time, pulling a deep groan of male satisfaction from her vampire.

Phantom.

Whatever he was now.

She didn't care which it was, he was still Grave, could still drive her mad with little effort on his part, knew exactly the right place to lick or breathe upon, or tease with his fangs.

A shudder wracked her as he delved lower, tongue probing her core, and her legs tensed, pressed against the sides of his head. He loosed another growl, hooked his hands over her thighs, and pulled them apart. He used them as leverage at the same time, a way of anchoring himself in place as he pushed her closer to the edge, making it impossible to shove him away.

Her belly heated, fire the temperature of a volcano's molten core blazing there, and she strained for more, rocked her hips against his face and rode his tongue as he thrust it into her, mimicking sex, fuelling the fantasy building in her mind.

The desperate and wild need.

"Grave," she murmured, voice throaty and deep, echoing that need.

He groaned and licked her harder, pressed his tongue against her nub and stroked it fiercely as it clenched and unclenched.

She twisted his hair tighter between her fingers and raised her hips, lost in the moment, consumed by her impending release, thrust beyond all control into a wild state where only feeling existed and the only thing that mattered was sating the need to climax.

Grave wrapped his lips around her bundle of nerves and gave a hard suck.

Isla cried out, hips jacking up. Stars sparkled and leaped through every inch of her, shattering her awareness of the world and replacing it with a swift blinding light and heat that travelled through her, flowing back and forth along her trembling limbs.

Dear gods.

She had been with males in her phantom form before, but none of them could compare with Grave. Being with him in her physical form had been exhilarating enough, but in her phantom form every inch of her was more sensitive, and as she sagged and struggled for air, she had the feeling he knew it and knew exactly how to take advantage of it to bring her to shattering releases that had her thinking twice about wanting a corporeal form again.

If Grave could make being a phantom this exciting and thrilling, could make her feel this much, then maybe she wouldn't be sad if Elissa couldn't find a way of making her corporeal again.

Grave kissed along her thigh and she wriggled as it tickled, just as it would if her form was solid.

If his form was solid.

That thought sobered her up, made the residual bliss from her climax fade away. It wasn't only her body on the line. If Elissa couldn't find the right spell, Grave would remain incorporeal too, and she still wasn't one hundred percent certain that mating would stop them from eventually fading. She wanted to be certain, and that meant finding the spell, and gaining a physical form again, together with Grave.

He didn't belong in her world.

Her beautiful, noble and deadly vampire belonged in his world, one where he led his Preux Chevaliers that were so important to him and could be part of his family again, the same as them. She wanted to go to that world with him. He was her family now, together with Frey.

Grave shattered all thoughts of other males as he kissed up her belly, his sides brushing between her thighs, and she moaned as he reached her breasts. He tugged the corset of her white dress down, exposing her nipples, just as he had back in the inn.

He stilled, lifted his head and frowned down at her. "What is wrong?"

She tried to smile. "I keep thinking about when we have been together in a more… physical way."

His pale blue eyes softened, but the hunger steadily building in them didn't go anywhere. It only grew as he raked his gaze over her, his pupils dilating as he took in her ghostly body.

"It does not feel any different to me." He lifted his eyes back to her and the sincerity in them touched her.

She wanted to feel that way too, wanted to believe he didn't care that he was a phantom now even when she knew that he found it strange and disconcerting.

"I miss the leather though," he whispered and lowered his head, teased her breasts with his lips, his breath cool against her skin.

It was strange to feel that, to feel anything so strongly when in her phantom form. Maybe it was because it was Grave. She knew the feel of him so well, the way his breath felt on her skin, his lips on her flesh, and his body under her hands, that the memory was enough to boost what she felt in her phantom form, bringing it close to how it had been when she had been solid.

"At least your clothes do not change when you are phantom." She tugged at his shirt, pulling him up to her so she could kiss him.

His lips claimed hers before she could seize them, and she moaned into his mouth as he kissed her, delved his tongue between her lips and battled hers for dominance.

Something else that was new. Normally when she did anything with males while in her phantom form, she was the one in control, always in control, taking what she needed from them and then discarding them.

Perhaps it was more than just how well she knew Grave that made it different this time. Maybe it was her time in a corporeal form that had changed her, had altered her to her very core, and was responsible for how differently she thought about things and approached them now. She wouldn't dream of using a male as she had before now, wouldn't be able to do such a thing, knowing that she was condemning them to a life as a phantom, using them and destroying their lives.

"Come back," Grave whispered against her lips and she realised she had gone still beneath him. He sighed, smoothed his hand across her brow and over her hair, and rested on his other elbow, propping himself up above her. She looked up into his eyes and found them soft and warm, laced with the love she now knew for certain he held in his heart for her. "You keep drifting away."

"I am sorry." She smiled and pushed her sombre thoughts aside. "Thinking about my past... when I should be thinking about my future."

He smiled back at her, and she couldn't breathe as she looked up at him, caught up in how beautiful he was.

"Gods, I love you," she whispered without thinking, the words escaping her lips before she could consider what she was saying.

She had never said those words to him before.

The soft look in his eyes turned to one of shock, and then something that resembled happiness, and his lips were back on hers, stealing her heart in a kiss that was so warm and tender that she wanted to cry.

She tore at his shirt, the desperate need that he had quelled building again as he kissed her, as she thought about how much she loved him and how much he wanted to be her mate again. She wanted that too. She needed it with all of her heart.

When the buttons of his ghostly shirt refused to give under her trembling fingers, she let loose a snarl of frustration and yanked the two sides apart, spraying buttons everywhere.

Grave arched an eyebrow at her. "That was my only shirt."

"I will make it up to you." She slid her hands between the two sides of his shirt and he groaned as she skimmed her palms over his hard pectorals and up to his shoulders, pushing the shirt off them. "Besides, it will be whole again by the time I am done with you. Phantom clothing repairs itself."

Because it was the only damned thing they could wear. She had ripped her dress a thousand times, but it always became perfect again in a matter of hours, slowly repairing itself before her eyes. She hated her drab white dress with a fierce passion, but it was part of her and she couldn't shed it or replace it with anything else, just as Grave's clothes were a part of him now.

He sat back and shrugged off his shirt, and Isla followed him as her gaze caught on the pendant around his neck and sat up on the bed.

"Why did you keep it?" She took hold of the delicate silver knot and lightly brushed her thumb over it, feeling the pattern, every intricate line of it, a ribbon of love and protection that had no end, was infinite, just like her feelings for the male she had given it to.

He looked down at the pendant, the hunger that had been building in his eyes abating again as he studied the knot, and then up into her eyes. "Because I love you."

Those were the words she had needed to hear. They melted her heart, the one that belonged to him, and she slid her hands over his muscular shoulders and drew him to her again, caught his lips in a kiss she hoped conveyed just how much those words meant to her.

How much he meant to her.

When he leaned into the kiss, she used his position against him, easily rolling him onto his back when his weight was off centre. He grunted as he landed on his back beneath her, but didn't fight her as she kissed him, her tongue tangling with his before she stroked his fangs with it, running the tip down the length of one.

He shuddered and moaned, clutched her backside through her dress and gripped it tightly.

Isla kept up her teasing, mercilessly driving him to the edge of reason, to the point where she knew he would lose control again. When he was close to it, she eased off and kissed down his jaw, following the strong line to his neck and from there charting a familiar path down his throat to his shoulder.

He moaned as she kissed a trail across his hard pectorals, following the line of one scar as it darted from the top of his pectoral near his right shoulder across the valley between them, to end near his left nipple. When she reached it, she swirled her tongue around the small bud, teasing it to hardness, and then gave it a brief, hard suck. He grunted again, fisted his hands in the material of her skirt and trembled.

She loved it when her powerful, deadly vampire shook as he was now, at her mercy, compliant when he was usually defiant, a slave when he normally ruled.

Her King of Death.

He shuddered, another moan escaping him as she trailed her lips lower, over the ridges of his stomach to the sensual dip of his navel. She looked up the length of him and couldn't stop herself from trembling too.

Her vampire had been sculpted by the gods, carved from the finest marble, honed to perfection.

She wriggled her hips, squeezed her thighs as best she could with his legs between them, and moaned at the thought of kissing every inch of him.

The darkness entering his eyes, devouring his pale blue irises, warned he didn't have the patience for such a leisurely and torturous exploration. He needed her. She could feel it drumming in his blood, the same way that it quickened hers.

Isla shifted further south, shuffling her knees down so they were closer to his, and he huffed as her backside slipped beyond the reach of his hands. That frustration faded as she lowered her mouth and followed the dusting of hair that led down from his navel, and her hands found the waist of his trousers.

She popped the button and then tackled the others, slowly eased his fly apart, and he was swift to lift his hips enough that she could tug the tight material over his backside and down his thighs. She slowed the pace as she walked her fingers along the waist of his trunks, kissing up the ridge of muscle over his right hip at the same time.

Grave snarled down at her, a commanding edge to it, one that had her smiling secretly against his cool skin. She did love to tease and see how far she could push him. Her vampire had never had much patience. He always got what he wanted, when he wanted it, but gods, she loved to make him wait as long as she could before giving in to him.

She hooked her fingers into the elastic waist of his trunks and slowly edged them downwards, her lips following to explore the skin she exposed, drifting back towards the trail of hair.

Grave lifted his hips again, his breath coming a little quicker, soft pants that mingled with hers in the tense silence.

She raised her head and eased his trunks over his cock, setting it free. Her eyes immediately darted down to it, a breathless moan escaping her as she took in the rigid shaft, from the thick base, up the ridge on the underside to the darker blunt tip. He trembled as she stroked her hand down it, feeling the velvet and steel combination that had always made her ache for him, had always sent whatever thrill she had been feeling shooting high into the stratosphere until she was close to begging him to fill her.

As she eased her hand down, she revealed more of the lush dark head of his cock, and she couldn't resist the temptation. She lowered her head and tongued his slit, savoured his grunt and the following groan of pleasure as she teased him, drawing a bead of moisture from him. His right hip shook beneath her other hand as she planted it against it, holding him place, and wrapped her lips around the sensitive head.

"Isla," he barked and moaned as he tensed beneath her, hips thrusting up towards her as his backside clenched. "Gods."

She moaned in time with him and took him deep into her mouth, intent on driving him as wild as he had driven her, torturing her with bliss and pleasure so intense her climax had almost blinded her.

Her right hand closed around his shaft and she held him firm as she sucked him, taking him so deep he touched the back of her throat before rolling up his length until he popped free of her lips.

Grave writhed beneath her, but in this form, she was stronger, easily able to keep him in place and at her mercy.

She devoured his moans as she devoured his cock, ignored his whispered pleas for mercy and the delicious way he begged for release in a broken way. She kept up with her torture, taking him so deep she could almost swallow around him, and his hands shot to her shoulders, gripped her fiercely enough that it hurt, but she didn't care.

All that mattered was making her mate wild, giving him a release he would never forget.

Isla lowered her right hand to his balls and tugged on them before rubbing the spot below them. Grave's hips jacked up, thrusting his cock deep into her mouth, and she moaned as she swallowed it, sucked and teased it, and he grunted and groaned again, began pumping into her mouth in a desperate way, lost to his need for release, overwhelmed by it.

When she felt his balls draw up, could sense he was on the brink of climaxing, she eased back and released his cock as she sat up.

He growled at her, flashing fangs.

Her wicked and wild male.

She had him exactly where she wanted him, where she needed him in order to make this mating happen.

She needed him so lost to his need that he wouldn't care about what they had to do to form a bond between them again, exactly as he had been when they had first bound themselves to each other a century ago.

Back then, he hadn't known what he had been doing, because he hadn't known what she was or what he had become. She had triggered the bond by stealing a piece of his soul through a kiss and his phantom instincts had responded, and he had taken a piece of hers into him without ever knowing it.

This time, he would be aware of what was happening, and she wanted him so crazed with need that he wouldn't panic, wouldn't care when it happened. He had been upset when she had mentioned feeding on souls to him. He had hidden it, but she had seen it in his eyes, had been able to read it in the subtle changes of his body language, so in tune with him that he hadn't been able to conceal the fear from her.

She didn't want him to be afraid.

What they were going to do was beautiful, not terrifying.

Grave went to reach for her but stilled when she lifted her skirts and eased up his body. His hands fell to her legs and he stared down at her thighs as she positioned herself over him, the hunger in his eyes growing as he watched her take hold of his length. He groaned in unison with her as she nudged the blunt head inside her and pressed down, slowly taking his long rigid cock into her. Gods, he always felt so good, stretching her and filling her so beautifully.

"Isla…" he whispered and she pressed her fingers to his lips, knowing the fear he wanted to voice. He was close. She had pushed him too far and he wasn't likely to last long, but she didn't want a slow session of lovemaking. That wasn't their style.

She needed it as wild as they always were, as frenetic and consuming as it was every time they came together like this.

She leaned over him, grasped the back of his neck and kissed him as she began rocking on him, lifting herself off his cock before sliding back down its length until his pelvis hit her sensitive bundle of nerves, sending a thrill shooting through her.

He groaned, grabbed her backside and began moving her on him, guiding her and setting a wild pace, one that had her panting hard against his lips, her breath mingling with his as he pounded into her.

Gods. She had missed this.

She had missed him.

She moaned and grabbed his hair, yanked his head back and kissed him harder. His fangs brushed her tongue as she delved it between his lips, and the tinny taste of blood flooded her senses.

Her blood.

She hadn't thought it possible for him to bite her in this form, even when she had known he still possessed his fangs, but the thought that he could sent a sharp thrill through her, roused a fierce hunger to feel them sinking into her flesh.

Grave groaned, shuddered and then he was on her mouth like a man possessed, seizing control. He rolled her onto her back, pinning her beneath him as he pulled her hips into the air and thrust deep into her, taking her body as he took her mouth. His fangs caught her lower lip, spilling more blood, and she shuddered as he closed his mouth over hers and stole every drop.

"Isla," he murmured between kisses, breathless and wild in her arms, untamed and beautiful. Her savage, wicked vampire.

He plunged deeper still, his thrusts rough and hard, just what she needed as she soared higher and felt as if she could almost reach the stars. She kissed him deeper and focused on her phantom powers, drawing them to the surface. Her breath cooled, bouncing back at her from Grave's lips, and his soon joined it.

His thrusts faltered but she wrapped one leg around his waist to keep him where he was, where she needed him to be.

"Do not fear your instincts," she whispered as he pulled back, awareness shining in his blue eyes, mingled with a trickle of fear. "You will not hurt me… it is only a small piece… enough to bind us."

The fear that had been building in his eyes immediately dissipated, replaced with a hunger that startled her.

His lips found hers again, cooler now, sending a deeper sort of thrill rushing through her. She had never felt anything like it. Every cell in her body sizzled with awareness, blazed with energy as she kissed Grave and he moved inside her, and the pleasure rolling through her only grew in intensity, becoming a mind-numbing tingling as she felt her power draining from her.

She immediately responded, feeding from his lips as he took from hers, stealing the piece of his soul. The coolness that had been running through her turned to liquid heat, lava that rushed through her veins and through Grave's too if his strangled moan was anything to go by, or the way his thrusts deepened again, gaining strength and pace as he kissed her.

The tingles racing over her skin and running through her blood pooled between her thighs and on her back, and she burned where they settled, the fire growing in intensity and temperature as Grave thrust deep into her, filling her with every hard inch of his cock. She clung to him, gripping his shoulder with one hand and the back of his head with the other, holding him to her as the mark on her back began to blaze.

Her whole body felt as if it was on fire.

The sensations bombarding her, building within her, reached boiling point and she broke away from Grave's lips and screamed as every molecule in her body seemed to explode, her core clenching and quivering as release shot through her and the lines of her mark pulsed with new life.

With a new bond.

Grave arched above her, thrusting his cock deep into her core, and roared as his own climax took him, his length throbbing wildly as it shot warm jets of seed into her.

His eyes slowly widened, and she knew why.

She could feel it too, the awakening of their bond, the threads that twined them together gradually gaining strength as the mark on Grave's back appeared. Light sparkled from above his shoulders, pulsing in time with his cock, and that same light glowed in his blue eyes as he lowered his head and looked down into hers.

Together with love.

His lips twitched into a smile and then he dropped to his elbows and kissed her softly, tenderly, stealing her breath away all over again.

Isla wrapped her arms around him and idly traced the pattern of his mark, savouring the connection to him, one that was precious to her. She had been an idiot, had done so many foolish things, but that ended now.

Grave had wanted a fresh start for them. He wanted to do things right this time.

She wanted that too.

She wouldn't live in their past anymore.

Their future started now.

She pushed at Grave's shoulders, needing to tell him that she loved him and that they would do things right this time, they would have the forever both of them wanted.

A sound like thunder boomed overhead.

The entire building shook and dark power spread like an oily tide down through the layers of it, chilling her as it touched her phantom form but making her burn at the same time.

The demon prince.

Fury rose to consume her as the thought she would finally have her vengeance speared her mind and roused her soul. Her senses reached outwards, scouring the building for the bastard, and her blood burned as she pinpointed him on the roof.

It chilled a second later.

When a baby wailed and a woman screamed.

"Helena!"

CHAPTER 23

Grave led the charge, tugging up his combat trousers and fastening them as he raced barefoot for the bedroom door. He grabbed his sword as he passed it, yanked the wooden door open and broke into a dead sprint as soon as he hit the corridor on the other side.

"Grave." Isla entered the hallway behind him and began closing in on him. "You are stronger now. The piece of soul you took from me to bind us… it will give you strength."

She was right. He could already feel it, a power that flowed through him just beneath the surface of his skin, chilled him in places but didn't sap him of strength as cold normally would. This icy chill only made him feel stronger.

The power of a phantom.

He reached the end of the corridor and looked up the staircase, and the world streamed past in a white blur. He appeared on the turn in the stairs on the next level and heard his cousins thundering along the corridor there, but didn't wait for them to catch up.

He focused again and appeared at the open door onto the roof.

Sera stood just metres in front of him, her short red dress fluttering around her thighs and her blonde hair streaming behind her in the night breeze.

On the other side of her, across the broad expanse of flat roof, the demon prince stood gazing down at the delicate white-haired baby in his arms, his polished black horns twisted and curled like a ram's ones, sharpened at the ends, and huge black wings extended from his bare back.

The male dared to lift a gauntleted hand and stroke the back of a black razor-sharp claw along the baby's cheek.

"Get your fucking hands off her." Grave darted out into the open and the male lifted his head, stared across the roof at him without a shred of compassion in his black eyes.

The demon's pupils stretched into thin vertical slits in their centres, blazing gold in the darkness.

"Helena," Sera whispered, voice cracking, and Grave looked back at her and issued a silent warning to remain where she was.

He knew she needed to reach her child, but the demon was too powerful for her to fight and he was liable to kill Helena if she attempted to take her back.

The demon slid his fiery gaze from Sera and back to him. "You appear… different… disappointingly so."

"You son of a bitch!" Isla screamed and burst onto the roof, a blur of white that suddenly took form on the opposite side of the roof to Grave.

She was flanking the demon with him, dividing the male's attention to gain the upper hand. The strong moonlight made her glow and that glow grew brighter as her hair fluttered around her shoulders and began to rise upwards, and the skirts of her white corseted dress danced around her ankles. Her blue eyes blazed, ethereal and blood-chilling, affecting even Grave as her demeanour changed, her face turning dark, and his senses warned of danger.

"I will kill you for what you did." Isla launched her hands forwards.

The demon prince reared back, giving Grave the opening he needed.

He focused on Helena and white streamed past him. When the world came back, he was standing right in front of the baby, already turning solid. He snatched her from the demon's hands and used his preternatural speed to get away before the bastard noticed that Isla's attack had been nothing but a charade to gain his attention.

The demon prince looked down at his empty arms and then his gaze shot to Grave as he stopped beside Sera, and the male roared at him, the sound deafening as it rolled across London like thunder.

"You have taken enough family from us... I will not allow you to take any more," Grave snarled at the demon prince and then quickly checked on the squalling bundle in his arms.

Helena's blue eyes opened and she calmed as she saw him, and relief rushed through him as he saw that she was unharmed. He handed her to Sera, who immediately bundled the baby up into her arms and backed away towards the roof exit. Antoine was there, wrapping her in his arms and pulling her into the shelter of them.

Snow stood beside him, a picture of wrath as he stared down the demon prince.

The male stared back at him, calm and cool, but Grave spotted something that gave his confidence one hell of a boost and almost made him smile as he faded back to his phantom form. The sight of so many powerful adversaries had rattled him.

It wasn't only Antoine and Snow who had joined them.

Aurora stood beside her mate, her strange green-to-blue eyes locked on the demon, glowing in the moonlight. On the other side of Antoine, Payne had appeared together with some other males and females Grave didn't know. When he spotted Night through the throng, Lilian held close to him, he shook his head, silently commanding his brother to remain out of the battle.

This wasn't his fight.

Grave had brought this down upon his family, and he would be the one to deal with the demon prince.

Snow stepped forwards, making it clear that it was his fight too, and the look he slid Grave said that he wouldn't listen to anything he had to say on the matter. He nodded, accepting his cousin's help, and turned back to face the demon prince.

The male growled through sharp teeth and held his hand out before him, and the pommel of a black blade rose out of the roof. The huge broadsword slowly travelled upwards, the blade seeming to go on forever as it materialised out of the black tar, and then it finally tapered to a point and the demon twisted his hand, took hold of the black-and-red hilt, and snarled as he hefted it in front of him, pointing it at Grave and Snow.

And Isla.

She drifted closer to them, her twin curved blades drawn and clutched tightly in her hands.

A war cry left her lips that warmed Grave's blood and had his heart beating harder.

"Nulla Misericordia!"

The demon turned on her with a roar and she launched herself at him, turning solid as her twin blades clashed with his sword, blocking it and driving it back. She lashed out at the huge male who towered over her, catching him across his armoured thigh with one blade and just above his hip with the other. A thin ribbon of red formed where she had cut him, and the male twisted, planted his left foot behind him and swept his blade upwards, slicing through the air.

Snow was there before it could reach Isla, his own sword striking the black blade, sending it back the way it had come and filling the night with the ring of metal clashing with metal.

The demon shifted his focus to Snow.

Grave launched his own attack, drawing his katana and rushing around behind the demon. He focused hard, but it took little more than a thought to turn himself solid, and he snarled as he slashed up the demon's back, catching one wing and ripping the leathery membrane.

The male flapped those huge wings, battering Grave with them and driving him back.

He let go of his solid form and the wings went straight through him. The demon growled and turned on him, lashing out with his claws, swiping them through the air. They passed harmlessly through Grave's throat, tearing another feral roar from the demon, this one filled with frustration.

Grave grinned at the bastard as he attacked again, meeting with the same result. Every blow he tried to land went straight through Grave. Gods, he had hated the idea of being a phantom before, but he was loving it now, embraced it as it made him feel invincible.

He had thought it would weaken him, making it impossible for him to fight and defeat the demon.

He had thought wrong.

It made him stronger, gave him the edge he needed over the demon prince, and for the first time he felt as if he could win.

He could protect his family because of what Isla had done to him, turning him into a phantom.

Grave sought her and his heart beat a little harder as she majestically shifted from phantom to solid in the middle of an attack, her right blade clashing with the demon's left gauntlet and driving his arm upwards, and became a ghost just as he thrust at her with his broadsword, so it went straight through her stomach.

She sidestepped, leaving the demon's sword behind, and twirled her weapons in her hands, so her thumbs were against the hilts and the metal blades ran along her forearms.

The demon beat his wings, turning quickly as she came up beside him, her right hand flying up in a fast arc, cutting towards the male's side. The demon snarled and slammed the flat of his hand into her arm, and she cried out as it snapped back, and quickly became ghostly again. The male was catching on.

Damn it.

"Antoine, get everyone out of the theatre." Snow didn't take his eyes off the demon as he issued that command.

"I am not leaving," Antoine snapped.

Snow grimaced, huffed and then sighed as he readied his blade and the demon turned on him. "Please. I need to know you are all safe. Think of Helena."

Grave could almost feel the glare Antoine directed at his older brother for using Helena as a means of getting him to leave a fight he clearly wanted in on, and Grave couldn't blame Antoine for wanting to be a part of taking the demon prince down. If someone had threatened his child, he would have wanted to butcher them too.

But Snow could sense what he could, that Antoine was too close to the edge, in danger of rousing his bloodlust and giving it a firmer hold over him. Neither of them wanted that, so Grave weighed in on Snow's side.

Besides, it wasn't as if it would ruin any relationship they had.

Antoine already hated him after all.

"Take the females and children, Antoine. It is your duty to protect them now." Grave held the demon prince's gaze as he circled him, trying to keep the male's focus on him and away from the more vulnerable members of the group behind him. "Payne… you can teleport. Take them all somewhere remote. Somewhere safe."

The demon's glowing gaze slowly inched towards Payne and the others.

"The cabin," Payne said and Snow grunted in agreement as he launched at the demon.

The two collided, solid muscle hitting solid muscle, and both staggered as they grappled with each other, Snow somehow managing to get hold of the demon's forearms to hold in him place and stop him from teleporting to the others.

On a mighty roar, Snow threw his head forwards and cracked his brow against the demon's one, tearing a muffled grunt from the bastard and making him lose his balance. Snow landed on top of the male and hammered him with his fists, knocking his head left and right, his knuckles growing bloodied as he kept up his savage attack. The male let out a slow, low growl that rolled into a roar, and bucked up, dislodging Snow.

His cousin quickly sprang to his feet and launched back at the demon.

The male teleported before he could hit him and Snow ran straight through the spot where he had been and staggered to a halt near the edge of the roof.

"I would not," Aurora said and Snow swiftly turned, wild red eyes seeking her, and Grave snapped his focus to her and the group too.

Aurora stood between the demon and the group near the exit, her arms outstretched, her white dress and the soft waves of her raven hair fluttering in the cool breeze.

"You know what I am." Her voice was low, a warning in it, and her eyes glowed brighter as she stared at the demon and he at her.

He growled through his fangs and stalked towards her. "A little fallen angel does not frighten me. You belong to Snow... so you will die first."

"Sorry, but you are wrong." Aurora whipped her right hand through the air and a white blade appeared in it. The demon slammed to a halt. "I am not technically fallen."

She kicked off, launching towards the demon, and swept the blade up as she neared him, a swift and brutal attack the male didn't have time to dodge. The demon threw his head back and bellowed in agony as the white sword sliced up his chest, sending him staggering backwards, and the rich smell of his blood flooded the air.

"I will help," an unfamiliar female voice put in, a slightly disappointed edge to it that didn't quite dampen the teasing lightness of it when she continued. "Although, helping out the incupire isn't normally my style... so you know I still hate you and I'm just doing this to keep me in the lead on the 'who's awesomest' scoreboard, right?"

Payne chuckled, the sound out of place in the thick night air. "I still hate you too, Succubus, but this time you're going down."

"I like going down... but I also really hate missing a good fight, so let's make this quick and then we can come back and kick arse. Race you!" The female was gone from his senses a moment later. Sera, Antoine and Helena disappeared with her.

Payne muttered something and he too disappeared, together with Night and Lilian.

"I will go too... but I will be back, and I will not hear a word against it." Aurora's normally soft voice brooked no argument, but that didn't stop Snow from huffing and pulling a face that said he wanted to go ahead and tell her that she had to stay away with the others.

She disappeared, taking three with her.

Grave sensed Payne reappear below him in the theatre, and then disappear, taking more with him. Aurora and the succubus did the same, until the building was empty.

The demon stomped around the roof, growling as he held one arm across his chest to stem the flow of blood that ran in thick rivulets down his bare stomach and flexed his fingers around the hilt of his broadsword. A trail of crimson followed him, dark in the moonlight. It ran down the plates of the armour encasing his legs and hips too, turning the dull black metal shiny in places.

He beat his wings and Grave could sense his fury mounting as he circled him, his blade at the ready, monitoring his every move.

Blazing gold eyes slid towards Snow.

He was singling out the weakest in their group.

Big mistake.

Snow couldn't turn ghostly, but he was hardly the weak member of their trio.

His cousin's lips peeled back off huge fangs as he snarled at the demon and hunkered down, lowering his big body into a crouch, his muscles coiled tight beneath his black jeans and t-shirt.

The demon twisted on his heel and kicked off, raising his broadsword as he closed the distance between him and Snow.

Snow waited, crimson eyes almost glowing in the moonlight, his lips twisting in a savage sneer as the demon approached.

The male roared, gripped his sword with both hands and raised it over his head. He brought it down hard as he beat his black leathery wings, increasing his pace and therefore the intensity of his strike.

Snow didn't move until the last possible second.

He swiftly lunged to his right, rolled and came onto his feet just as the demon's blade struck the black tar where he had been, slicing deep into the roof. Snow loosed a feral roar of his own and launched at the demon, his crimson eyes blazing like the fires of Hell as he swept his blade down at his side and then brought it up in a devastating arc.

The demon glared at him and disappeared.

And didn't reappear.

Grave turned in a slow circle, his senses stretching around him, mapping everything. No godsdamned way the demon was gone. He was injured, but Grave knew the look that had been in his eyes, because it was the same look he gave his enemies on the battlefield. He wouldn't back down. He couldn't.

It was death or glory.

He licked his fangs, itching for the demon to reappear, and flexed his fingers around the hilt of his sword.

Even in his phantom state, his bloodlust still affected him. It slowly rose within him as he waited, silently goading the demon into returning. Gods, the bastard could bring an army right now and he would take them all down.

His heart pounded, pumping darkness through his veins. He felt Isla's gaze on him but refused to look at her when his bloodlust gripped him, because he feared it would go away, tempered by his beautiful female. He had seen the way Aurora could calm Snow, and he had the sinking feeling Isla did the same to him.

He didn't want calm. Not right now.

He wanted a tempest, savage and glorious. He wanted to ride the storm brewing inside him, the wild and wicked craving for bloodshed and death, and harness it, creating a force that would carry him to victory.

Grave stoked the black fire in his veins, fed it with thoughts of battling the demon, sinking his fangs into the bastard's flesh and ripping into him, spilling blood and painting the rooftop with his entrails. He would tear the male apart, and only once he was scattered in a thousand pieces would he be satisfied.

Isla gasped.

Snow roared.

Grave didn't hesitate.

He focused on the spot where the demon had reappeared and the world streamed past in a white blur. He thrust his sword forwards before he even landed at the male's side, his senses guiding him. They were a little off. He turned solid as he appeared, but rather than his sword turning solid through the demon's chest as planned, it turned solid through his shoulder.

The male grunted and slammed the flat of his palm against Grave's chest, and the world twisted around him as he flew through the air. He landed hard on the rooftop near the exit, rolled and ended up face down. He groaned, planted his hands against the black roof and pushed himself up slowly, giving his brain time to stop spinning.

Grave growled as he sat back and looked down at his now ghostly body.

His sword was gone.

He scanned the roof for it as Snow and Isla took on the demon, working in tandem to keep him off balance, forcing him to turn one way and then the other to block their attacks.

His eyes drifted back a few feet and he huffed as he saw his sword resting against one of the roof vents. He pushed onto his feet and gritted his teeth as pain spread through him, streaking outwards from the centre of his chest.

Grave looked down at his bare chest and curled his lip at the four deep puncture wounds that formed a crescent above his heart, visible even in his phantom form.

The demon had taken the opportunity to sink his claws into him while pushing him away.

He was going to pay for that.

Grave staggered towards his sword and his legs gave out, sending him crashing to his knees.

No. They hadn't given out.

They were solid and he hadn't been prepared for it.

He pushed onto his feet and his legs turned incorporeal again, and then they were solid once more. What the hell was going on?

He raised his hands in front of him as they switched between ghostly and corporeal, and frowned at them. The sudden shift was dizzying, messing with his mind as his body tried to keep up.

He wasn't doing it.

The demon sent Isla flying through the air and she landed in a heap a few metres from Grave.

And remained solid.

"Isla." Grave rushed to her side and helped her up, and she stared at him with wide blue eyes that held a note of fear.

"I cannot control myself." She looked him over, and the panic he could feel in her grew stronger. "You too?"

He nodded and wracked his brain for a reason, and then his eyes caught on two puncture wounds on Isla's chest. He reached out and brushed his fingers across them, his eyebrows drawing down as he studied them, and then looked across to his left at the demon where he fought Snow.

"He did something to us." It was the only possible explanation. "He was gone for too long. He went somewhere and got something that affects us... to give him the advantage."

If they couldn't control their phantom forms, they could only attack when they were solid and even then they were in danger of turning into a ghost during those attacks. On top of that, they couldn't turn incorporeal at will, meaning the demon could attack them and land blows.

Grave touched the puncture wounds on his chest and brought his bloodied fingers up to his nose. He inhaled deeply and frowned as he caught a sweet note among the tang of his blood.

"It must be some sort of spell," Isla said and edged closer to him, her slender fingers flexing around her blades.

One the demon had administered to them when he had clawed them.

"If he thinks this gives him the advantage, he does not know who he is dealing with." Isla straightened, flipped her blades in her hands and stared at the demon, her blue eyes flashing like lightning in the night, matching the colour of her leathers. She slid her gaze across to him. "Nulla Misericordia."

Gods, his mate was wonderful.

"Nulla Misericordia." He picked up his own blade and Isla broke away from him, circling around the other side of the demon, flanking him.

Snow grappled with the towering male and managed to sink his fangs into the demon's shoulder. His cousin growled as the male bellowed, and ripped his head away, cleaving vicious deep grooves in the male's flesh. Snow grinned, flashing bloodied fangs, and brought his knee up, landing a hard blow between the male's thighs.

The demon doubled over and Snow swept around him, grabbed his left horn and pulled his head back, forcing the male to bow forwards.

Grave roared and ran at him, sword aimed for the demon's stomach. He cut a fast hard arc towards it and growled in frustration as he turned phantom just as it struck, and all he could do was watch it harmlessly pass through him. This was going to be more annoying than he had thought.

Isla didn't seem dissuaded by his failure. She sprang into the air and sailed through it on a war cry, her twin blades pointed downwards towards the demon. Her right one turned ghostly but she sank the left into the male's right hip.

The demon unleashed another bellow and swung his arm out, catching Isla and sending her flying through the air again. She landed hard at the edge of the roof and rolled into the small wall that surrounded it.

Grave checked her with his senses, reassuring himself that she would be fine, and then launched his own attack, striking hard at the demon male. The male shook Snow off and blocked Grave with his forearm, so his blade struck the black metal gauntlet that protected it.

He pulled his sword back, shifted his feet to move his weight to his right leg and struck again, and this time he put all of his strength into it and actually aimed for the male's raised forearm. The force of the blow drove the male to one knee on the roof and the demon snarled as he shoved upwards with that arm, knocking Grave's sword away.

The demon beat his wings but Snow grabbed one, sinking claws deep into the membrane and puncturing it so he could grip the connecting spur of bone. The male tried to turn on him but Snow kept behind him and growled as the demon tried to batter him with his other wing. His cousin blocked each attempt with his arm, and between each one tried to grab hold of the wing.

"These are fucking annoying," Snow growled as he finally got hold of the second wing. "I think they need to go."

He pressed his knee into the demon's back and heaved backwards, pulling on the male's wings. The male roared and arched forwards, and for a moment it looked as if Snow was really going to tear the wings off a demon.

But then they disappeared, shrinking out of Snow's grip, and the demon turned on him so quickly his cousin couldn't evade him, his eyes blazing with gold fire and his horns flaring forwards as he brought his right hand up in a fast blur.

Snow roared in agony as the demon's clawed fingers ripped into his left side, tearing through his flesh. The rich scent of his blood flooded the air and he staggered backwards, his hands quickly coming down to cover the wound as he pulled away from the demon. Blood pumped from between his fingers and Isla rushed over to him, catching him as his backside hit the roof.

Darkness poured through Grave's veins, blacker than he had ever felt it, and he knew from the look on Isla's face that the red in his eyes had been almost completely swallowed by that darkness, leaving only a ring of crimson around his elliptical pupils.

With a vicious roar, he ran at the demon's back.

He dropped his sword along the way.

The only weapon he needed was his bloodlust. He harnessed it, stoked it and embraced it, let it flow through his body and soul and claim hold of him. His claws extended into sharp points and his fangs bit into his gums as he growled through his clenched teeth.

The demon slowly turned to face him.

Not fast enough.

Grave kicked off and launched at him, landed heavily on the male's back and didn't give the bastard a chance to react. He struck hard, sinking aching fangs into his neck, and snarled as he pulled on the male's vein. Thick, rich blood burst into his mouth and, gods, it sent his bloodlust spiralling higher, consuming more of him, demanding more from him.

He dug his claws into the male's shoulders as he tried to dislodge him, clawing and grappling with him. He didn't feel the pain as his flesh tore open, couldn't feel anything but the powerful need for more blood. More violence. More death.

He sank his fangs in deeper, barely bit back the moan that bubbled up his throat as he sated that hunger with the male's blood. It flowed into him, gave him strength even as the demon took it with each blow he landed and every slash he cut into Grave's body with his claws.

He needed more.

The bastard demon slipped through his hands as they turned ghostly and blood pumped from the wounds beneath his pale lips but refused to go down his throat.

His bloodlust roared for more, but he couldn't feed it, not in this form.

Every instinct he possessed screamed that he could, and he obeyed it, couldn't stop himself as the need to feed, and to destroy, overwhelmed him.

Grave swept around the demon, coming face to face with him, and the male snarled at him, flashing razor sharp teeth.

He planted his mouth on the demon's bloodstained lips and the male bellowed as heat poured into Grave, dark and potent, making him hazy all over. His bloodlust purred in approval and he surrendered to it, feeding deeply from the male, pulling that power he possessed into him and claiming it for his own.

The male's cry stuttered and then died as he dropped to the floor at Grave's feet, his skin ashen and almost blue in the moonlight.

Grave stared down at him, feeling nothing as warmth consumed him, filled him up and made him feel alive.

Gods, he wanted more of that high.

"Grave?" Isla's soft voice drew him back to the world and he frowned as he looked at the demon below him and his senses detected no heartbeat.

No sign of life.

The darkness pouring through his veins slowly began to ebb away and clarity rolled in to replace it, a sickening sort of awareness that sent a shiver through him.

"We do not tell anyone what I just did." Because his reputation would be ruined if word spread about the fact he had killed a demon.

By kissing him.

He shuddered and ignored Snow's deep chuckle. His cousin would keep this a secret, although Grave suspected he was going to tease him about it for centuries.

Isla drifted up beside him, her ghostly white corseted dress flowing around her ankles, and a mischievous smile curved her lips. "You are positively glowing."

He scowled at her. "Not a word, Phantom. Not a word."

She only smiled wider.

He huffed and looked back down at the demon. Dead. Not exactly the way he had planned on killing the bastard, but he would take it as a victory.

The demon was dead. His family were safe. Isla had carried out her revenge.

Everything was looking up.

He turned towards her and raised his hand, needing to feel her beneath his fingers and unable to curb the desire to touch her.

His hand disappeared.

His arm followed it.

"Grave!" Isla grabbed his cheeks, her panic lancing him too as weakness went through him, cold and startling in the wake of feeling so powerful. "Do not fade."

His arm and hand slowly reappeared, ghostly but more translucent than before. They weren't safe. He had thought they were now that he had become an ordinary phantom. The look in Isla's eyes said she had thought the same thing, had truly believed they could exist as phantoms for however long it took to find a spell to make them corporeal again.

He raised both of his hands and held Isla's cheeks as she clutched his, a desperate and wild edge to her eyes that begged him not to fade. He didn't want to, but he wasn't sure he had any say in it.

He clung to her as she clung to him, feeling normal again while she touched him, and whispered, "Never let go of me then."

She smiled shakily and stepped into his arms, pressed her cheek to his chest and wrapped her arms around him. "I will not... I am never letting you go again."

He looked at his right hand, fearing it would fade again and the rest of him would go with it, and he wouldn't come back.

"Aurora." Snow's deep voice broke the quiet and Grave realised that the ex-angel had returned. He looked across at her and she rushed to Snow. Snow waved her away when she tried to fuss over him. "Get Elissa and Lilian... now."

She nodded and disappeared.

When she reappeared a moment later, the two female witches were with her. Elissa's silver hair sparkled under the moonlight as she hurried over to him and Isla, her eyes dark in the low light.

"What happened?" she said as Isla shifted between solid and phantom in his arms.

"I am fading… we are still fading." Grave hated saying those words, because it felt as if by admitting it aloud he was condemning them to do exactly that.

He was making it real.

"But Isla is…" Elissa broke off as Isla switched forms again, going solid for a few seconds before returning to her ghostly body.

"We need that spell, Elissa," Grave snapped as Isla trembled against him, her fear flowing through him. She didn't want to fade. To die. He didn't want that either. He hadn't found her again only to lose her. He wanted a long life with her. Centuries at the very least. "We need it now."

"Bossy boots… if you let me finish!" Elissa planted her hands against her jeans-clad hips and glared at him, sparks of lightning flashing in her eyes. "Why is she switching like that?"

"She cannot control it. The demon hit us with something…"

"What?" Elissa's eyes lit up with a strange sort of excitement, as if he had said something wonderful not simply informed her of what had happened.

The reason for her excitement slowly dawned on him and a trickle of that emotion went through him too.

"A spell." He set Isla aside and crouched beside the demon, grabbed his arm and raised it. "It is on his claws. It affects us… makes us unable to control our bodies. We keep turning solid against our will."

Against their phantom instincts.

Elissa was beside him in a heartbeat, crouched and sniffing the demon's claws. She closed her eyes, frowned and was silent for so long he wanted to shake her and make her say something.

Her eyes pinged open, sparkling with silver stars.

"I think I can save you both."

CHAPTER 24

Isla drifted up through the quiet theatre, smiling as she passed Kristina and Callum, and their twins on the stairs. The female werewolf returned the smile with one of her own, but the male vampire had his hands full with a boisterous youngling, wrestling to keep the boy still in his arms and stop him from falling.

The sight of the child drew tears to her eyes and thoughts of Tarwyn to her heart, and she lowered her head, using her fall of white hair to conceal her face as she struggled with the sorrow building inside her. Tarwyn and Melia were gone, but they would always live on in her heart. She would carry them wherever she went, and she would never forget them.

She had avenged them, and as soon as she was able, she would relay that to Frey, setting his mind at ease.

Her focus shifted from that male to another as she neared the roof, seeking the only one who had the power to chase the cold from her heart and ease her hurt.

Grave appeared in the doorway to the roof as she rounded the corner in the staircase, frowning down at her. "What is wrong?"

He went to step down towards her, but she shook her head and drifted up to him, not wanting him to leave the quiet of the roof just yet. She found it peaceful up there, just as he did, scanning the mortal world and soaking it all in, all the life and the colour.

"I was just thinking about my family." It wasn't hard to admit that to him, to let him beyond the barriers and reveal her pain to him, not anymore.

He held his hand out to her and she slipped hers into it, even though she couldn't truly hold it right now. They were out of sync again, Grave enjoying a temporary solidity while she was a phantom. She moved her hand in such a way that it looked as if they were holding hands and followed him onto the roof, careful not to ruin the illusion.

When he stopped near the southern edge of the roof, she halted there with him and watched the quiet streets. Even this late in the night, buses and taxis were moving around the city, ferrying mortals home or to their next location.

Isla looked from the street to Grave's hand, and then up at his noble profile. His eyes remained fixed on the world stretching before him, moonlight turning his skin milky white but his eyes an incredible shade of blue that almost glowed.

She moved closer to him and he looked down at her, smiled and placed his arm around her shoulder, and she smiled at the gesture. He couldn't touch her, and it was probably a pain to hold his arm out at his side without being able to rest it on anything, but she appreciated it, and his comfort and support. It was strange to have him like this again, so attentive to her, not fighting or hating her.

Strange in the best way imaginable.

As if all her dreams had come true.

All except one.

She was about to make that dream happen.

"Elissa is almost ready." She sensed Grave tense as he heard those words and felt the relief that went through him, laced with happiness.

The witch had managed to locate the spell after she had analysed the liquid that had been on the demon's claws, and had been rushing between fae towns hunting for the ingredients since then. One of those ingredients, the one that should have been the hardest to source but had in the end been the easiest, was strong demon blood.

She hated the idea of using the demon prince's blood in their spell, but in a way she supposed it was fitting. He had brought her and Grave together again, united them in a common cause, and now he would be pivotal in keeping them together.

Forever.

"You promise not to annoy her?" She looked up at Grave and he glared down at her, but she knew he didn't mean it.

He had gone to the roof after he had tried helping Elissa find the spell and had kept getting under the witch's feet and on her nerves. Elissa had banished him from the room. He hadn't been happy about it, had pointed out rather brusquely that it was their lives on the line and they had a right to be part of finding the solution.

Isla had convinced him to take in some fresh air and had promised to tell him whenever there was a breakthrough.

She had come to him and told him when Elissa had found the spell, and part of her had expected him to come back down and help, but he had been quiet and contemplative, and she hadn't had the heart to force him back into the theatre. She had left him to his thoughts, and that had plagued her during the hours that had passed since then.

She wanted to know.

Needed to know.

"You have been thinking a lot." She studied his profile and he sighed, his shoulders heaving with it beneath his black shirt. "About us?"

He nodded, glanced at her and then up at the faint stars. "Do you have big plans after this?"

"Yes." She schooled her features when his head snapped down, eyes locking on her.

"What plans?" There was demand in his voice, an order, but also nerves, and she wanted to laugh at how foolish her vampire was, fearing things that were never going to happen.

"I plan to make your life hell." She drifted out from under his arm and around his back, and he slowly turned to track her movements, his eyes narrowing on her. "I think it is high time your sunny little home had a female touch."

He huffed at her. "I thought we agreed you would stop calling it sunny?"

"You painted it yellow... not me." She smiled as he reached for her and she drifted backwards, evading him. "Of course... I will need my own quarters and a rank."

He scowled, but then his handsome face softened, the darkness lifting from it, and his eyes brightened. "You have quarters... mine... and a rank... my mate."

"A mate is not a rank." She twirled on the spot. "I was thinking... second in command."

The frown returned and he folded his arms across his chest. "Asher would not be happy about that. He worked hard for that position."

"And for your love." She ignored the way his eyes darkened again at that and kept smiling. "So, not second in command... chief advisor then."

Her smile faltered, the jest leaving her as she thought about Melia and the First Realm, and the time she had passed there with her family.

"What is wrong, my love?" Grave closed in on her again, concern etched on his face and in his feelings that flowed through their bond.

"Advisor was the rank Melia assigned me. One I still hold with Frey's legion in the First Realm."

Grave's scowl came back full force and crimson ringed his irises.

"Frey? Who the fuck is Frey anyway? You speak of him as if he means something to you... you are close to him?" He stalked towards her, a predator on the prowl, and a thrill bolted through her in response to the sensual and wicked way he moved, all darkness and danger. "I will kill him. You are mine now... mine forever."

Isla bit back her smile as it tried to return, her heart lightening again as Grave's jealous streak reared its head. Gods, it was wonderful to see it, to have it reassure her of his love and how fiercely he needed her. More than the demon she had mentioned and the First Legion needed her.

"My brother-in-law... and current king of the First Realm." She drifted around Grave again and the scowl stayed as he tracked her.

"I hate him already."

"Of course... our being mated could possibly be construed as making him a relation of sorts to you... so if I were to live with you... you would have to promise not to make war against the First Realm." She felt awful for pressing him into it, using his love for her against him, but she needed to know that there would never come a day when Frey became her enemy.

He was her brother. The closest thing she had to one anyway.

Grave huffed and folded his arms across his chest. "Fine... but if he needs assistance, he still has to pay for it. The Preux Chevaliers do not work for free.

If I am going to face death and look the bastard straight in the eye, then I am going to be paid for it."

It was wrong that she loved it when he spoke like that, all fire and spit, and fury. She regretted the things she had said to him a few nights ago, stomping all over his pride and his beloved Preux Chevaliers, and had apologised a thousand times over. Each time, Grave had shrugged it off, but she knew she had hurt him with her thoughtless words so she would keep apologising until he accepted it.

"Frey has plenty of gold in his coffers, but little war on his lands."

He shrugged. "Everything can change in the blink of an eye, Isla. Peace never lasts."

Gods, he sounded like Frey when he spoke like that, so eager for battle and bloodshed, to test his mettle against the next powerful foe. She supposed she was the same deep in her heart. She loved the fight, the thrill of dancing with death, because it made her feel alive.

Just as Grave made her feel alive.

"You will be my advisor now… first female of the First Legion." Grave's expression soured. "Gods, Asher will think you have my balls in a vice."

Isla chuckled and he smiled, his blue eyes lighting up, as if he loved the sound of it and she had given him pleasure.

She was about to tease him by asking if she didn't already have his balls in a vice, when a shiver went through her and she sensed Payne reappearing below her, together with Elissa.

A moment later, the blond incubus-vampire appeared on the roof beside her. "It's time."

She nodded, her belly fluttering at the thought that soon she wouldn't have to worry about fading and neither would Grave. They would be safe, and all of her dreams would have come true.

Grave held his hand out to her and she slipped hers into it, and followed him into the building and down the stairs.

Everyone was waiting for them in her room on the second floor down. Antoine and Snow greeted Grave and she gave them a moment alone, because she knew they needed it. When the time came, everyone but the ones involved would have to leave so Elissa and Lilian could concentrate.

Payne and Night were talking in one corner, watching their females work. Elissa and Lilian were busy preparing the bed, spreading leaves from a plant around it that looked familiar. She recalled seeing them around her when the mage had performed the spell on her.

Elissa had talked in depth to her about the spell when she had been putting together the list of ingredients, telling her that it might be different to the one the mage had cast on her but not to worry. There were many ways to do the same spell and the witch was confident it would work.

She stepped forwards, but Grave's hand caught her wrist.

She looked down at his ghostly hand on her and then up at his pale face.

"I can do it," he said and she shook her head.

She appreciated him wanting to go through the spell for her, because only one of them needed to do it to turn both of them solid as they were before, but she had to be the one to do it. She had brought him into her world, and got him into this mess, and she had to be the one to fix it.

Even though it was going to hurt like hell.

She had kept that part from him, and he wasn't going to be happy when he realised that the spell was hurting her, but by then it would be too late and Elissa would have to keep going.

She had hurt Grave enough. She never wanted to hurt him again.

Isla raised her arm, removed his hand from her wrist and then stepped up to him and kissed him. He was quick to respond, a slightly desperate edge to his kiss as he leaned into it and sought more from her, relaying his fear to her. He didn't have to worry. She wasn't going anywhere. Nothing about this spell could take her from him.

It could only bring them together.

She drifted away from him and up onto the bed, and lay with her head above the pillows and her hands on her stomach. Nerves fluttered in it but she breathed slowly to keep her heart steady and calm herself as best she could.

Antoine and Snow left.

Elissa stood on one side of her and Lilian moved to the other, and Grave drifted to the foot of the bed. She could feel his eyes on her and she looked down at him and smiled to reassure him that everything would be alright. She had been through this once for him, and she could do it again.

Payne and Night filtered out of the room and closed the door, leaving her alone with the two witches and Grave.

Elissa closed her eyes, held her hands out over Isla and began to chant. Lilian mirrored her. The candles around the room flickered and then burst to life, filling the space with warm golden light.

Isla kept her focus on the two witches, and on allowing their words to flow over her. Colourful ribbons of magic swirled around their outstretched hands, beautiful and dazzling, stealing her focus away from the pain steadily building inside her, making her feel as if she was being squeezed into a container, restrained and restricted.

When the pain became so intense that even the bright magic couldn't distract her, her eyes sought Grave. He had moved closer to the end of the bed, his steely blue eyes fixed on her and her alone.

Elissa picked up something from the side table and splashed it on her. Her skin burned wherever it touched, blazed red hot and she grimaced as she tried to keep from crying out. The witch bent over her, slipped one hand under her head and lifted it up as she brought the cup to her lips. Isla swiftly drank the contents, not wanting to draw anything out.

The second she swallowed, an inferno swept through her, fire that crushed her inwards, compressing her, and she arched up off the bed and screamed.

"Isla!" Grave's voice penetrated the fierce fiery darkness consuming her, a light that she reached for, and her throat burned, her voice giving out as she exhausted all the air in her lungs. "I am here, Isla."

Cool fingers touched her toes and a chill swept through her, dousing the fire and giving her relief.

She breathed hard through the pain as Elissa and Lilian continued to chant, sagging back against the bed and struggling for air. Gods. She writhed and screwed her face up, wanted to claw her way out of her skin as it pressed down on her.

Caged her.

Fresh pain rolled through her as Lilian stopped chanting, leaving Elissa's as the only voice for her to focus on, and she tried to bear it, panted through it and told herself over and over again that it was worth it.

She would bear pain a thousand times worse than this to be with Grave.

Elissa finally fell silent, so the only sound that filled the room was her own fast breathing.

And then Grave, his voice a low snarl.

"Gods… I think we should do something about this before anyone comes back in… I might kill them."

She frowned but before she could open her eyes, a blanket was covering her, and she realised her transformation from phantom to corporeal hadn't brought her clothes with her this time and she was naked.

Warmth spread through her cheek as his palm pressed against it and she rolled towards him as he sat on the bed to her right. "Isla?"

She slowly fluttered her eyes open and flinched at the brightness of the room. The lights dimmed and she struggled to focus on Grave. He was a hazy blur above her. She stared up at him and slowly he came into focus. Concerned blue eyes held hers, darting between them, and then relief flooded them when she smiled and managed to lift her hand and place it over his on her cheek. That relief coursed through her too as she took in the sight of him, solid again just as she was.

"How are you feeling?" Elissa popped into view beyond Grave, her silver hair falling to her left as she canted her head to see past him. "You look pretty solid."

Isla smiled up at the witch. "I feel pretty solid."

"Well… we should probably let you rest now… but remember, you will have to take regular doses of medicine to stop your problem from reoccurring."

Grave frowned at that, turned and looked at the witch. "What medicine?"

Elissa waggled a silver eyebrow. "The sort that makes a bond between mates stronger."

A beautiful blush stained his cheeks, drawing a smile from Isla, one that fell away as he shifted to gaze down at her and the heated look in his eyes scalded her.

Gods, she was all too happy to start that course of medicine right now.

"Rest," Elissa ordered, but she wasn't listening to the witch, and it seemed Grave wasn't either.

He leaned over her, his focus dropping to her mouth.

Out of the corner of her eye, Isla saw Elissa grab Lilian and drag her out the door. It closed behind them with a soft click.

Grave stopped with his lips just a bare millimetre from hers and whispered against them, "Have a nice rest."

She growled, grabbed his shoulders before he could even think about leaving, and pulled him down onto the bed, rolling him onto his back and landing on top of him. He chuckled and planted his hands on her bare hips, his eyes darkening and turning serious as his laughter died and he looked her over, taking in her nudity.

His hungry gaze drifted back up to hers. "I am weak… I think I need medicine."

She rolled her eyes, wondering how many times he was going to use that excuse each day to get her into bed with him.

And how many times she was going to use it to seduce him.

"I think I have just what you need." Isla pressed her hands to his chest, feeling his heart beating strongly against her palms as she leaned over him, lowering her mouth towards his.

He lifted one hand from her hip and brushed her hair behind her ear, and stole her breath.

"You are all I need, Isla." He feathered his fingers along the line of her jaw, his eyes darting between hers. "You were all I ever needed."

Gods. Her heart leaped into her throat at the sincerity in his eyes and the love behind those words, and she kissed him, losing herself in him as he wrapped his arms around her and held her close to him.

The love she had felt for him a century ago, the love they had both tried to deny and destroy, had conquered her all over again and it had done the unimaginable too. It had conquered the vampire beneath her, a male who never lost a battle, a male who was hers now and would be forever.

He was everything she wanted.

He was everything she needed.

Her dreams come true.

Her love eternal.

Her King of Death.

The End

ABOUT THE AUTHOR

Felicity Heaton is a New York Times and USA Today best-selling author who writes passionate paranormal romance books. In her books she creates detailed worlds, twisting plots, mind-blowing action, intense emotion and heart-stopping romances with leading men that vary from dark deadly vampires to sexy shape-shifters and wicked werewolves, to sinful angels and hot demons!

If you're a fan of paranormal romance authors Lara Adrian, J R Ward, Sherrilyn Kenyon, Gena Showalter, Larissa Ione and Christine Feehan then you will enjoy her books too.

If you love your angels a little dark and wicked, the best-selling Her Angel series is for you. If you like strong, powerful, and dark vampires then try the Vampires Realm series or any of her stand-alone vampire romance books. If you're looking for vampire romances that are sinful, passionate and erotic then try the best-selling Vampire Erotic Theatre series. Or if you prefer huge detailed worlds filled with hot-blooded alpha males in every species, from elves to demons to dragons to shifters and angels, then take a look at the new Eternal Mates series.

If you have enjoyed this story, please take a moment to contact the author at **author@felicityheaton.co.uk** or to post a review of the book online

Connect with Felicity:
Website – http://www.felicityheaton.co.uk
Blog – http://www.felicityheaton.co.uk/blog/
Twitter – http://twitter.com/felicityheaton
Facebook – http://www.facebook.com/felicityheaton
Goodreads – http://www.goodreads.com/felicityheaton
Mailing List – http://www.felicityheaton.co.uk/newsletter.php

FIND OUT MORE ABOUT HER BOOKS AT:
http://www.felicityheaton.co.uk

CPSIA information can be obtained
at www.ICGtesting.com
Printed in the USA
LVHW021051291218
602142LV00002B/603/P